WHEN THE SUN GOES DOWN

ERIN NOELLE

*Lorin
Love what
you live
~Erin Noelle*

When the Sun Goes Down

Published by Erin Noelle

All rights reserved. No part of this publication may be reproduced, stored in retrieval systems, copied in any form or by any means. Electronic, mechanical, photocopying, recording or otherwise transmitted without written permission from the author/publisher, except by a reviewer that may quote brief passages for review purposes only. This book is licenses for your personal enjoyment only. This eBook may not be resold or given away to other people. If you would like to share this book with another person, please purchase an additional copy for each participant.

This is a work of fiction. Names, characters, places, and incidents either are products of the author's imagination or are used factiously. Any resemblance to actual events or locales or persons, is entirely coincidental.

All publicly recognizable characters, settings, etc. are the property of their respective owners. The original characters and plot are the property of the author of this story. The author is no way associated with the owners, creators, or producers of any previously copyrighted material. No copyright infringement is intended.

Cover Graphics & Design: by Hang Le

Editing by Kayla Robichaux and Mandi Gibala

Formatting by Kassi Cooper

For my favorite Nessy ~
This is what I do with a good idea

Contents

Prologue i
Chapter One 1
Chapter Two 7
Chapter Three 15
Chapter Four 18
Chapter Five 26
Chapter Six 30
Chapter Seven 34
Chapter Eight 36
Chapter Nine 41
Chapter Ten 44
Chapter Eleven 53
Chapter Twelve 62
Chapter Thirteen 63
Chapter Fourteen 66
Chapter Fifteen 72
Chapter Sixteen 80
Chapter Seventeen 86
Chapter Eighteen 92
Chapter Nineteen 97
Chapter Twenty 106
Chapter Twenty-One 108
Chapter Twenty-Two 118
Chapter Twenty-Three 123
Chapter Twenty-Four 127
Chapter Twenty-Five 129

Chapter Twenty-Six	130
Chapter Twenty-Seven	131
Chapter Twenty-Eight	134
Chapter Twenty-Nine	139
Chapter Thirty	141
Chapter Thirty-One	149
Chapter Thirty-Two	156
Chapter Thirty-Three	158
Chapter Thirty-Four	163
Chapter Thirty-Five	166
Chapter Thirty-Six	169
Chapter Thirty-Seven	175
Chapter Thirty-Eight	183
Epilogue	190
Acknowledgements	193
When the Sun Goes Down Playlist	195
About the Author	197

Eight Years Prior

"We the jury, find the defendant, Robert Allen Green, *not guilty* in the sole count of the crime of murder in the first degree."

The words *not guilty* echo throughout the courtroom like a shot in the night. Everyone is stunned to silence, including the man on trial and his team of attorneys. The young, teen-aged girl sitting in the front row jumps up, tears streaming wildly down her face as she screams, "I saw him do it! I watched him kill my mom with my own eyes! How can this happen? What is wrong with you people?"

The judge bangs his gavel and calls for order in the court, while the adults surround the girl, pick her up, and carry her out of the courtroom. Right before they get her through the door, she turns over her shoulder and calls out in a choked sob. "*You* will pay for this! I will get revenge!"

Chapter One

Trina

(Mysterious Ways — U2)

"Miss Foster! Miss Foster! Is today puh-cussion day?"

"Miss Foster, can I play the bongo drums?"

"No, I want to play the bongos, Josie! Girls play the triangle!"

"Paul, you should play the bells, 'cause you're a ding dong."

Chuckling to myself at the last comment, I attempt to get the class under control. "Okay, boys and girls, everyone take a seat on a colored circle and calm down. There will be plenty of opportunities for each of you to play all of the instruments today." I don't scold Josie for calling him a ding dong, even though I should; I have a hard time reprimanding students who speak the truth. Thankfully, all of the children listen and do as they're told, without even an argument about who sits on which color.

I look around at their eager seven-year-old faces and my heart is filled with warmth. I love my job. The innocence of childhood is one of the few things that still brings joy to my life. Music is another… if only I could spend all of my days, here in the classroom, surrounded by these two untarnished things in my life. Unfortunately, that's not the case, but I make sure to soak up every moment while I'm here. Turning my attention to the ten or so instruments I've set out for today's lesson, I begin the hour long class.

Three classes later — all of which are second graders today — it's time for lunch. I make my way down the hall to the teacher's lounge and grab my food out of the refrigerator. My leftovers from the night before are almost finished heating up, when I hear an all too familiar voice screech behind me.

"Trina Foster! There you are, woman!" Her arms slip around my waist as she hugs my back, and I flinch just a bit.

"Hiya, Lauren. How's your morning?" I ask, pulling my chicken and rice out of the microwave. I turn around to face her cute little freckled face and can tell by her expression that it hasn't been a good one. "Uh oh, what's wrong?"

She motions for me to follow her to one of the sofas. We both plop down after I set my food on the table nearest to me. "First, tell me about your spring break. Did you do anything fun? Go on any hot dates?" she asks hopefully.

I shake my head and laugh. "Boring, no, and no. Okay, your turn. What or who has got you all upset today?"

"Oh, just a bunch of shit. I found out that prick Jason is dating like four other girls, my rent is increasing a couple hundred dollars when my lease is up in the summer, I'm so pathetic I spent the majority of the week off at my parents' house, and my kids are refusing to listen today." She flashes a big, cheesy, fake smile at me. "So not much, really."

I push my glasses up on my nose a bit and tilt my head at her. "Screw Jason, find a new place to live, be thankful you have parents to visit, and they're kids; be patient. It's the first day back after vacation." Smiling sweetly at her, I take a bite of my lunch.

"Well, don't you have all the answers? I think I'll just call you Alex Trebek," she teases, then takes a long slurp from her diet shake thing that she always drinks for lunch.

"No, no. I don't look like an Alex at all. I could never pull that off — my boobs prevent me from being a boy-Alex and I'm not nearly exotic enough to be a girl-Alex," I reply deadpan.

We both burst out laughing to the point I think she's going to choke on her drink. Everyone in the room looks at us like we are crazy, and I immediately get quiet. I hate to bring attention to myself here at work. I don't need anyone passing judgment on me or assuming they know anything about me. I'd prefer they not think about me at all.

"Shh, Lauren, people are staring," I urge her to stop making a scene.

"Oh, who cares, Trina?" she asks waving her hand in the air. "They're all a bunch of old fogeys. We really need to get you to loosen up some."

I simply shake my head and gather up my containers, leaving her sitting on the couch to go throw my trash away. We've had this conversation way too many times, and I really don't want to do it again today.

"You are nearly twenty three years old. You need a life outside your job. It's not healthy," she hisses into my ear a few seconds later. "Come out with me tonight or one day this week... just one drink and we will be home early."

Groaning, I turn around and stare at her, my face expressionless. "I appreciate your concern for my health, but my primary care physician, gynecologist, and psychologist all seem to think that I'm just fine. I like my life the way it is — easy and drama-free. Now, if you'll excuse me, I have a classroom of budding musicians waiting for me."

I walk past her, leaving her standing there, mouth wide open. I don't want to be rude to one of my only friends, I don't like to hurt people's feelings, but I don't know any other way to get her off my back about my social life. No one understands.

As I grab the door knob to exit the lounge, she calls out, "I'm not giving up, Trina! I will break you eventually!" I pause for a moment, closing my eyes and shaking my head. I contemplate turning around and saying something back, but I'm sure we have an audience at this point. Instead, I turn the knob and push the door open... right into someone's face.

"Crap! That hurt!" I hear a male voice say seconds after I feel the door make contact.

"Oh my goodness! I'm so sorry!" I squeak as I move to see my victim.

Standing there — holding his nose as blood streams out like he just climbed out of an MMA octagon — is a guy around my age, that I've never seen before, dressed in khakis and a white polo.

"You're bleeding! Oh, I feel awful! I'm so sorry; I didn't know you were standing there," I squeak out an apology, unsure of what to do.

He laughs softly and I bring my eyes to meet his. They are the most unusual eyes I have ever seen — one is sky blue, while the other is a light brown. In any other circumstances, I would comment on the uniqueness of it, but right now I'm too flustered.

When he speaks to me, I look away, realizing that I've been staring. "I should hope not, or I'd be really offended."

"Excuse me?" I ask.

"I hope you didn't know I was standing there and hit me on purpose," he explains. "Then, I may think you don't like me."

I blush and continue to keep my gaze far from his. "I don't know if I like you or not; I don't know you. I've never seen you around here before."

"That would be because today is my first day here. I'm taking over for Ms. Jordan who's on maternity leave for the rest of the year. Ya know, I would love to continue this conversation at a different time when I could actually shake your hand and not be covering my face, but I should probably clean up and get some ice on this," he says, his voice softening a bit.

I nod my head. "I'm sorry again about your nose and your shirt. If you bring it to me I can get those stains out for you."

He looks down at the blood stains on his shoulder and chest, and instead of getting angry or frustrated, he laughs. "Okay, Miss; I'm sorry I didn't get your name."

"Miss Foster," I reply quickly, still looking down at the ground. "And I really should go, my kids will be waiting."

"Yes ma'am, Miss Foster. I'll take you up on that offer." I nod again and raise my head up to his chest level, so it doesn't appear that I'm completely rude. "My name is Lucca, or Mr. Ellis, if we're sticking with last names. And despite the circumstances, it was a pleasure to meet you." I hear the playful tone in his voice; he knows I'm embarrassed, but he's trying not to make me feel more uncomfortable.

Spinning on my heel, I hurry back to my classroom and try desperately to forget about the lunch encounter over the remainder of the afternoon classes. The kids make it easy to get lost in their excitement over beating on some drums and making as much noise as possible. It's not often they get to do this without getting yelled at about it. When the final bell rings a little after three o'clock, I say goodbye to my last class of the day and begin to clean up the room. Being Monday, it's hot yoga day, and I'm really looking forward to a session of sweaty planks, downward dogs, and cobras.

I'm bent over putting away the last of the drums when I hear someone clear their throat at the door. I sigh aloud, assuming that it's Lauren, and without turning around, I say, "I'm not going out with you tonight or any other night. It's just not happening. Ever."

"Our initial introduction wasn't ideal, I agree, but I think you're being rather harsh," that same throaty voice that had danced in my ears earlier in the day retorts.

Snapping upright and turning around sharply, my entire face enflames. "Oh my goodness, Lucca, or uh Mr. Ellis, I'm so sorry... again." I shake my head, hardly believing what an idiot I can be. "I thought you were someone else. I didn't mean to be so rude. I wouldn't say that... I mean, it's not that I *do* want to... I mean, I didn't..." I just stop talking since nothing is coming out right.

He continues to stand in the doorway, grinning like a fool, obviously enjoying the fact that I'm rattled. "You were saying?" he asks.

Now that he's not covering his face, I can't help but to notice how handsome he is... even with the bandage on his nose and the beginnings of a black eye. His hair is as dark as mine is light and he's got that style where it's sticking up every which way, like he just rolled out of bed, yet it still looks perfect. He's got the kind of smile that makes most girls go weak in the knees. Thank God, I'm not most girls. I mentally pull myself together to find my voice and my inner calm.

"I apologize for those remarks; I honestly thought you were someone else. And again, I'm sorry for the collision earlier," I say softly. "I'm usually not so rude as to give someone a black eye and verbally accost them within the first day of meeting. Now, what is it that brings you by this afternoon?"

He leisurely walks over to where I stand, smirking the entire way. I don't like the way he makes me feel, and I really don't like the way he's looking at me right now. "Well, Miss Foster, if I remember correctly, you offered to take care of my shirt for me." He pauses and pulls the shirt over his head, leaving him standing in just his pants less than three feet from me. Instinctively, my eyes are drawn to his tight chest and abs like fingers to a cello; his torso is perfect instrumentally. I force myself to pull my stare up to his face, to those exquisite eyes. He's still got that shit-eating grin on his face, and he knows exactly what he's doing. He holds the shirt out to me and I snatch it from his hands.

"I'll return it to you soon," I force out in my sweetest possible voice and then turn away to walk towards my desk. I don't want to give him the satisfaction of knowing that he's getting to me. I hear his footsteps walking towards the door, but before he leaves, he calls out, "Yes ma'am, Miss Foster, I'll see you tomorrow."

My entire body flinches at his words.

Chapter Two

Kat

(The Only Time — Nine Inch Nails)

Drying off after my nightly bubble bath, I lather up my freshly shaved, now extremely smooth skin in my favorite Kanebo Sensai body cream. My skin feels like pure silk and smells like a whiff of heaven after I apply it from head to toe. There truly is no other lotion or cream on the market that is even close to this stuff. I'm not sure what it is about it, but something in the plants and extracts that they use, make it worth every dollar I spend on it — all four hundred of them.

I slide into my black, silk robe, not even bothering with the tie that dangles around my waist, and make my way to the kitchen. I grab the open bottle of 2011 Chevalier-Montrachet out of the wine chiller and pour myself a healthy glass. After the first sip of the expressive chardonnay, my taste buds come to life and I moan aloud in delight. The hint of spicy floral mixed with a zest of lemon is an impeccable combination, and much like my lotion, is irreplaceable in my nightly ritual.

Leisurely making my way back to my bedroom with my vino, I saunter into my closet to decide what I'm going to wear tonight. Typically, I wear all black on Monday's, but after the day I've had, I'm feeling a little like breaking the rules tonight — even if they are my own rules. Shaking my head and laughing softly at myself, I grab my new sapphire-blue fitted dress off of its hanger with a pair of silver stilettos and throw them on my oversized bed.

I head back into the bathroom and climb up on the marble countertop, yelping as my bare ass hits the cold surface. I have to sit up here to put my make up on; it's like it doesn't apply correctly if I don't. It's similar to when I have to fix my hair standing in front of the left sink instead of the right. There's a certain way and order that everything needs to be done in, otherwise my inner balance gets thrown off and I spin a little out of control, and nobody wants that to happen.

Smiling at myself in the mirror, I begin to apply the dark charcoal eyeliner that frames my crystal blue eyes, then I follow it up with several thick coats of mascara. I'm blessed that I have naturally long lashes and don't have to go through the trouble of falsies; unfortunately, they are just very pale, like everything else on me. After a little blush and all over shimmery powder, I overlay my naturally ruby lips with a thin coat of cherry lip gloss and blow myself a kiss in the mirror. Seriously, who could resist this face?

I hop off of the counter and move over to the hair station, bringing my now half-finished glass of wine with me. I release my long flaxen blonde hair from the clip that's been holding it on top of my head, allowing it to cascade down my back. Thirty minutes with the straightener and I'm good to go. I stare at my reflection one last time before turning to get dressed. Perfect ~ just enough make up to accent my eyes and lips and my hair looks better than Duchess Catherine's. I have mastered the concept of sexy without slutty. People have always told me that I have the face of a porcelain doll, and truly, I must agree. Unfortunately for them, I share the same emotional capacity as one of those dolls in my bitter, frozen heart.

I take off the robe, hang it in its designated spot on the back of the bathroom door, and then prance naked over to my wardrobe to choose my lingerie for the evening. This is probably my favorite part of the entire getting ready process. A woman's undergarments truly say so much about her mood and intentions. For example, a woman in a white cotton bra and panties probably isn't thinking about getting fucked, and even if she is, she doesn't care much about impressing her partner. Whereas a lady in sheer black lace is at least hoping that someone will get a peek at her without clothes on. The fabric and color of my intimate apparel most definitely affects my attitude and disposition; plus, it's the basis on which an entire outfit is built around.

When The Sun Goes Down

Seeing that I'm completely going against my better judgment and wearing blue and silver tonight, I opt for my grey metallic demi cup bra with the matching thong. Sitting on my bed, I carefully slide my iridescent thigh highs up my perfectly toned legs and hook them to the grey garters. Stockings and garters are a must for me anytime I leave home after sunset. This is one rule that *can't* be broken. When I slide the sleek, delicate material onto my body and attach it to the clasps that perfectly frame my tight ass and sweet pussy, a switch goes off in my head — a switch that locks away any sliver of goodness left in my soul and turns me into a fierce predator with only one goal in mind ~ to dominate and destroy.

I glance at the clock and see that it's a few minutes past ten, which means that I need to get a move on. I quickly slip into my dress and shoes, then take one last look at myself in the full length mirror. I should feel bad for the men who cross my path tonight. Too bad I don't. I swallow down the last of my drink as I walk towards the front of the apartment. Stopping to rinse out my glass and placing it in the dishwasher, I then grab my clutch off the table and head out the front door.

Emerging from the elevator, I give Andres, the nightly security guard, a quick smile and tip of my head, before escaping into the cool March night. Leo is waiting for me with the SUV, just as he is every night, and I hurry into the backseat of the black Range Rover. He closes the door behind me and hurries around to slide in the driver's seat.

"Where are we headed tonight, Miss Kat?" he asks as we pull away from my building.

"The World Bar Trump Towers. I'm feeling feisty tonight and need some international blood." I reply in a sharp tone. He glances up into the rear view mirror and catches my eye. His expression speaks volumes, but he's smart enough to not say anything.

I raise my eyebrows at him. "Do you notice anything different about me tonight, Leo?"

"You're not wearing black, Miss Kat," he says without even having to think.

"You're always so observant. I really don't pay you enough."

"You pay me more than enough, but thank you for the compliment."

He smiles at me in the mirror, and I allow myself to return the friendly gesture. Being in his presence calms me like no other. He is the only male in my life that I never intentionally want to hurt, but I know that I still do. Daily. Our relationship is unconventional and most definitely unhealthy. He is the closest thing I know to love, yet it's still so fucked up that I'm not even sure that's the correct terminology for it. I know he loves me, and I care about him as much as I can, but that's not saying much.

Before I can spend any more time thinking about Leo, we pull up to the building and he hops out of the car to come open my door. I take his offered hand and slide down off of the black leather seat. As my feet hit the ground, I give him a quick peck on the cheek. "This shouldn't take long," I tell him, and he simply nods knowingly. I stride confidently though the door, and once inside, I scan the room swiftly before making my way to the lit up marble bar. Every person present, both male and female, watches as I make my way across the room. I feel their eyes on me, and instead of making me uncomfortable as it would many people, I feed off the attention.

The bar is quite crowded for a Monday, which pleases me immensely — more of a menu to choose from. I select the open chair in between two men who both appear to be there alone. The one on the left is a little old for my liking, but the one on the right caught my eye immediately. The bartender, dressed in his white tux, scurries to greet me.

"What can I get for you to drink this evening, ma'am?"

"Grey Goose Martini. Dry, dirty, and with a twist, please." He nods his head with a smile and steps away to make my drink.

"There's nothing sexier than a beautiful woman who knows how to order a drink," the older gentleman says to me. I refrain from rolling my eyes and swallow back the words that I want to say. It's time to play the game.

I look over at Grandpa and grin. "How sweet of you to call me beautiful; thank you so much." One good look at his face and I know that even if his age didn't rule him out, his uni-brow would've. Thankfully, the bartender arrives with my drink at the perfect time to end this conversation that's barely started. I thank him and take a sip of the cocktail. Perfection.

"That has to be the poorest attempt at a chat up I've ever heard," a deep voice with a thick British accent murmurs in my right ear.

Smirking, I turn slightly to get a better look at the other guy sitting next to me. I do a quick assessment ~ early thirties, attractive face, full head of medium brown hair, nice teeth, not overweight. Yep, I think I found a winner... or a loser, depending on whose point of view you're considering.

"A chat up, eh?" I ask playfully. I lean in close to his ear and whisper, "Something tells me that a 'chat up' isn't what he is really looking for."

He chuckles and shakes his head, then takes a long drink of the amber liquid in his rocks glass. "Something tells me that you're a smart girl."

I smile my most innocent smile and lock my eyes on his. "I'm fucking brilliant," I say with a serious face. He stares at me for a second, almost as if he can't believe I just dropped the F-bomb, and then bursts out laughing.

"Well bloody hell, aren't you the best thing I've met since I've been here?" I beam back at him. He rearranges his body position slightly so that his knee is gently resting against mine before continuing. "I'm Benjamin, by the way."

"Nice to meet you, Benjamin. I'm Chloe," I lie.

And... game over. I win. The victories aren't always this easy, I actually prefer when they put up a little more of a struggle, but tonight I'll take it. Over the next forty minutes, I entertain him by pretending I care about his important marketing job and his growing up in London while sipping on my drink. I laugh when I'm supposed to, touch his arm and leg here and there, and pretend that I don't notice him staring at my boobs. Finally, he asks if I'm interested in sharing a night cap at his place. After explaining that I'm not the kind of girl that goes to a stranger's place, I suggest a hotel room. As his eyes light up and he adjusts his crotch, thinking that he's sealed the deal, the disgust rolls through my body. They are all the same.

Benjamin pays for both of our drinks and we walk out of the bar, hand in hand. Leo is waiting and ushers us into the vehicle. The surprise is evident on Benjamin's face, but he refrains from saying anything. By the look of his clothing and the Hublot timepiece adorning his left wrist, he's no stranger to luxury, but I'm guessing that he wasn't expecting this from me. Once we are both securely in the back seat and on our way to our destination, I twist in my seat and place my hand high up on his thigh.

"Benjamin, would you be interested in playing a little game?" I ask, my voice dripping with sugary sweetness. He first looks down at my hand and then slowly brings his gaze up to my face.

"Absolutely, my pretty little Chloe," he replies with a shit-eating grin. His words make me want to vomit, but instead, I scoot my hand up a bit on his leg and bite my lip suggestively. He leans into me and lightly kisses my exposed neck. "Whatever you want to do, I'm good with," he murmurs against my sensitive skin.

I reach underneath my seat and pull out a piece of heavy black fabric. Crawling onto his lap and straddling his thighs, I gently brush my lips across his before tying the blindfold around his eyes. I feel him tense a little bit as I take away his sight and the excitement begins to bloom inside of me. Next, I retrieve the metal restraints and cuff his wrists together behind his back.

"You're a kinky little thing, aren't you?" I can hear a trace of fear in his voice but the bulge in his pants that continues to grow tells me that he's eager for what he thinks is about to happen.

"You have no idea, Benjamin," I respond in a husky voice. Seeing him so vulnerable, without the ability to see or move his hands, has my body humming. "You won't forget this night for quite some time." I look over my shoulder to get Leo's attention and twirl my finger in the air, indicating that I just want him to drive around. This isn't going to take long; I'm losing interest in this guy before the fun has even started. Briefly, I question what is wrong with me, hoping I'm not growing soft, but then I look down at my dress and I know… I should've worn black. It's my own fault for breaking the rules.

Turning my attention back to him, I lazily begin to unbutton his dress shirt to expose his chest to me, followed by unfastening his belt and dress pants. I skillfully pull his pants and boxers down over his hips until they are around his ankles. His medium-sized cock is standing at complete attention and I can see his pulse racing in his neck. I climb back on his lap, pulling my dress up around my waist and begin to grind my panty-covered pussy on his bare cock. The neckline of the dress pulls down easily along with my bra, so I pop my boobs out and stick them up to his mouth. He needs no words of encouragement; he quickly draws one of my nipples into his mouth and begins sucking forcefully. I increase the speed and pressure of my movements while he devours my breasts; my pussy's growing more and more wet as I anticipate what's about to happen.

Suddenly, I pull my hardened nipple from his mouth and turn around in his lap. My back now to his chest, I roll my hips around so that his jumping cock is nestled in between my ass cheeks and my clit is firmly pressing down on his tight balls. I reach down and slide two of my fingers into my slick opening, rubbing my juices all over my mound. I know he can smell my excitement, and with the way he's writhing around underneath me, I know that he's dying to touch me. He keeps lifting his hips up to press further into me, but each time he does, I stop moving until he relaxes back into the seat.

I continue the torturous treatment for several minutes, bringing myself closer and closer to my release, but never following through. I lift my hand to my breasts — pinching and pulling on my nipples — making them even harder than they were. I catch Leo watching in the rearview mirror and I smile at him, knowing that he's enjoying the show. Nearing the end of my playtime, I dip my fingers inside my hot core once again and lean back onto Benjamin.

"Taste me," I instruct him as I place my fingers on his mouth. Like a starved animal, he opens his mouth and begins sucking and licking my sweet juices off of my hand.

"Fuck, Chloe, you taste even better than I imagined," he growls. "Please, bury my cock inside of that sweet pussy. I'm dying here." I pull my hand from his greedy mouth and evilly laugh as I climb off of his lap. The SUV comes to a gradual stop in an unpopulated alley.

"Funny choice of words, asshole. Unfortunately, you have no idea what dying really feels like, but you and your blue balls are sure to be uncomfortable while hanging out in the cold." The door opens and Leo grabs him by the arms, pulling him out of the car. He's yelling expletives and thrashing around, but he's pretty helpless without the use of his hands and not being able to see. Before I close the door, I call out to him, "I'm sure you've fucked over a female in your life at some point. Consider this payback."

Moments later, we're speeding away from his pitiful ass and on our way to my Central Park apartment. I continue to play with myself the entire drive back, not caring in the least that Leo watches; he always does.

We pull into my parking spot and he escorts me up the elevator and through the front door. Once inside, he undresses me in my lust-hungry state, and then licks me until I cover his face with my sweet cream. He really does the most amazing things with his mouth — lapping, curling, sucking, and nipping until my body quakes violently with relief. Then he carries me to bed and tucks me in, kissing me on my forehead.

"Goodnight, Leo. Thank you for taking care of me," I mumble sleepily.

"Yes ma'am, Miss Kat. I'll see you tomorrow."

And he disappears.

Chapter Three

Trina
(In the Fade — Queens of the Stone Age)

I arrive at work early Tuesday morning so that I can leave Mr. Ellis' now stain-free Polo on his desk, without having to see or talk to him again. Visions of his bare chest and abs have been dancing through my mind for the better part of the morning and its really starting to irritate me. I'm still mad at myself for not yelling at him for that stunt. How dare he take his clothes off in an elementary school? What if one of the kids would've come back in because they left something? He obviously is an immature, egotistical ass that doesn't care about keeping the job that he just started. Just thinking about it infuriates me.

Slamming the car door without meaning to, I hurry across the blacktop as the sun is just beginning to peek out over the horizon at this early hour. This is not the best of neighborhoods and walking alone outside — especially in the dark — is not recommended and something I rarely do. As soon as I reach the building, I release the breath I'm holding and slip inside the door. I quickly make my way to Ms. Jordan's classroom only to find the door locked. Shit! I didn't think about this. I try using the several school keys that I have, including the one to my own room, but unfortunately, none of them work. Frustrated and even more irritable, I trudge off to the lounge to grab some coffee.

Thankfully, there isn't anyone else in there so I'm not forced to make small talk. I hastily make a quick cup, add my milk and sugar, and head out to my room. I've just about made it to my safe haven, or at least it had been until yesterday, when I hear someone call my name from behind me.

"Miss Foster? Is that you?" I know who that annoying, nasally voice belongs to without even turning around. Groaning internally, I plaster on my fake smile and spin around on my heel.

"Good morning, Principal Matthews. How are you today?" He makes his way towards me, sucking in his gut and puffing out his chest as if it makes a difference in hiding his awful personality.

"It's great to see you here so early. I love when my teachers are so eager to please." It's not just the double meaning of the words he uses, but the disgusting tone behind them as well, that makes me want to hurl all over his shoes.

Before I have a chance to reply, he looks down my body, probably to stare at my boobs, and asks, "Bringing a change of clothes to work?"

Confused, I look down at the shirt draped over my arm. "Oh, no, this is Mr. Ellis'. He needed me to get some stains out of it for him," I explain.

He raises his eyebrows at me and smirks. "Wow, Trina, you work fast... yesterday was just his first day. I knew you were hiding something behind the big glasses, bun, and frumpy clothes you wear every day. Maybe you and I can go out for happy hour one afternoon," he suggests, placing his hand on my shoulder.

I step out from under his touch, keeping the smile on my face even though I really want to throw my hot coffee on him and knee him in the balls. "No sir, you've completely misunderstood; I gave Mr. Ellis a bloody nose yesterday by hitting him in the face with a door. However, you are right, I am hiding something... a team of attorneys that wouldn't think twice about suing you and the school system if you imply anything such as you just did or touch me ever again," I say in my sweetest voice possible.

He sniggers, "You're an elementary school music teacher; you couldn't afford one attorney much less a team. Not to mention, it would be my word against yours. I've been a principal for over fifteen years and never had a single complaint; you're a second year teacher with no family or friends." My eyes widen at his statement. *How the hell does he know anything about my personal life?* "You look surprised. I've done my research, Miss

Foster, and I know more than you think. You should tread carefully if you want to keep your job, and meeting me for a drink one afternoon would be a step in the right direction." He reaches up and strokes my cheek before turning around and walking away, whistling *You Are My Sunshine*. I hate him. And I hate that song.

I slink into my room as tears begin to fall down my cheeks. I had a bad feeling about that man when I interviewed for this job, but there weren't many openings available, so I accepted the position and have tried my hardest to just go unnoticed. Most men make my skin crawl, but he... after what just happened, he makes me murderous. I set the shirt and mug down and sit on the edge of my desk. I can't help it, I begin sobbing to the point I'm shaking. It's more than him just coming on to me, I'm petrified about what he's learned about me and my past. I bury my face in my hands as I try to hide the tears and regain my composure when two strong arms wrap themselves around me. Frightened, I peek out over the tops of my fingers into two different colored eyes overflowing with compassion and kindness. *Lucca.*

Chapter Four

Kat
(Destrokk — MGMT)

I can't get in the bath fast enough this evening. I need the jets to power wash away my awful day and the bubbles to carry me to a happier place. It's only Tuesday and it's been one of the worst weeks that I can remember in a long, long time. The icing on the cake was the phone call from my step-mom this afternoon.

"Hello, Viv. What does he want?" I answer the phone, thankful I didn't grow up in the pre-caller ID generation.

"Well, aren't you delightful, as usual," she replies in her snotty voice. "You're father wants to know if you've come to your senses and are going to come visit your little brother."

Sighing loudly in her ear, I tell her the same thing I've told her for the last six months. "Look, I'm sure he's a real cute baby, and nothing against him, but he's not my brother... just like your husband is not my father."

"You're an ungrateful, little spoiled bitch, you know that? I'm not sure why Bobby even tries with you."

"Touché" is my only response before I disconnect the call.

There are so many things I want to say to her. The fact that she's only a couple of years older than me and talks to me like I'm a child is probably what drives me the most crazy about our conversations. She's a gold-digging, power-hungry whore that got all of her prayers answered when *he* got her pregnant. I would tell her that again, but it really does no good, and I've just stopped caring. They are not a part of my life.

Turning on my iTunes before I climb into the oversized tub, I try to push the conversation out of my head as I begin my nightly routine. *Destrokk* by MGMT is the first song that comes on and I quickly find myself lost in the music. Singing at the top of my lungs, "As you're falling down, your blood is all around you now," the dark lyrics lead me to my happy place and I begin thinking about my plans for the night. I'm in the frame of mind to kick my usual activities up a bit. I've been getting a little bored to be quite honest, and with this shitty ass day, I really need something to improve my mood.

After soaking for a while and shaving myself smooth, I step out of the bathtub and into my hot pink robe. Putting lotion on my body is damn near orgasmic; I may be slightly obsessed. It's Tuesday, so its pink day, and I learned last night not to fuck with the days of the week/ color mojo. Tuesday/ pink day is actually one of my favorite days because there are so many shades of pink that I can work with. Light baby pink can come off as sweet and demure, Barbie pink is playful and flirty, and a dark fuchsia tends to be more sensual and luxurious. I haven't quite decided yet which route I'm taking tonight.

From the bathroom to the kitchen, I pour a glass of wine and return to my bedroom to get ready. Along with it being pink night, Tuesday's (as well as Thursday's) are my college dive bar nights. In addition to the well-known NYU and Colombia campuses, there are a ton of other small community schools and specialty colleges in the city, which provide a breeding ground for a bunch of stupid, drunk college boys. It's actually not even fair to most of them since they prove to be the easiest conquests of the week time and time again, but I enjoy giving them a reality check and it does wonders for my ego. Standing in my closet, deciding what to wear, I opt for the innocent school girl look tonight. Not that many guys can resist my charm, or my angelic face and devilish body for that matter, but wearing a short pleated skirt with knee socks is like cashing in a lottery ticket.

The wine goes down easily as I finish my first glass while putting on my makeup. I hurry to the kitchen for a quick refill because I can't get ready without having something to drink. Again, it messes with the cosmso. Back in the bathroom, I blow dry and straighten my hair, then French Braid a section of my blonde locks into a headband across the front of my head. Pleased with the way it looks after just the first try, I hang my robe up and skip into my bedroom naked.

Deciding on my bubblegum pink satin bra and crotchless panty set that has silver sparkles sprinkled across the fabric, I slip them on. Pink and black argyle socks that come to right over the knee are next. This is one of the few exceptions when I don't wear a garter belt, but the naughtiness of the panties makes up for it. I admire myself in front of the full length mirror since it really is a shame I have to wear clothes over this look. Not to worry, I won't have them on long. I swallow the last drops of wine in my glass before sliding the black skirt up over my hips and the pink cashmere sweater over my head, careful not to mess up my hair. I finish the look with my black, low-top Chucks and head out the door.

Andres sits in his usual spot behind the security desk, watching the surveillance cameras and playing on his iPad. "Have a good night, Miss Kat. Be safe; there's a bunch of crazies out there," he says jokingly.

I smile politely and even laugh softly at his joke; however, I'm laughing because I know that I *am* one of the crazies. I'm the girl mom's warn their babies about, the wolf in sheep's clothing, the one with a black heart. Of course I don't tell him this. To be quite honest, I have no clue what he, or any of the other building staff, thinks about me. I'm always courteous and respectful to them, but never go out of my way to be overly friendly or chatty. Privacy is a huge deal to me, and one of the main reasons I live here, other than the fact it's a super posh, luxury apartment located directly next to Central Park, is that the security and anonymity that they offer. I know at least two of the city's superstar athletes call the building home, and I've heard rumors that several actors and actresses have places here too. It's not that paparazzi are hounding me, or even know who I am for that matter, but that's the way I want it to stay.

Leo waits for me with the car door open. The small smile that tugs at the corner of his mouth when he sees me doesn't go unnoticed, but I treat him with the cool, aloof demeanor that I always do. After he slides into the driver's seat, I greet him. "Evening, Leo. I hope your day was better than mine."

"Evening, Miss Kat," he replies with a concerned tone in his voice. "What happened today that was so bad? And where are we headed tonight?"

"I woke up to begin with, that's usually enough to piss me off," I say half-jokingly. "But it was when *the bitch* called this afternoon asking me to come over and visit, that the day really took a nose dive. Oh, and The Edge on East 3rd in between 1st and 2nd. I feel like corrupting some young boys tonight." I look out the window not wanting to see his reaction to my statement. I'm not sure how Leo feels about my sperm donor, his child-bride, or their newest addition; I fucking hate all of them — well, except the baby — but just give them time to warp his mind and I'm sure I'll add him to the list at some point.

The city flies by through the car window — the thousands of people out on the streets, the bright lights illuminating the night's sky, and the sounds of car horns and shouting voices. I don't think I could ever live anywhere else, even if it would mean escaping my past. New York City and all of its chaos and madness is what keeps me sane. I can easily hide in the millions of people, all of them caught up in their own lives; I just pass by as another pretty face on the street, except for the unfortunate few that take a chance on me at night. Laughing softly, I feel no remorse. They all deserve it, and night after night, person after person, I grow more confident in my abilities to seduce. Soon I will begin to tear apart *his* empire, piece by fucking piece, and I will have my revenge.

The Range Rover pulls up outside the bar, and Leo hops out before I can stop him. Several young people are outside smoking under the awning, and the fact that I have a driver that opens my door makes them take notice. I simply smile as I walk past them and through the glass double doors. The place is a dive; there's no other way to describe it. It's rather dark and dingy, with numerous pool tables and dart boards scattered about. The bar itself is just a wooden slab, with a good selection of beers on tap. Overall, it looks like the stereotypical college bar hang-out, which is just what I was hoping for.

As I walk to the bar to grab a beer, I feel the entire population of the place turn to stare at me, similar to the effect I have most times I enter a room. Older crowds usually do it in a more discreet way whereas college aged kids are much more open at their gawking. In addition to feeling their eyes burning a hole in me, I hear the whispers and murmurs. The girls call me a whore, a rich bitch, and a slut out of jealousy and immaturity; the guys talk about "tapping that" or bending me over a pool table, only hoping they could be so lucky. Their words don't upset or anger me because I stopped having fucks to give about nine years ago; instead, they fuel my fire, and to be quite honest, it turns me on a bit.

The bartender greets me and I order a draft pear cider. After he hands me the chilled pilsner glass, I turn around to assess the prospects tonight. A good sized crowd surrounds one of the pool tables, watching two guys who are either really good, extremely competitive, or both. I can't get a good look at them because of the pack around them. People continue to gaze over at me, but when I lock eyes, they look away. Their lack of confidence boosts mine and I love to feel in control of the situation. I continue to scan the room, noting a few guys that catch my eyes, but no one that really jumps out at me.

Loud cheers from the pool match draw my attention back to that side of the room. Apparently it's over, because all I can see is money being exchanged all over the place. Moments later, two guys emerge from the mob, talking and laughing as they walk towards the bar. They actually look pretty similar; both have short brown hair, are well-built, and are dressed in fitted t-shirts and jeans with visible tattoos covering their arms. They both look me up and down as they step up to order their drinks and give me a smirk. They carry themselves as if they are something pretty special, at least they think so. The fire inside of me is lit. The game is on.

An hour later, I send Leo a text that I'm ready to be picked up. The game ended up being child's play; the boys unable to think with more than their cock. After they invited me over to their table to "teach" me how to shoot pool, I let them think I had no idea what I was doing, so that they could lean me over and press their bodies against mine while I held their "sticks." It really took everything inside of me not to roll my eyes on numerous occasions, but the death stares that I was getting from all of the females in the bar made it worth playing along. A few minutes later, I exit the bar with not one, but both of the guys. I usher them into the backseat of the SUV and then crawl over one to sit in between them.

Leo gets behind the wheel and asks, "Where to this evening, Miss?"

"To the Hyatt at Union Square, and make it quick," I snap at him. He simply nods and pulls away from the curb.

The guys on either side of me — which I honestly can't even remember their names at the moment except that they both start with a J — are breathing heavily and I can see their erections bulging in their pants. Neither of them has said a word nor even attempted to touch me since we've walked out of The Edge; just with the appearance that I have money and authority, I've taken control of the situation. They sit silently, waiting for my instructions.

As we make our way to the hotel, I put one of my hands in each of their laps, unzipping their jeans and reaching inside to free their cocks. Both of them let out a series of moans and hisses as I grab their shafts and begin to slowly move my hands up and down. They refuse to look at each other's cock even though they are less than eighteen inches from one another, which gives me a great idea for the night. The guy on the right, who I decide to call J1, finally gets the nerve up to place his hand high up on my thigh just before we reach our destination.

I release them as we pull up in the valet drive. "Make yourselves presentable until we get in the room," I instruct. They quickly tuck themselves back in their pants and zip up. I grab my fun bag from under the seat as we exit the car. I lead them through the lobby without stopping at the front desk, straight into the elevator and to the suite that I keep a key to. *What can I say? Money is powerful.*

Ushering the guys into the room, I waste no time to get to business. "Strip and get on the bed," I order them as I place the bag and my purse on the table and slip off my shoes.

One of the J's decides he's going to test my authority. "Why do you get to make all the rules?"

Without turning around, I pull my sweater over my head and unzip my skirt, allowing it to pool at my feet. I bend over to slightly to step out of my skirt and give them a nice view of my exposed, bald pussy before standing back upright. My back still turned to them, I say calmly, "If you want a piece of this sweet ass, you will strip, get on the bed, and not question me again. If you aren't interested, you can leave now; my driver is waiting outside the door and can take you back to the bar. The choice is yours." I hear the swishing of fabric followed by the slight creaking of the mattress. Game over... I win again.

I see the fear in their eyes when I finally turn around with blindfolds and cuffs in my hands. I smile innocently as I stroll over to them. Setting the toys down on the white comforter, I climb up on the bed and begin a quick dance for them. It's amazing what a guy will let me do to him as I'm rubbing my more-than-a-handful boobs in his face and my swollen cunt on his throbbing cock. Five minutes later, they are both properly restrained to the headboard, and their eyes are covered with heavy black sashes. I hop off the bed to let Leo into the room. Tonight I need him for more than just watching, I need a photographer. Even I have to admit as I walk back into the room that the two guys are pretty nice specimens of the male species, physically speaking. *Too bad all I care about is fucking with their world.*

I grab each of their phones out of the pockets of their jeans and toss them to Leo with a wink. I rejoin them on the bed and pick up where I left off in the car. I play with their cocks for a bit, getting them nice and excited. After a little bit of dirty talk, I tell them that there's a contest on who can eat my pussy the best. I take turns sitting on each of their faces, and surprisingly, they are both pretty good. They struck me as guys that didn't care much about getting their girl off, ones that thought most things revolved around them. To reward them both, I lick up and down their shafts at a tantalizing slow pace. I think they are both close to exploding and now it's time for *my* fun. I scoot off the bed and grab the key to the handcuffs. I undo the one hand that's closest to the other.

"I want to see you jack off for me," I tell them. Without additional prodding, they both grab their own erections and begin going to town. "No! Stop! I want you to jack each other off."

Immediately, they scoff at the idea and begin to tell me no. I dip my fingers inside of my wet, juicy slit then smear my sweet juices across their lips. "If you want to know what this tight little cunt feels like wrapped around your cock, you will jack each other off for me. Now." Hesitantly, J1 reaches his hand out towards his friend. Beaming with my conquest, I help guide his hand until he's got a hold of his buddy's rock-hard shaft. J2 flinches a bit at the initial contact but it takes less than thirty seconds before he begins to relax and enjoy the sensation. I grab his free hand and move it over to J1's cock, and minutes later, they are both lost in the lustful ministrations.

The entire scene playing out in front of me is turning me on more than I thought it would. Before I get too caught up in it, I gingerly move off the bed and Leo gets straight to work, quietly snapping photos and shooting videos while I get dressed. It doesn't take long before they are moaning and groaning as they explode on each other's hands.

I take the phones from Leo, text the photos and videos to everyone listed in their favorite contacts, and we leave them nude and cuffed to the bed. Making my way back downstairs, I nod at the woman behind the front desk as we walk out, giving her the signal that someone needs to go free them in about ten minutes. I'm even nice enough to pay for a taxi back to their cars.

Leo drives me home and neither of us says a word the entire trip. After parking the car, he walks me up to my apartment where his tongue and hands fuck me until I come all over his face. Then he carries me to bed and tucks me in, kissing me on my forehead.

"Goodnight, Leo. Thank you for taking care of me," I mumble sleepily.

"Yes ma'am, Miss Kat. I'll see you tomorrow."

And he disappears.

Chapter Five

Trina
(My Same — Adele)

Finally, it's Friday; I don't think I could take another day of this week. I've managed to hide from Principal Matthews since our encounter on Tuesday, but Lucca has been a different story. It's like he's everywhere that I am, even when I'm where I'm not supposed to be. After witnessing my breakdown Tues, the aftermath of the principal's inappropriate advances, he tried to get me to tell him what was wrong. Now, I think he's made it his purpose in life to either get me to open up about my issues, or to drive me crazy in the process; too bad for him that the first isn't ever going to happen, and the latter already did — he's late to that party.

 Lauren hasn't been much better either. She refuses to stop hounding me about my social life, or lack thereof, and now she's curious about why Lucca is following me around. If I didn't absolutely adore the kids in my class, I'd walk out of this place in a heartbeat, but I can't do that. I'm completely and utterly attached to the bright smiling faces that I'm greeted with every morning and afternoon. Most of these kids have parents that work two or more jobs and aren't home to spend much time with them, or they have parents that are lazy, selfish pieces of shit that shouldn't have had children in the first place. Being able to give these little ones some much needed time and attention makes me feel incredible. Add in the fact that I'm spreading the love of music to them, and it's a position I can't walk away from, which leads me back to my original problem of dealing with the other aspects of the job... one of which just walked through my classroom door.

"Trina, this is the third day this week that you've eaten lunch in your classroom." Lauren's high-pitched voice pulls me from my salad. "If I didn't know better, I'd think you've been trying to hide from me."

Looking up at her pouty face as she crosses the room, I give her a soft smile. I really do like her, despite the fact she can be a bit overbearing and dramatic. She's the only friend I have really, even if our friendship is kept to weekdays between the hours of eight and three. "It's not *you* that I'm hiding from. You know how I feel about the whole teacher community thing — just because they work in a school, doesn't mean they have to act like they're still in school."

Her face eases a bit as she pulls up a chair to my desk and grabs her nasty shake out of her cooler. She ignores my comments about the other teachers because she knows I don't want to talk about the issue at hand. Regardless of my aversion to the teacher lounge gossip, I've never made a habit of eating my lunch in my class. "So when are you going to tell me why the hot new teacher follows you around like a lost puppy?" I love how she gets right to the point. No one can ever accuse her of pussy-footing around a topic.

Sighing, I reply quietly, "He doesn't follow me around like a lost puppy."

She screeches in delight at my response. "So you do at least acknowledge that he's hot?"

"I'm an introvert, not blind."

"Well, you must be if you haven't noticed him everywhere that you are."

I don't say anything. I know she's right, but I really don't want to discuss this with her. She takes my silence as an invitation to keep talking. "The weird thing is I never see him talking to you. It's almost as if he's just watching over you. It's got a protective feel to it, which is just weird considering he doesn't know you." She stares into my eyes. "He doesn't know you, right?"

"Lauren, I met him for the first time in my life on Monday when I slammed a door in his face, so I doubt he's trying to protect me. If anything he's probably keeping his eye on me to stay out of my way so I don't give him another black eye," I retort. "Now can we please talk about something else?" I shake my head and take a long drink of water; this entire conversation is making me uncomfortable.

She ignores my last sentence completely as she's now pretty much talking aloud to herself. "What if he's one of those guys that likes to be dominated? Ya know, like a submissive pain slut?"

Water comes spewing out of my mouth at her words; I can't believe she just said that. "Oh my God... are you crazy? You really need to stop reading those damn books, and I am officially putting an end to this conversation." I look at her with sincerity. "I know you desperately want me to have a life that includes drinking, males, and fun times, but please accept it; that's just not me."

She smiles and nods like she's got it all worked out. Standing up to head back to her own room, "You're a lesbian; I knew it. It's okay, though, I still love you the same... well, not the same like that." She hugs me before turning to walk out of the room. "This changes nothing, Trina. Now we just need to find you a sexy woman."

I shake my head and turn around to put up my lunch container in my tote bag as she prances out into the hall. *What am I going to do with her?*

"A sexy woman, eh?" I close my eyes as that deep, male voice that has been playing in my mind for the last four days calls out to me from the doorway.

I pivot on my heel to see Lucca leaning against my door frame with a smirk spread across his face. He's wearing dark jeans and a plaid button down shirt with the sleeves loosely rolled up to just below his elbow. He causes the strangest feeling inside of me when he looks at me; I hate it and like it all at the same time. I really don't have time for this distraction in my life.

"I have no idea what she's talking about," I say, acting aloof. "She's desperately trying to make my life exciting, and unfortunately, that's just not happening."

He wanders into the room, my body temperature rising with each step that he takes closer to me. "So if you don't like sexy women, then men are your thing?"

Rolling my eyes, I sigh overdramatically. "*People* aren't my thing. I'm fine by myself, thank you." I move around him to rearrange the instruments that really don't need rit.

"I don't buy that, Miss Foster. Everybody wants to feel wanted." His eyes follow me around the room, the heat from his stare causing my entire body to flame.

Standing upright, I turn to face him as his words slice to my core. "I know what it's like to feel wanted, Mr. Ellis, and believe me, that's *not* what I want. Feeling wanted and being loved are two completely different things." I stop before I say anything else to reveal information that I don't want anyone else to know, especially the guy that enlivens things inside of me I didn't even know existed. "My students will be back from lunch soon, so please excuse me as I set up."

"You'll never know what being loved feels like if you don't allow anyone to get close to you, Miss Foster." Running his fingers through his messy hair, he walks out of the room. "I'll see you around." His voice is calm and collected, and the words he speaks are true. I'm just not ready for anyone to be close to me. I know if I let someone in, they'd run away scared once they found out who I really am, and my heart would break all over again. I just can't.

Chapter Six

Kat

(Ain't No Sunshine ~ Bill Withers)

I have a love/ hate relationship with the weekends. Like most of working America, I take the weekends off, which for me means that I don't go out on the prowl on Friday and Saturday nights. Instead I enjoy some down time for watching movies, listening to music, and reading books, it also gives me time to think. Typically, when I start thinking, no matter how hard I try not to, I end up recalling a lot of old memories; and my memories, unfortunately, send me into a deep, dark place of malevolence, spite, and vengeance.

Tonight, however, I'm prepared for the bitterness and hostility that I'm going to dredge up, because I'm developing my plan of attack. The past week has tested me in more ways than one, making me second guess my end goals and resolve. I've been working towards this for almost two years now, and I finally feel comfortable enough with myself to move on. Now is the time, before anything or any*one* gets in my way, myself included.

I thought about inviting Leo over for dinner and asking him for strategic advice, but I don't want to infringe on his time off, nor am I sure that I want him to know exactly what I'm planning to do. He knows my issues; he knows more about me than anyone else in the world, especially considering he's been my personal attendant-driver-babysitter-lover since I was thirteen and has known me since I was an infant. Well, he didn't become my lover until I was seventeen, and that was only because I basically forced him to.

The party had turned out to be lame as shit with her parents there watching our every move, and I was ready to go. I called Leo to let him know I was ready to be picked up, and as usual, he was there within five minutes. I wasn't sure if he was always lurking just around the corner from where he dropped me off, but I appreciated his promptness and attentiveness. He pulled up in the silver convertible Mercedes SLK 55 AMG that the sperm donor had given me for my sixteenth birthday. I'm sure driving my car around was one of the perks of the job, not to mention he and his mom, Rosa — who had been my family's housekeeper since I was born — lived in our guest house which was bigger than what ninety five percent of people in the New Jersey area resided in.

"Early night, Katie-bug?" he asked as I slid in the front seat next to him.

Rolling my eyes at the ridiculous nickname he had given me as a child, I groaned. "Yes, Yvette's parents were there and thought we needed chaperones, I guess. And would you please not call me that anymore? I'm going to college in two months, not kindergarten."

He laughed and pulled out of the driveway into the sultry night. "No problem, princess. Where to now? We headed home?"

His smug attitude and shitty "princess" comment coupled with the disappointment of the failed party aroused the darkness that had lurked inside of me for a few years — ever since I had basically become an orphan.

I looked over at him with a mischievous glint in my eye. His good looks were not lost on me — his naturally tanned skin and big brown eyes affected me like no other guy I had ever met; all of my friends had crushed on and flirted with him since we realized boys didn't have cooties, but I had always refrained... he was just my Leo. They were all green with envy that he catered to my every need, always with a smile on his face, as if I was his precious little sister. Truth be told, he would probably prefer to be out with people his own age, but in addition to being paid an obscene amount of money, I think that he felt sorry for me and the entire circumstances known as my life. I decided that night that I didn't want his pity; I just wanted him.

I wanted to prove to him that even if he was eight years older than me, I controlled our relationship.

"Yes, I think I'm ready to go home. I'm not feeling so well anyhow," I said with a pouty look on my face. "And I'd prefer if you'd call me Miss Kat."

The drive home was pretty quick without the daytime traffic that usually clogged the expressway. As he pulled the car into the garage, I turned to him with water eyes. "Leo, can you come in with me? I hate being all alone in that big house. I'd love if you stayed with me until I fell asleep. Unless you have plans to go out with your girlfriend or something..." My voice trailed off as I climbed out of the passenger seat.

He didn't respond, but instead just followed me into the main house as opposed to crossing the backyard to his home. I stopped to grab us a couple of sodas before heading upstairs to my suite. I set the drinks on the nightstand and tossed the TV remote at him. "Here, watch whatever you want while I take a shower, and why didn't you answer me?"

He took his shoes off and plopped down on my bed as he turned the television on. Leo hanging out in my room was nothing new for us; he had probably spent more time in here with me growing up than he did in his own room. "You know I don't have a girlfriend, Miss Kat," he replied.

"Then why don't you stay here with me anymore?" I whined.

"You always have company over. It's like a co-ed slumber party here every other night. It's not like you need me watching over you and your friends. I stay in my and Ma's house, and I make sure I'm here if you need me. I understand you're growing up and have a social life, so I just want you to have room to breathe."

"I have people over because I'm lonely! Ever since Momma died, I've lived here by myself. He hasn't been here in over a year and a half! Do you know that he didn't even call me on Christmas or my birthday this past year? Not that I want to ever talk to him again in my life, but you would think he would at least try to be civil to his only child considering he took my mom away from me!"

Again, I got the look of pity from my best friend. Frustrated that I had lost control of both my feelings and the conversation, I pulled my tank top over my head and unzipped my shorts, letting them fall to the floor. Standing in front of him in just my bra and thong, I saw him swallow hard and redirect his eyes to the show on TV. "I'm going to take a shower," I stated authoritatively, "and I don't want to talk about this anymore. You can stay or go to your place... it's whatever. I'm used to being abandoned."

Fifteen minutes later, I exited the bathroom to find Leo in my bed, dressed in just his undershirt and boxers, with a bowl of my favorite kind of ice cream waiting for me. His sweet smile greeted me and told me everything I needed to know. He loved me, even if it was in an unconventional way, and he would always be there for me.

An hour later, I was writhing my tight seventeen- year-old frame underneath him as he worshipped every inch of my body like I had never experienced before or since. He wasn't happy as he slid his rock hard cock inside of my tight slit and it met the resistance of my virgin body — I may have led him to believe that I wasn't one -but by then, we were at the point of no return.

After we cleaned up and I got back in bed, he lay down and held me until I began to drift off. He kissed me on my forehead and I mumbled sleepily, "Goodnight, Leo. Thank you for taking care of me."

"Yes ma'am, Miss Kat. I'll see you tomorrow."

And he disappeared.

Thinking back to that day, I realize that I've been using men for well over five years now. I used Leo back then to feel wanted and loved, much like I use him to this day. I do love him, in the only capacity that I can love, but I will never be his, even though he is always mine. The day my father shot my mother for walking in on him with his whore, I lost the ability to love completely. If Leo can't break through my heart of darkness, I don't think anyone will be able to. And even though I know that nothing I can do will ever bring her back; the time has come for me to get my revenge on the bastard that stole the sunshine from my life.

Chapter Seven

Trina

(Addicted to Love — Skylar Grey)

Every Saturday I spend pretty much the entire day watching movies on Netflix, and today is no different. I wake up early and cook myself a prosciutto and cheese omelet with a side of rosemary potatoes. Cooking is my other love, besides movies and music, but cooking for one can be a bit depressing. I've thought about having Lauren over to cook for her one evening, but I don't want her to know where I live. It would just bring way too many questions along with it — questions that I don't want to answer — not now, not ever.

Sitting down with my yummy breakfast on the oversized leather recliner, I pull up the guide and scroll through the options. An hour and a half into the movie, my belly is nice and full, but I'm wondering what in the world I was thinking when I chose to watch *Her*. Expecting to watch an uplifting love story to brighten my spirits after this mentally-draining week, I instead find myself lost in this poor guy's devastatingly heart-breaking story. Most people would probably be surprised to find out that I actually prefer watching and reading tales of the heart more than any other genres considering my aversion to real-life romantic relationships, but I find comfort and fulfillment in watching the happily-ever-afters that I will never experience.

Once the movie is over, I quickly wash the dishes and grab a fresh cup of coffee before beginning the next flick. Eager to remove the awful emptiness and sadness left inside of me, I dive right into another film. *Endless Love* is much more what I am looking for. Boy meets girl... girl is too good for boy... boy and girl fall in love anyways... girl's family gets in the way... well, you know what happens from there. Typically, I would've cried happy tears, made notes of good music from the soundtrack, and been thoroughly pleased with the improbable fairy-tale ending; however, as I watch the movie, I find myself visualizing Lucca as David and me as Jade more than I care to admit. As soon as the credits are rolling, I turn the television off and jump up. I need to get out of the apartment quickly. That boy is doing something to my mind and I don't like it one bit. There's no room in my life for feelings, and there's even less room for Lucca Ellis.

Chapter Eight

Kat
(Sail ~AWOLNATION)

Sunday is upon me before I know it, and I still need to work on the specifics for the evening's plans. After extensive research on Friday night, I'm now well acquainted with all of the members of my sperm donor's political team, as well as his close and personal friends. I've decided that I'm going to start at the bottom and work my way closer to him.

I grab my iPad and type into the search engine: *Robert Allan Green*. In addition to being the recently elected Governor of the state of New York, my sperm donor was also a pro-bowl quarterback for the Giants nearly fifteen years ago, which makes him not only loved and borderline worshipped by most people in this area, but extremely easy to investigate.

As soon as the search results are displayed, pictures of him pop up on my screen. I'm so used to seeing his face on the TV, newspapers, and internet, it hardly affects me any longer. It's not that my loathing of him has decreased any over the last nine years; in fact, every holiday that I spend without my mom, it grows even stronger, but I'm almost numb to looking at him. But when photos of him and my mom — and even ones including me when I was young — are staring at me, recollections from my childhood inundate my memory.

Daddy didn't make it home for dinner for the third night in a row, and even though Momma acted like it was no big deal, the disappointment hung heavy on her face. Even when sad, she was the most beautiful woman I had ever seen. She had the same long, naturally blonde hair that I did, her eyes were bluer than the Caribbean Sea, and her skin was so flawless that it looked as if it had been airbrushed. That night when she had tucked me in to bed, she sang 'You Are My Sunshine' to me just as she had every night since I could remember.

When she finished, I asked her why she always sang the same song, and she answered, "You are the light that keeps me from being afraid of the dark." She smiled brightly as she leaned over and kissed my forehead before leaving me to drift off to dreamland.

I remember thinking how silly her answer was — I was the little kid that was a scared of the dark, not her. If anything she was my sunshine instead of the other way around.

Tears stream down my cheeks at a steady pace as I pull myself from the bittersweet memory. Tragically, the darkness destroyed her despite me being right next to her side. Now, I must focus on avenging her death.

When I sifted through his current staff a couple of nights ago, I found a guy named Daniel Saunders who is his current head of communications. After a little further research, I found that he recently married Claudia Roberson, the daughter of the mayor, who also just so happens to be one of Robert's best friends. Daniel seems to be trying to work his way up the political ladder and is the perfect target for me to kill two birds with one stone. It really couldn't be any more perfect.

I pick up my phone and call my friend, Travis, hoping he has the information I requested.

"Hey, gorgeous. What's up?" he groggily answers the phone.

"Hi, Trav. Sorry if I woke you, but it's after noon, so get your ass up," I say playfully.

I hear him grumbling and moving around as he whines, "You know I don't go to bed before six... ever."

"Yeah, yeah... the life of a New York socialite is so hard, I know. You get into any restaurant or club you want without waiting, eat and drink for free, and party with all the beautiful people. I feel your pain. Really, I do."

Chuckling, he retorts, "I don't party with you, and you're one of the most beautiful people in the city, Miss Kat."

"Oh, shut the fuck up. My idea of a party is a little different than yours, and you know damn well the last thing I want is to be around all of those paparazzi that you have a love affair with. Now, tell me what you found out about my latest project."

"Hold on one second while I pull up my notes..." his voice trails off for a moment, "and how do you know I don't share your idea of a good time?"

"Unless you've started batting for the other team here recently, Trav, I'm pretty sure my body parts aren't what you're looking for anymore."

He snorts out a laugh before acting offended. "Sex isn't required for us to have fun. You know people do other things besides that when hanging out. We could have dinner and drinks, go dancing, or God forbid just talk about our lives. I'm beginning to think you're just using me."

Growing slightly frustrated with him, I growl, "Did you get my info or not? You're worse than a damn female."

"Yes, I did... and I'm just trying to be friendly," he huffs before giving me what I want. "Okay, it appears Mr. Saunders is a regular at *Provocateur*, especially when the wifey is out of town, which according to my sources, she will be this Tuesday through Thursday. I have a contact at the club, so I can get you on the guest list for Tuesday night, if you'd like?"

"Yes, perfect! Thank you so much!" I smile into the phone. "You're the best."

"Mhmm. A minute ago I was 'worse than a damn female' and now I'm the best?" he jokes.

"You know I love you and all you do for me, just like you love me and all the money I pay you to do it," I respond sassily. "Just remember this conversation goes nowhere. I'm going to need your assistance quite a bit here in the near future."

"Just promise me you aren't murdering anyone; I don't want to be an accomplice, even if it's unknowingly."

"I promise, Trav, I'm not killing anyone." Feeling a little guilty for my stretched-truth, I add before ending the conversation, "And anytime you'd like to come over for dinner, I'd love to cook for you. I'll see if Leo wants to come too, if you'd like?" I knew I wasn't playing fair with that last line. It was no secret that Travis has been crushing on Leo since he had met him five years ago, and I loved to tease him about it.

"You are evil, woman... pure evil," he says with a chortle. "But I'll most definitely take you up on that offer. Make sure *he's* there."

I hang up the phone feeling a little disappointed; I was really hoping to get my hands on Danny-boy before Tuesday. I know that it's only two days away, but I'm an instant gratification kind of girl, and thinking about what I'm going to do to that man is going to consume me for the next forty eight hours.

I attempt to keep myself busy over the next few hours with a book but fail miserably. Finally, it's time for me to begin my evening preparations before going out, and I can't get in the bubble bath fast enough. Soaking in the tub, I allow the highly-powered jets to work my overly tense muscles. After about twenty minutes, I climb out, dry off, and lotion up before pulling my robe on. I head to the kitchen for my glass of wine and then back to my bedroom for the rest of the routine.

Nearly an hour later, my make-up is on, hair is fixed, and I'm standing at the dresser choosing my lingerie. It's Sunday, which is all white day, and no, the irony is not lost on me. I grab my lacy white push-up bra with matching panties and garter belt. As I slide the silky white stockings up my leg and connect them to the clasps, the switch flips- it's time to make some bastard pay. I quickly throw on a white and gray plaid skirt with a fuzzy white sweater blouse and then head downstairs to meet Leo.

Punctual as always, he waits for me with the car door open and a huge smile on his face. I take a brief moment to take in the true specimen that Leo is; he truly is like sex on a stick. I know that I'm incredibly lucky to not only have him as my driver-slash-bodyguard, but also as a dear friend that would do absolutely anything for me.

"Good evening, Miss Kat," he greets me pleasantly as he takes a seat behind the wheel.

"Evening, Leo. I hope you had a nice weekend," I reply as he looks back at me in the rearview mirror.

"I did, thank you. Now where are we headed tonight?"

"I dunno. Surprise me... nothing too fancy and something pretty close to the hotel," I answer nonchalantly. I still can't pull my thoughts from Tuesday night enough to care about making important decisions like that.

"Is everything alright, Miss Kat?" Leo asks immediately, his voice heavy with concern. He knows that it's very unlike me to relinquish any of the control, especially during night hours.

"Yes, I just have a lot on my mind. I had a busy weekend."

He doesn't say anything else; he just nods and drives.

Within two hours, I've found some married tool that spends too much time at the gym and bars, rather than at home with his wife. I take him to the hotel where I shackle him to the bed and make him beg me to fuck him; then I leave him with a raging erection and the cuff keys just out of his reach. Driving home with Leo, I feel completely dissatisfied with the entire encounter.

Just as he does every night, Leo escorts me into my apartment and performs the best oral sex imaginable. It takes me a little longer than usual to come tonight because my mind is still a bit preoccupied, but he is relentless and doesn't stop until the only thing running through my mind is that it should be a sin to be able to use one's tongue and mouth like that. Then he carries me to bed and tucks me in, kissing me on my forehead.

"Goodnight, Leo. Thank you for taking care of me," I mumble sleepily.

"Yes ma'am, Miss Kat. I'll see you tomorrow."

And he disappears.

Chapter Nine

Trina

(Can't Get You Off My Mind — Lenny Kravitz)

It's Monday yet again, and I *really* don't want to go to work this morning. I wish they could just bus all the kids to me and let me teach them at my apartment so I wouldn't have to deal with the adults at the school. Between inquisitive and overly caring Lauren, creepy and disturbing Principal Matthews, and can't-get-him-out-of-my-mind Lucca, I'm not sure who I need to hide from most. Sighing heavily as I get out of my car, I hurry into the building and head straight for my classroom.

Surprisingly, the morning classes go by quickly and without any unwanted visitors. The students have now been back a week after Spring Break, so they've calmed down a bit, and they're truly enjoying the diverse music I've been playing for them. I like to introduce them to all different kinds of music, not just the traditional children's songs that I find boring and outdated for the most part. In the short time that I've been doing this, I'm amazed at how positively the kids respond to classic musicians like The Beatles and Elvis, but if I told them who it was and how old the songs were beforehand, they wouldn't be interested. Most of them are exposed to pop music and hip-hop on a daily basis, so hearing songs like *Yellow Submarine* and *Blue Suede Shoes* is both different and fun for them.

At lunch, I decide not to be a complete hermit by eating in my room again, so I venture out to the teacher's lounge. Lauren meets me in the hall with her usual chipper smile and happy-go-lucky attitude.

"Hiya, Trina!" she says as she bounces up next to me. "How was your weekend?"

"Hey, Lauren. It was fine. I actually got quite a bit of stuff done that I had been planning to do. How about you?"

"It was really good!" She pauses as we enter the break room, and then picks right back up once we're seated on the couch with our lunches. "I finally told that asshole Jason off Friday night, which felt great, and then I met a new guy at a barbeque on Saturday. I'm not really sure yet where that's going, if anywhere, but we exchanged numbers and he texted me yesterday."

As I look into her smiling face, I want to scream at her that her happiness shouldn't depend on if she's met someone or dating, but I don't. It's pretty evident that I'm not the happiest person around, so what do I know really? Instead, I do what every good friend should do, and I smile back and nod my head. "That's awesome, sweetie. I'm happy for you."

"Speaking of new men, where's your fella today? I haven't seen him hovering around you."

Gritting my teeth, I snap, "I don't have a *fella*, Lauren. Just stop. You're trying to make nothing into something."

She slurps her shake through her straw, smiling mischievously, obviously not listening to a word that I say. We both remain quiet for a few minutes. Finally breaking the silence, she asks, "Trina, do you consider us friends? Like, *real* friends?"

I try to be as sincere as possible with my reply. "Lauren, you are the closest female friend that I have. That's the truth."

"Then why don't you ever want to do anything with me outside of work? If it's because you live in a bad area or are embarrassed or something, that's okay; I don't judge. We can even meet up at like a restaurant or something if you don't want me to see your place. It's not like my apartment is anything to write home about."

Shaking my head, I'm at a loss for how to respond and I'm running out of excuses. "Lauren, it's not that. I just don't have a social life, nor do I want one. Those who have one invite drama into their lives that I'm not interested in. It's the same reason I don't date."

"But all you focus on is the possible negative outcomes of social relationships; you fail to account for the positives: the fun, the camaraderie, trying new things, and getting dressed up! All of that." She tries hard to convince me, and I know that she means well. I also know that she's such a genuinely nice person, and there truly are so few of them left in the world, that I feel guilty for ever befriending her.

"I tell you what," I say, against my better judgment, "I'll meet you out for dinner and drinks one night."

Squealing, she hugs my neck tight, and gushes. "Oh, yay! You have no idea how happy you just made me! This is going to be so much fun! When do you want to go?"

Without me even realizing that he had come into the room, Lucca joins us on the couch, sitting on my left side so that I'm squished in between the two of them. My heart rate increases at just the sight of him, and when the scent of his cologne hits my nose, I feel my body temperature rise as well. "And just where do you think you lovely ladies are going?"

Lauren doesn't even give me a second to tell him that it's none of his business; she can hardly contain her excitement. "After nearly two years of pleading and damn-near begging, Trina has finally agreed to go out to dinner with me."

He looks at me with those captivatingly unique eyes and smirks. "Two years, eh? That's quite a hold out. I hope she's worth it, Lauren." She laughs at his silly little joke and I really want to roll my eyes at him, but I can't pull my gaze from his.

"Oh, I have a feeling once I get her to lose the bun and change out of *teacher* attire, she'll loosen up quite a bit."

Still staring at me, he responds to her, "Mhmm. Wouldn't I love to see that? You think you could take pictures for me?"

She's giggling so hard that she can't even talk, and my face is now burning hot, not just from the way he makes my insides flip around but with frustration at the two of them talking about me as if I'm not sitting right here. Unable to take it anymore, I stand up abruptly and stomp over to the sink to rinse out my container. Just as I finish drying it off, I feel him move right up behind me and I freeze; he's completely invading my personal space. Leaning in further towards me, his warm breath tickles the sensitive skin of my neck, just below my ear, and he whispers, "I promise, you won't hold out two years on me." He pauses for a moment to brush his nose against my ear lobe. "Don't fight the inevitable, Miss Foster."

And he disappears.

Chapter Ten

Kat
(Better Living Through Chemistry ~ Queens of the Stone Age)

The last forty eight hours have been absolute hell. I'm an impatient person naturally, but knowing that the plan of vengeance I've been dreaming about for years is finally about to be put in motion, has me on edge. I decide to go shopping on Tuesday afternoon to buy a special outfit for the night. I've never been to *Provocateur* before, it's really not my style, but I know it's where the pretty people go to be seen. If I want Daniel Saunders to not only notice me, but be willing to cheat on his wife with me, then I best look damn good. I'm honestly not sure if he's the straying type or not; I wasn't able to dig up much dirt on him, but if he likes to go out clubbing as soon as the Mrs. leaves town, I'm willing to bet he'll be easily persuaded.

Prior to drawing my bath, I saunter into the kitchen and pull out the bottle of 1949 Macallan Scotch Whisky from my liquor cabinet, along with a tulip-shaped glass. I've been waiting for the right occasion to open this beauty up, and I can't think of a better one than tonight — not to mention, I need something to release the tension built up inside of me. I'm a ball of nervous energy and could use some liquid relaxation. After pouring a small amount of the caramel-colored liquid into the glass, I swirl it around and allow the single-malt spirit to breathe, as a film thinly coats the sides of the crystal and then slowly descends back down. I bring the glass up to my nose, inhale deeply, and then set the glass down before bringing it back to my nose to breathe in the scent again. The second and subsequent inhalations are where the true aromas and flavors are evoked. I've had this specific scotch only once before, and as the firm and spicy fragrances tease my senses, the memory of that day floods my mind.

It was my college graduation and the only people that came to see me receive my diploma were Leo and his mom. My sperm donor was on his honeymoon with his new trophy wife, and I never thought for a minute that it was a coincidence she planned their wedding the same weekend of my commencement ceremony. They sent me a bottle of this Scotch instead, how incredibly thoughtful of them, right? So after Leo and Rosa left me alone that night in my apartment, I cracked open the bottle and sat around scheming of different ways I could kill the bastard. Leo, knowing me as well as he did, came back over after taking his mom home, and held me as I cried and lashed out until I finally fell asleep in his arms. When I woke up the next morning, he was still holding me tightly up against his chest. It was the first night that he ever refused to have sex with me, and it was the only night that he didn't disappear.

I take a small sip from the glass, drawing in just enough that the whisky teases my taste buds without overwhelming them. Finally, I swallow the liquid and find great pleasure at the burning sensation as it travels down the back of my throat and into my chest. Parting my lips slightly, the lingering afterglow that sits on my tongue is just heavenly. I close my eyes and remind myself that I need to be cool, calm, and collected if this plan is going to work. Much like drinking whisky, there are specific steps that must be taken in order for the end result to be glorifying. I open my eyes and smile, feeling relaxed and in control. Now, I'm ready.

Bath, lotion, makeup, and hair — the same routine that I do every night, except tonight I spend a little additional time pampering myself and making sure I look absolutely perfect. Once I am one hundred percent pleased with my reflection in the mirror, I pad into my bedroom where I've laid out my new clothes from my shopping trip earlier in the day. It is Tuesday, which means it's pink night, and I don't stray from the schedule.

First, I put on my new bra and panty set which is hot pink satin topped with a layer of black lace and lined in tiny rhinestones. The bra pushes up my naturally perky C breasts up to form the perfect amount of cleavage, and the thong and garter belt frame my toned ass impeccably. My stockings are black with hot pink bows at the top seam — in both the front and back — which adds a sprinkle of innocence and playfulness to the entire ensemble. My dress is simple yet sensual — a dark pink Dolce & Gabbana with three-quarter length sleeves, a plunging neckline, and a hem that hits about mid-thigh. It fits my body like it was made specifically for me, and I feel absolutely amazing in it. I slide my feet into my favorite black Gucci stilettos, grab my matching handbag, and head out the door.

I grin and say hello to Andres as I walk through the lobby before greeting the waiting Leo. He blinks and swallows hard as I approach the car, and I know by his reaction that I've accomplished the look I was hoping for. Once we are both in the car, he turns over his shoulder and says, "Miss Kat, you are stunning tonight. I must admit that I'm reluctant to take you anywhere looking like that. It's just not fair to the rest of the people there."

Smiling, I reach out and rub the back of my hand across his cheek. "Your words are too nice for a girl like me, Leo, but I appreciate the compliment. Let's hope Mr. Daniel Saunders feels the same way."

"Daniel Saunders?" His face contorts with confusion.

Leaning forward, I rest my lips on his in a gently kiss, mumbling against his mouth, "Nothing for you to worry about, just wish me luck."

Then, I sit back in the seat and instruct him where to go. "*Provocateur* at Hotel Gansevoort. While I'm in the club, I need you to get a suite in a fake name and wait for me in there. Text me the room number."

He nods and acts like he's about to say something, but thinks better of it. He spins back around, puts the transmission into drive, and pulls out into the night. Traffic is worse than usual for a Tuesday night, but I'm enjoying Leo's music selection of a little Iron & Wine. Over half an hour later we pull into the valet parking area of the hotel, and I can feel the nerves rolling like dark thunder in my stomach. Once we are ushered out of the car and into the hotel, Leo briskly kisses my cheek and tells me that he'll see me in just a bit.

Entrance into the club is easy thanks to Travis. I walk past the lengthy line of hopeful partiers, straight to the doorman, and tell him my name. He doesn't even check the list in his hand; he takes one look at me and motions for me to enter. The place is pretty crowded and the violet-hued lighting is rather dim, but I've spent all day staring at the face of the guy I'm searching for so that I'd be able to easily pick him out in a setting like this. Heads turn to look at me as I cross the room. I'm sure most of these people run in the same social circles and at least know who one another is; to them, I am an outsider — a threat to the women and a conquest to the men.

As I walk towards the bar, I scan the room diligently without appearing as if I'm looking for someone. I've mastered this act in all of my nights out hunting for my own prey. A group of people, mostly men, sitting around one of the plush booths catches my interest. There are a few females sitting between the men, looking way too interested in what the guys are talking about to be their significant others. My eyes quickly sweep over each of the faces, but none of them are him. Just as I'm about to move my search to a different area, a guy approaches their table and bends down to whisper something in the ear of one of the girls. She laughs and scoots over on the bench to make room for him to join her. He sits down and then looks up in my direction and our eyes lock. *Bingo! Target located.*

He gives me a quick nod of the head and a sly smile — both of which I return — before he turns his attention back to the giggling redhead, and I continue my path towards the giant angel wings adorning the top of the modern bar area. It takes me a few minutes to work my way through the crowd and reach a bartender.

"What can I get you, love?" the buxom blonde asks from behind the bar.

Sticking to the whisky theme from earlier in the night, I request, "Johnnie Walker Blue neat, please."

She goes to pour my drink when I feel someone move up behind me. Assuming it's only another bar patron trying to get a drink, I scoot to the side to make room for him or her without paying much attention.

"A beautiful woman that knows how to order scotch... now that's not something you see every day," a deep, masculine voice says in my ear.

Plastering on my best fake smile, I twist around expecting to have to get rid of some dipshit, but am pleasantly surprised to find *him* standing right next to me. The smug smirk on his face tells me all I need to know about how highly he thinks of himself... and how easy this is going to be. My fake smile quickly becomes my flirty, playful one; I'm *really* going to enjoy this.

The bartender hands me the glass, and I go through an accelerated but somewhat provocative version of my swirl, sniff, taste, and finish as he stands and watches me intently, the grin never leaving his face. I then tilt my head a little closer to him. "I not only know how to order it, but I know how to appreciate it as well."

Cocking his head, he lets out a short laugh. "That is quite apparent. I think that may be the sexiest thing I've ever seen."

Subtly running my tongue across my bottom lip, I ask him teasingly, "Would you like me to do it again?"

"Absolutely, but let's go sit down and get out of this crowd. Would you like to join me and my friends over there?"

Unsure if any of his friends were also coworkers, I decide it's better to not meet any of them. "Actually, would you be okay if we grabbed a table alone? I'm a little apprehensive in big groups," I say, putting on my best innocent act.

"Not a problem at all. Follow me," he replies with a smile. He grabs my free hand without asking and leads me to one of the few open tables in the room, which thankfully is set off in a corner.

Once we're sitting, I finally have a chance to get a good look at him. I already know his name, that he's thirty one, he was born and raised in Virginia, graduated from Yale, and of course his occupation and marital status. He's better looking in person than his pictures; he's actually quite attractive with short dirty blonde hair and big brown eyes. He's dressed in designer dark grey slacks with a light grey button-down shirt. His wedding ring has been moved to his right hand, and I have to consciously keep myself from laughing at the lame move.

"So, Miss Whisky Drinker, do you have a name?" he asks once we're settled.

I think about using his wife's name just to see how he'll react, but I don't want to scare him off. "Alexis, but most of my friends call me Lexi," I lie.

"It's a pleasure to meet you, Lexi. I'm Daniel, but most of my friends call me Danny," he replies. "I hope it's okay that I'm putting myself into your friend category so soon."

"Of course, Danny, I don't share tables with people who aren't my friends."

He beams at me, his gaze moving back and forth between my face and my boobs. "What brings you to a club like this all alone? Are you meeting some friends later?"

"No, actually, I'm just in town on a business trip, and I'm staying here at the hotel. They don't have clubs like this where I'm from in Indiana, so I thought while I was here, I'd come check it out. I love to dance." His eyes light up when he learns that I'm not a local, obviously excited that if we do hook up, I'll be leaving town shortly after.

"Once you finish that drink, I'd be happy to take you out on the dance floor and show you how we like to party in the city."

We make small talk for the next fifteen or twenty minutes until I indicate that I'm ready to shake my ass. At first I act a little unsure of myself — so that he'll "show" me how to move — but by the second song, we are grinding our bodies all over one another, both of us turning into an erotic, sweaty mess. After two more songs, I tell him that I'm ready for a break. As we walk back towards the table we were sitting at, I stop mid-stride and look up at him. There's no point in dragging this out any longer.

"Danny, I'm already getting a bit tired, and I have an early flight tomorrow," I say through heavy lids. "Would you like to come up to my room with me to hang out for a while or do you need to go back to your friends?"

"No, I came by myself. We all just met here. I'd love to go up with you," he replies with a huge smile, like he's one the pervert lottery. "You lead the way."

Making our way out of the club, I check my phone inside my purse for the room number and then head to the elevator bank. Four floors later, we head down the hallway to the suite where Leo waits for us. I knock on the door and explain, "Sorry, I left my key in the room. My friend will let us in."

Moments later, Leo opens the door for me and a very confused Danny. "Oh, I'm so sorry. I didn't realize your boyfriend was here," he stammers as he eyes Leo and tries to take a step back.

I cling tightly to his hand. "No, no... he's not my boyfriend, and everything is fine. *Paul* was just leaving, weren't you?" I say to Leo in a sugary sweet voice. I want to make sure he knows not to use my name, as I don't want there to be any way that this can be traced back to us.

Playing along with it, he smiles and agrees. "Of course, I was just headed out for a few drinks. Please don't rush on account of me. I'm a big boy; I can entertain myself," he says as he lets himself out the hotel door. "See you guys later."

Once the door closes, I turn back to Danny and smile as I walk towards him. "Sorry about that, but now that he's gone, let's get you a little more comfortable." Standing just inches from him, I reach up to his shirt and slowly begin unbuttoning it. Seconds later, it slides off of his shoulders and hits the floor. I then make quick work of his belt, pants, and boxers, and they fall to the floor. Kneeling down in front of him, still fully dressed myself, I help him step out of his shoes and his pants. He's allowing me to control the entire situation without saying a word, which works just perfect for me.

I look up at him and notice that his cock is already hard without me having even touched him. Chuckling to myself, I stand up, allowing my body to brush up against his shaft as I do, and look him dead in the eye. "What would you like me to do to you, Danny?" I ask.

The poor guy can barely speak. "Everything," he chokes out.

Smirking, I lean forward and kiss him softly, yet seductively, sucking gently on his lip as I pull away. "Your wish is my command."

I take one step back from him, so that he can see my body completely, and unzip my dress. The pink fabric slides down my slender body, pooling at my heels, and his jaw drops open as he gapes at me standing in my lingerie and heels. I grin and tilt my head, "It's your lucky night, Mr. Saunders," I tease. I fail to mention it's a night of *bad* luck. He can only nod his head. "Get up on the bed, in the center with your back leaning against the headboard." Obeying my command, he quickly scrambles onto the bed and sits, waiting for me.

I kick my heels off and begin the routine that I now have mastered — dancing on the bed... doing a seductive strip tease... allowing him to grope me... stroking his erection a bit... then breaking out the blindfold and cuffs. At this point he's so horny and worked up, he'll agree to almost anything, just as long as he thinks that he's going to get to come either in me or on me.

Once I have him securely restrained to the bed, I text Leo to come knock on the door. I jump up when I hear the rapping and him call out "Room service," and pretend I'm telling someone that they have the wrong room, as I let him in the room and hand him my camera. I rejoin Danny on the bed, silently instructing Leo to take pictures of me posing with him in all sorts of positions. Luckily, he has his fraternity symbols tattooed on his shoulder, so there will be no question of his identity despite the blindfold. Danny is still unaware that Leo is with us, so I unhook one of his hands to allow him to touch me. I'm afraid that if he's completely bound in the photos, he could say he was drugged and taken advantage of; I want it to be apparent that he's a willing participant in this.

Leo continues to silently snap away as I suck Danny's cock and he violently finger fucks me; then I move to where we are in the sixty-nine position, and allow him to delve his tongue into my sweet cunt. When I feel confident that we've got enough pictures, I tell Danny that I'm going to cuff his free hand again so that I can ride him until he explodes. Once he's re-cuffed, I hurriedly put my clothes back on. Just before we exit the room, I say, "Sorry, Danny-boy, I gotta run. Tell your wife, Claudia, I said hello." As the door closes behind us, I hear him calling out, "Wait! Where are you going? Get back here, you bitch! Who you are?"

Leo and I make our way down to the lobby in no hurry, as to not bring attention to ourselves. I don't even bother letting anyone know he's in there; someone will find him eventually. After we're securely in the car and on our way back to my place, he turns around and looks at me sternly.

"I know who that was, Kat," he says disapprovingly. "You play with fire and you're gonna get burned."

"I know what I'm doing, Leo. Don't get involved," I reply with exasperation. "The less you know, the better. All I need is for you to do what I tell you, and if anything ever happens, you won't be accountable for anything."

"I'm going to say it again. Let the past be the past. Move on, be the better person. I know what *he* did — what he took away from you — but he's not worth spending your life in jail."

I ponder his words for a moment before I respond. "No, but she was. And I have to do this for her. Please don't be mad at me, you're all that I have left." He sighs, but says nothing else for the rest of the ride.

Once we get in the apartment, I swiftly strip out of my clothes, leaving the discarded garments on the floor as I lead Leo into the kitchen. I hop up to sit on the granite island top and motion for him to stand in front of me. Leaning back on my elbows, I bring my feet up to the surface and open my knees to give him a full view of my hairless pink pussy lips. I can feel how wet I am from the earlier events in the night combined with the anticipation of his mouth on me. He's either over our disagreement in the car or has accepted the fact it's an argument that he'll never win, and he loves me too much to stay mad at me long. Lifting his eyebrows to ask permission to begin, I nod eagerly as I suck my bottom lip in.

"Wait," I say, stopping him. "I want you naked too. It's been way too long since I've seen your beautiful body."

His lips unfurl in a lopsided grin as he begins to disrobe. First, he removes his already loosened tie from around his neck and sets in on the counter next to me. He then steps out of his shoes, as he unbuttons the dress shirt. The shirt comes off, followed by the slacks and boxers, until he is standing in front of me, as gorgeous as a male model, ready to worship my body.

"That's much better," I proclaim.

Then, as he does nearly every night of the week, he brings me complete ecstasy as his hands and mouth devour my body. He doesn't stop until I am completely satisfied and exhausted, and he then carries me to my bed, tucking me in and kissing me on my forehead.

"Goodnight, Leo. Thank you for taking care of me and everything else tonight," I mumble sleepily.

"Yes ma'am, Miss Kat. I'll see you tomorrow."

And he disappears.

Chapter Eleven

Trina

(Head Full of Doubt/ Road Full of Promise — The Avett Brothers)

Despite my better judgment, I agree to go out to eat with Lauren on Wednesday evening. I figure it's best to get it over with sooner rather than later so that I don't have to listen to her talking about it every day at work. We're meeting at seven o'clock at Extra Fancy in Brooklyn — a restaurant of her choosing — and I'm trying to figure out what to wear. At lunch today, she made me promise to wear my hair down and not "dress like a teacher." I couldn't help but laugh out loud when she said that, quipping back with, "But I *am* a teacher."

I try on several different outfits before I settle on a lavender sweater with black leggings and black knee high boots. I really don't want to put make-up on and fix my hair, but I apply a little mascara and lip gloss to appease my friend, as well as allowing my straight, long blonde hair to cascade down my back. Leaving about forty five minutes before our set meeting time, I take off from my apartment and head towards the subway.

At just a little after seven, I walk through the door of the red-bricked Williamsburg bar and eatery and look around for Lauren. The place is quite busy, but I immediately recognize her curly auburn hair sitting up at the bar that lines the left wall of the room. I make my way over to her, chuckling to myself that she's already engaged in a friendly conversation with the guy sitting on her right, and grab the empty barstool on the opposite side.

She feels my presence as I sit down and twists around to say, "I'm sorry, I'm saving that... Oh, Trina, you came!!" Her sweet voice turns into a scream once she sees my face, and she jumps off her stool to engulf me in a hug. Taking a step back, she scans my body up and down, taking in my entire appearance. "You look beautiful! I knew you would!"

Feigning hurt feelings, I frown and reply, "Are you saying that I'm not beautiful every day?"

"No, of course not! I've just never seen you with your hair down and make up on," she exclaims as she climbs back onto her seat.

Once we're both situated comfortably, she introduces me to the guy she was talking to and we exchange small talk for a few minutes before he leaves to meet his friends at a table. The bartender finally makes his way over to where we're sitting and I ask for a draft beer. Not even thinking about it when he asks for my ID, I take it out of my wallet and slide it over to him. As he slides it back towards me, Lauren intercepts it to look at my picture.

She looks at it and then up at me and then back down at the photo. I cringe knowing that she's reading the information on it and I feel my protective wall crumbling around me. I knew there was a reason I never wanted to do this! I haven't been here five minutes and already the questions are going to start.

"Why aren't you wearing glasses in this picture?" she asks with a confused look on her face.

"I was wearing contacts that day," I reply, hoping she's not paying too much attention to the actual data that indicates I have no restrictions.

She looks up at me and cocks her head. "Why don't you wear contacts any other day?"

"They irritate my eyes, and honestly, I just prefer glasses."

Looking back down at the license, she murmurs, "You are more than beautiful, Trina. You're stunning. Why do you try so hard to make yourself frumpy and unnoticeable?"

I sigh in relief, thankful she's just focused on the actual photo. "I've had a rough past, Lauren, that I'd really rather not discuss. It brings up bad memories," I say softly. "I prefer my life this way, so please stop asking questions. I agreed to come out to dinner with you, which is *way* outside of my comfort zone, so can't you just be happy with that for now?"

A tinge of remorse sweeps across her face as she goes to hand the card back to me; however, just before I take it from her hands, she snatches it back. "Wait! You live at Central Park West?!?" she yelps. Her eyes find mine and the look of confusion has now turned to intrigue. She leans into me and hisses, "You're crazy rich aren't you? What the hell, Trina? Who *are* you?"

My heart is pounding, my teeth are clenched, and it feels as if a volcano has erupted in my stomach. I want to get up and walk out of the restaurant, but I know that will only make me look more suspicious and her questions will be waiting for me at work tomorrow. "It's not polite to ask people about their financial situation," I retort sharply as I pluck the license from her fingers.

After putting it safely away in my wallet, I look dead into her eyes. "I like you a lot, Lauren. As a matter of fact you're my only female friend. The fact that I'm even here with you speaks volumes. I know you don't understand why I am the way I am, and I don't expect you to, but until I'm ready to tell you about my past, please do not ask me questions about it or try to play detective and figure things out on your own." I pause for a moment and smile softly at her. "I'm not trying to be a bitch, but my privacy is very important to me. I'm asking you as a friend to respect that. I don't want this to be the last dinner we have together, okay?"

She nods understandingly and returns the smile. "I'm sorry for making it a big deal, I just would have never guessed, and I really would like to be friends. I promise not to push."

"Thank you so much," I reply. "And please don't tell anyone what you know."

"Don't tell anyone what?" a familiar male voice asks from behind me.

Spinning around hastily, my eyes confirm my suspicion of who has joined us. Lucca and his damn different colored eyes that haunt my dreams is standing there, looking sexier than I remember from just a few hours prior, dressed in a fitted gray thermal top with baggy jeans, black Doc Marten's on his feet, and a blue Mets cap on his head. The devilish smirk on his face tells me that he knows he looks good too, which irritates me even more.

"What are you doing here?" I snap. "How did you know?" I answer my own question before I even get the whole thing out. Whipping my head around to Lauren, I glare at her. "Why?"

"Please don't get mad, Trina," she begs. "I just wanted a fun evening with some friends from work. I thought you'd feel better if there was a group of us. Plus, Lucca can block any guys that try to hit on us." She smiles as she says the last sentence, obviously proud of herself for just coming up with that lame reason.

"I can leave if you ladies want to be alone. I'm sorry, I didn't mean to intrude on anything," he offers, still with that shit-eating grin on his face.

They're both looking at me, making it my decision to be the bad guy and tell him that he can't stay and eat dinner with us. Of course, I say it's fine, that he's welcome to hang out with us. I may have been raised with a silver spoon in my mouth, but my mom also made sure that I had proper manners. I will discuss this with my dear *friend* later.

Even though there's an empty seat on the opposite side of Lauren, where I assume Lucca will sit, she hops off her stool and moves down one. "Here Trina, you move over one too, so that Lucca can sit on your other side. This way you can be in the middle and we can prevent any weirdos from trying to talk to you," she explains.

I don't make a big deal about it. I know exactly what she's trying to do, and if I say anything, it will become more of an issue than it already is. "I think I'm surrounded by the two biggest weirdos in the place," I grumble as I change seats. They both laugh at my comment and I can't help but join them. Really what else can I do?

From that point on, the night goes by just fine... actually, much better than fine. I'm having a great time talking to the two of them, learning about where they grew up and their interests outside of work. Neither of them pressures me to talk about things I don't want to, but I do find ways to add to the conversation without revealing too much about myself. Since we are all rather young, college is still fresh on our minds and we all have funny stories to tell of the ridiculous things we did not so long ago.

Lauren was born and raised in Staten Island, so like myself, she's grown up in and around the city. She has a love for art, painting to be specific, that I never knew about. She actually went to school for it at School of Visual Arts in Manhattan, but seeing as there's an overpopulation of aspiring artists in New York, she's teaching elementary school while she continues to paint in the evenings.

Lucca, on the other hand, is originally from Florida. He left home to attend college and play baseball in Texas, where he just graduated in December. He joined the Teach for America Corp, a program that places you in a teaching position in an area of their choice that's in need of teachers, but in return assists with paying for your master's degree. Up until three months ago, he had never stepped foot anywhere north of South Carolina, and he's now getting a crash course in city life. He'll start working on his graduate studies in the fall at NYU, as well as being permanently placed in a school to teach at for at least two years, but until then he's just filling in at ours.

After hearing his story, learning that he's recently relocated and knows no one else here, I feel bad for the way I've shut him out and been borderline rude to him. I'm not sure why but at one point, I lean into him and whisper, "I'm sorry I've been such a complete bitch to you. I just don't really like people much... I don't trust them."

He scoots a little closer to me, his deliciously clean scent teasing my nose, and whispers back, "I don't think you're a bitch, you're just careful about who you allow to get close to you." His warm breath lingers on my neck, sending shivers down my back and causing my belly to tingle. I close my eyes and enjoy the sensation for a brief moment, knowing full well that Lauren is watching us out of the corner of her eye. Before he pulls away, he adds, "And I plan on getting *really* close to you, Miss Foster."

Thankfully, the bartender walks up with our meals just in the nick of time, or I may have stupidly said something back like "I want you close." Once he retreats from my personal space, I'm able to release the breath that I didn't realize I was holding. I focus on the plate that's been set in front of me and try to regain my composure. *Why do I let this guy who I barely even know get to me?*

Lauren starts talking as soon as the food is delivered, preventing any uncomfortable lull in the conversation. She and Lucca begin discussing different diets and work out programs, and I'm happy to keep quiet for a few minutes. However, he doesn't allow me too much time to retreat back into myself before asking about my exercise regiments. It doesn't take me long before I feel at ease with them again as we talk about the advantages and disadvantages between yoga and Pilates-type classes compared to aerobic exercises such as spinning and *Insanity*. I love the sanctuary I find in all different forms of working out, no matter if I'm moving fast and working up a mad sweat or if I'm focusing on my flexibility and core strength in dictated poses and stretches. It's when he asks where I work out that I feel the color drain from my face. I don't like to lie — I usually prefer eluding from the truth. "Oh, at a gym close to my apartment," I answer with a wave of my hand, acting as if it's no big deal.

"Where do you live anyway? I don't think you've ever said," he challenges me. I can tell by the look in his eyes that his first question was purposely setting up this one.

"I live in Manhattan. What about you?" I ask, hoping to turn the spotlight back on him.

"Oh, a fancy city girl, are you?" he teases, but I don't laugh.

Lauren cuts in, now knowing my sensitivity with the issue. "Lucca, you live here in Brooklyn like me, right?"

He's studying my face, I guess trying to get a read on why I don't want to discuss this. "Yeah, I'm just over in Park Slope with my cousin and another roommate. I came to visit him last summer, and he knew that I was getting ready to start the program, so he urged me to list New York as my first priority. They were looking to upgrade from their apartment in Bushwick, so when I was accepted here, it worked out for all of us."

"Oh yeah, I love it over there. You did luck out," she replies sincerely. "I'm here in south Williamsburg. I've been in my apartment with my college roommate now since we've graduated." She stops and chuckles. "I really don't stop to think about it, but she and I have lived together for almost six years now — all through college and the two years that we've been out. It sure doesn't seem that long. However, that's all gonna change here soon 'cause she's getting married at the end of the summer." Her face drops and I can see the sadness in her eyes, which tugs at the strings of my heart. If things were different, I'd share a place with Lauren. I think that we could make it work. Unfortunately, they're not, and I can't.

Inevitably, the conversation comes back to me. I know he's been dying to ask me something else to try and put together the puzzle that is me. "How long have you lived in Manhattan, Trina?"

"I've been in my apartment for five years," I answer honestly.

"Do you have any roommates?"

"No, I live alone."

"Wait a minute," he scoffs. "You're twenty two, right? And you've lived in your own Manhattan apartment for five years?"

I take a swig from my beer as I think about how best to word this. I don't want them going off to try and research me, so I tell them enough to hopefully appease their curiosity, at least for tonight. I look back and forth between the two of them. "As you both can tell, I enjoy keeping to myself at work, and that is no different outside of the school either. I would appreciate if anything that we do or talk about, both tonight and in the future, is kept between us. I grew up with a bunch of nosy bodies around me, and I've learned that it's best to keep a tight bubble of trust. I just don't like people in my business, plain and simple." I pause before going any further to make sure they are both in agreement. I then continue with an abridged and cleaned up version of my life. "I grew up in Jersey, but my family always had a place in the city for my dad's job. I was home-schooled the last two years of high school so it allowed me to start college at seventeen. When I began attending classes at NYU, I permanently moved to the city. Because I don't have much of a social life, I focused heavily on my studies and was able to finish in three and a half years. I graduated with my degree in Music Education about two weeks before my twenty-first birthday and began applying to schools immediately. I purposely only applied to schools in lower socio-economic communities because I feel like I'm providing more to those kids than the ones whose parents can pay for them to take specialized music lessons or whatever." I stop and shrug. "I love my kids and am very thankful for what I do. I don't ever want any of the students, or administration for that matter, to know that I come from a background different than theirs."

"Wow, I'm even more in awe of you now," Lauren says as she throws her arm around my shoulder and squeezes me in a sideways hug.

"There's nothing to be in awe over," I argue. "Believe me... And please don't treat me any differently. I'm still the same Trina that you've badgered and bothered for the last two years.

I twist to face Lucca and he's just sitting there with a goofy smile on his face. "I knew there was a reason I liked you, Miss Foster."

I playfully roll my eyes, desperately trying to lighten the mood. "Oh? And what reason is that, Mr. Ellis?"

"I need to keep you around to pay all my bar tabs. I've been looking for a sugar mama," he replies before busting out in a fit of laughter.

I slap his arm and start laughing along with the both of them. If anyone else had made that statement, I probably would've been offended and insulted; however, since it was him, for some reason, I know that he is purely joking. I admire him for having the balls to even say it, to be quite honest.

The next two hours fly by and before we realize it, it's after ten o'clock. We all have to be at work tomorrow morning at seven for a staff meeting, so we agree to call it a night. After quick hugs goodbye to Lauren, she takes off on foot to her apartment while Lucca and I head towards the subway. We walk in comfortable silence for a few minutes before he brings up our earlier conversation.

"I meant what I said earlier," he states matter-of-factly.

Not sure where he's going with this, I ask teasingly, "About having a sugar mama?"

He throws his head back laughing and then brings his gaze to mine. "No, not that."

He stops walking and takes a step towards me, closing the distance between us. Cupping my jaw with his large but surprisingly soft hands, he lowers his face to where it hovers just inches above mine, our eyes locked on each other's. I'm afraid he can hear my heart pounding in my chest or the wild zoo that has been let loose in my stomach, and suddenly I feel like a thirteen year old girl about to get her first kiss.

"I want to be close to you, Miss Foster," he whispers.

"You just want what you can't have, Mr. Ellis," I reply in a much more seductive-tone than I planned.

Slowly, he leans down until his lips graze mine, kissing me gently. I've never felt lips so soft and tender before, and as much as I thought I didn't want this, I wouldn't dream of pulling away. The kiss ends long before I want it to, but then again, I could've stayed this way forever. He draws back just a bit with a warm smile on his face and a light dancing in his eyes. Stroking the pad of his thumb across my bottom lip, where I can still feel the tingle of his kiss, he then presses his forehead to mine and says, "I can, and I will, Miss Foster."

The rest of the walk is a blur. I feel like I'm living in some fairy-tale dream; I know this isn't my life, but I'm going to enjoy it until I wake up. We walk the rest of the way hand-in-hand to where we have to part and he gives me another sweet kiss before I get on my train.

"Goodnight, Lucca. Thank you for a great evening," I mumble against his mouth.

"Yes ma'am, Miss Foster. I'll see you tomorrow." His smile speaks a thousand words.

And then, I disappear.

Chapter Twelve

Kat

(Been Caught Stealing ~ Jane's Addiction)

The day after my interaction with Daniel Saunders I'm afraid I'm going to explode at the seams with anticipation. I give Leo the day off because I don't feel like taking part in my usual routine nor do I want to answer the questions I know he's going to ask. I just need some time to work on my project.

As soon as I get a chance in the late afternoon, I pull the pictures up on my computer and begin editing them. I need to make sure that my face isn't visible in any of them, but that his tattoo is in order to identify him. I didn't even think about having him blindfolded and not being able to tell who he is. It's something I will have to consider modifying on the next step of my plan. I'm just thankful I got lucky this time with the ink in the location that it was. After a little over an hour, I'm satisfied with two of the photos. Now I have to determine when I should release them. The child in me wants to send them off immediately, but I know I need to be patient. Timing is everything.

Chapter Thirteen

Trina

(Calm Like a Bomb — Rage Against the Machine)

Thursday morning I wake up wondering what in the hell mess I've created. It was supposed to be an innocent dinner out with Lauren — one that contradicted my better judgment to begin with — and it ended up with me blabbing personal details and then later kissing Lucca. I don't do the whole hearts and flowers thing, especially not with coworkers. I think about calling in sick, but decide against it; I may be a lot of things, but a coward isn't one of them.

As I make the lengthy drive into work, I contemplate all of the different ways to handle the situation. I decide on telling him coworkers shouldn't get involved because when the relationship goes bad, it causes unnecessary problems. Surprisingly, I even admitted to myself that I do like Lucca. Just having a conversation with most men makes me sick to my stomach, yet I find being in his presence both enjoyable and exhilarating; however, I can't allow him to get any closer than he already is. I just can't risk it.

I get to school a little earlier than normal and head straight to my room, hoping to avoid any early morning confrontations with Principal Matthews, Lucca, Lauren, or anyone else for that matter. My plan seems to be working as I scurry down the halls; that is, until I get in my actual room where Lauren is already sitting at my desk waiting for me.

"Well, someone's here early this morning," I say as I lock my purse away in the desk and hang my sweater on its hook.

She smiles like she's hiding the biggest secret in the world. "We have staff meeting this morning, remember? Or did you forget while you were making out with pretty boy last night?"

Instantaneously, my face heats up and I know that my cheeks are blushing a crimson red. "Oh, right," I reply calmly, not taking the bait. "I did forget about the meeting... well, I guess I'm glad that I'm here early then."

Nodding knowingly, she stands up to allow me to sit down in my own chair. "Don't get too comfy there. We have to be in the auditorium in less than ten minutes. You want to grab a cup of coffee beforehand?"

I try to act normal, hoping that she gets the hint I really don't want to discuss last night whatsoever. "Yeah, that sounds good. Let me put up my lesson plans and I'm good to go."

She waits quietly for me by the door for the few minutes it takes me to get situated. I know she's dying to talk, the questions are multiplying in her head with each passing minute, but I'm not about to open that can of worms. We walk silently to the teacher's lounge, go in to make a quick cup of coffee, and head out to the auditorium. The silence is neither awkward nor comfortable. It just...is.

We take a seat towards the back of the auditorium, as we typically do. I don't want to talk to any of the other teachers and I want to stay as far away from Principal Matthews as possible. Finally, she breaks the silence.

"I really had a good time last night, Trina. I'd love to do it again sometime," she says softly, which is completely out of character for her.

I can't help but start to laugh. "You sound like you're reading a script from *What to Say After a First Date*."

Giving me a pouting face, she whines, "Well, what do you want me to say? I tried to talk about it with you in your room and you basically refused. You must've been miserable all night."

"Come on, Lauren, you know that's not the case. What I'm refusing to talk about is me and Lucca, especially here, but as far as hanging out with you both last night, I had a good time... you could even say I had fun." I smile brightly at her, hoping I've mended her hurt feelings.

"I had fun, too," Lucca says as he climbs into the seat next to me from the row behind us.

Turning to him, I act annoyed. "Must you *always* sneak up behind me and eavesdrop on my conversations? It's getting to be a bad habit of yours."

"No, I mustn't *always*," he replies with that damn silly grin on his face, "but it's so much more fun when I do because I like to hear you talk about 'me and Lucca' as if the two go together as a pair. Plus I really like that thing you do with your face when you get aggravated with me."

I scowl at him as I hear Lauren giggling on my other side.

"Yep, just like that." He leans over and pecks me on the cheek.

"What are you doing?!?" I ask angrily, my nostrils flare and my teeth grit together.

This is exactly what I was afraid of after last night. If anyone else saw what he just did, the rumors will be spread like wildfire around the school before lunch. Then, as if the moment couldn't get any better, Principal Matthews walks down the aisle next to us, heading to the front of the room to conduct the meeting. Of course he stops to greet us.

"Miss Dulles. Miss Foster. Mr. Ellis," he says as he nods his head slightly at each one of us. "It appears as if you three are becoming somewhat of a little trio. I guess Miss Foster has made quite the impression on you, Mr. Ellis." He turns his wicked stare to me, making my skin crawl. "She's a pretty thing and may act a bit gun-shy at first, but don't let her fool you; she's a feisty one." He winks at me and continues his path down the walkway, whistling *You Are My Sunshine*.

I want to kill that man.

I hear Lauren and Lucca asking me what that was all about, but I don't answer. I'm torn between the desire to get up and flee from the room and the yearning to end that sick fucker's life. I do neither. I sit there throughout the entire meeting, my face stone cold, as I watch him twirl his wedding ring around his finger as he talks. I can hear his voice but my brain refuses to process anything he's saying. I don't know who he thinks he is or what he thinks he knows about me, but I'm at my breaking point with him. And my breaking point isn't pretty, nor is it gun-shy.

Chapter Fourteen

Kat
(S&M — Rihanna)

By the time Thursday evening rolls around, I need to get out of my apartment in a bad way. I'm filled with anxiety and overall a bunch of pissed-off-ness, even if that's not a word. I've decided that I'm going to distribute the photos to the media on the following Tuesday when the governor has a scheduled luncheon with the Manhattan Young Democrats and Claudia, a.k.a. Mrs. Daniel Roberson, is a guest speaker at the Women's City Club of New York's Spring Charity Gala. It should be a good topic of discussion for both of them. The following day the mayor, Daniel's father-in-law, is scheduled to throw out the first pitch at the Yankees home opener. The news should get plenty of run on that broadcast as well. However, tonight, I just need a break from thinking about that and all of the other thoughts ripping through my mind, and a pompous ass college boy should do the trick.

As I soak in the bath and allow some jazz music to calm me, I focus on getting back to my routine of doing things. For well over a year and a half, I've followed the same schedule, never once allowing myself to get out of rhythm. Each day of the week has a specific color, a specific type of guy, a specific place I end up; and for all that time, I was content with what I was doing. The purpose was to practice my skills of seduction, to learn different ways of domination and control, and to prepare myself for the ultimate revenge. But in the last couple of weeks, I've allowed myself to stray from the schedule, and I've begun to question myself about so many things. *What is my true purpose in all of this? Is it solely for revenge? What happens once it's all over? Will I then be able to be happy? Will I ever be able to be happy?* Recently these questions and so many others torment me day and night. Most of them I don't know the answer to, but one thing's for sure, no matter what happens, I will never get my mom back. Even though as a little girl, I always thought it was my dad who was my shining star, she was always the light of my life. I didn't realize that until it was too late — until he took her from me. And ever since that day, the day the sun went down in my life, my soul has been a dark, dark place.

Standing up abruptly in the tub, I climb out and put my robe on. Anytime I start to think about my mom, the vivid memories from that night threaten to come storming through my mind, and I don't want to revisit them tonight. I don't need another night where Leo actually has to save a poor victim from my wrath. That's only happened on a couple of instances and it's always on a day when I've had some sort of reminder of what happened. I shake my head and look at myself in the mirror.

"Do not let anyone or anything control you. Only you have the power to decide what thoughts you'll think and what actions you'll take."

I have said these same two sentences to myself no less than a thousand times. It's something I learned in therapy as a teenager, and it's taken me years to actually believe them, but now, they are the words I live by. Ever since that day, I've allowed *him* to dictate how I feel or what I am or am not going to do, but once my plan is complete, I'll never have to worry about that again. I just wish these recent thoughts of me second-guessing myself would go away.

Over an hour later, I'm in the back of the SUV as Leo drives me to 1020 Bar on Amsterdam Avenue, a favorite of Columbia students. There's a tension between us that has never existed before. He's still doing and saying the same things he usually does, but I know something's off.

"Are you upset with me?" I ask him, unable to stand it any longer. I could give two shits if most people are upset with me, but Leo and I don't do *this*, whatever this weird feeling is.

"Yes," he answers solemnly.

I scoot up in my seat so that I'm leaning between the driver's and front passenger seats. "Do you care to tell me why?"

"No." Refusing to look at me, he keeps his eyes locked on the road.

"Leo, damn it. Tell me why you're upset. I can't handle you acting like this with me." I know I sound like a whiny brat, but I don't care.

He continues to drive in silence for a few minutes before finally speaking. "I know what you're doing, or what you think you're doing, and I don't like it," he says with a clenched jaw.

"*What I'm doing*?" I ask. "I'm doing the same thing I've done every Thursday for the past eighteen months. You've never said anything about it before."

"That's not what I'm talking about, and you know it."

"No, I don't know. Please enlighten me." I *do* know exactly what he's talking about, but I want to hear him say it.

"The Saunders guy — I know who he is. Don't play stupid. And then you last night..." He shakes his head disapprovingly as his voice trails off.

I knew he had figured out who Daniel was, but I wasn't sure what he meant about the previous night. "So you looked him up online and learned who he was," I begin.

"Yes!" His raised voice causes me to flinch and jump back a bit. Taking a deep breath, he starts over, "I'm sorry I scared you, but yes, I researched who he was to find out why you were so adamant about getting to him on Tuesday."

"Well, now you know."

"What are you going to do with the pictures, Kat?"

"That's none of your business," I snap defensively.

"It is my business," he argues. " You. Are. My. Business."

"Leo, I have to do this. You don't understand."

"I understand every bit of it. I was there, too. Remember?"

"I have to do this," I say again, more adamantly this time. "You aren't going to talk me out of it."

He turns slightly to look in my face. "At least let me know what you have planned, what you're going to do. That way I can help as much as possible and I'm not caught off guard by anything."

Staring into his pleading eyes, I want to tell him no — tell him that I can do this by myself — but I can't. I know he's right, it's best if he's prepared. I don't answer him verbally, I just nod my head.

"We'll talk about it later, okay?" he offers with a small smile and a tilt of his head towards the window.

I look outside and realize we're parked in front of the bar. Grabbing my clutch, I return the smile. "Yeah, we'll talk. I'll text you when I'm ready to go." I don't wait for him to get out to open my door; I jump out of the car and head inside, needing that release even more after that conversation.

I make my way to the bar to grab a beer; I'm really in no mood to play games. It takes about two minutes to scan the room and realize who the biggest egotistical douchebag without a female is in this bar tonight. Spotting him with no problem whatsoever, it takes less than thirty minutes before I'm texting Leo to come pick me and whatever-his-name-is up.

On the drive to the hotel, I don't waste much energy pretending I even like the guy. Neither he nor his wandering hands seem to mind though. Thankfully, it doesn't take long to get there, and I hastily usher him up to the room. At first, he attempts to take control of the situation, as I'm sure he does on most of his sexual conquests, but when I threaten to leave, his tune changes rapidly.

Once I get him naked and cuffed to the headboard, he decides to get a little mouthy. "Do you even know what to do with me now that you've got me here?" he asks with a smirk.

Laughing at his effort to continue to control the situation even after he's restrained to the bed, I climb up on him, still in my purple silk panties, and straddle his hips. He presses his erection hard up against me, I guess his way of showing me how manly he is. I slowly walk my fingers up his chest until they reach his mouth, and I tap his lips. Cocking my head with a sly smile, I say, "You seem to have already forgotten who's in charge here."

He chuckles and narrows his eyes. "*I'm* always in charge in bed. I'm just playing along so you can get your kicks."

This guy is dumber than I thought. I pat my fingertips on his lips again. "You want me to suck your cock, little boy?"

I feel his shaft twitch underneath excitedly me, despite his reply. "I'm no little boy and you *will* suck my cock, slut."

Without thought I slap him hard across the face, and again, his cock jumps with pleasure. "Oh, I think you liked that. You want me to do it again?"

"Get off me, slut, and unlock me."

I slap him again, even harder than the first time, as I simultaneously push down on his erection with my pussy. He moans and pulls against the restraints. Grinning as I lean down, I bite down hard on his shoulder before whispering, "I think you've got it all wrong, little boy. You're the one who's a slut." I bite down again. "A little pain slut."

Groaning and wiggling underneath me, I think he's probably harder than he's ever been. I can feel his cock pulsating through the cloth of my panties. He may come just from me hitting and biting him. I plan on finding out. I sit back up and look down at him. "Do you want me to hurt you?" I pray he says yes. He nods without hesitation, his eyes begging for more.

It takes no more than ten minutes of me slapping, pinching, and biting him, on pretty much every place except his cock, before he's squirting his sticky cum all over his own stomach. Typically, I don't like for the guy to get off, but I found an inexplicable calmness while abusing this kid, so I really don't mind. If I didn't have the self-imposed rule that I never prey on the same guy twice, I'd definitely enjoy playing with him again. Had I known how this night would turn out, I'd have brought a whip, some hot wax, and who knows what else. Nonetheless, I feel much better at the end of the session, and based on the smile spread across his face, I think he does too. I crawl off the bed and begin to put my clothes back on, leaving him to revel in his post-orgasmic bliss.

"Don't you want me to please you too, *slut?*" He can't help himself from laughing as he says the last word.

Turning around so that I can look in his face, I tell him honestly, "You did please me, *little boy.*"

Without another word, I walk out the door to the hotel room as he calls after me asking how he's going to get free or get back to his car. Leo waits for me outside the door and I tilt my head towards the elevators. "Let's go."

Once we're back in my apartment, he wastes no time in tearing away my clothes and consuming my body. From my neck to my toes and back up again, he kisses, licks, and nibbles like pleasing me is an Olympic event. I even make him call me *slut* as he does it, which drives me wild. And much like the boy from earlier in the night, I find my erotic release in a very short time. Leo wins the gold, no doubt.

Then as he does every night that he brings me home, he carries me to my bed, tucking me in and kissing me on my forehead.

"Goodnight, Leo. Thank you for taking care of me," I mumble sleepily.

"Yes ma'am, Miss Kat. I'll see you tomorrow."

"Leo," I call out to him as he's walking out of my room.

He stops and pivots around. "Yes, Miss Kat?"

"What did you mean earlier in the car when you said 'and then you last night'?"

"I followed you," he replies and then spins back around, not waiting for me to say anything.

And he disappears.

Chapter Fifteen

Trina
(Glad You Came -The Wanted)

Friday morning I want to call in sick even more than I did on Thursday. I don't want to deal with any of it. Thankfully, neither Lauren nor Lucca pestered me about the incident prior to the staff meeting or the events of our dinner the previous evening. They pretty much left me alone for the majority of the day, each of them sticking their head in once just to say hello, or most likely to make sure I hadn't run away. I have no idea what to expect today and I hate it.

I hate not having the control over my surroundings or the people in it. That's one thing that I love about being a teacher in an elementary school. Sure, kids are unpredictable and can act up, but when I'm in my classroom setting, the bottom line is I'm the adult and I'm in control. The oldest child I have in any of my classes is ten, and even as a petite twenty two year old female, I control ten year olds. But adults in a workplace environment are a completely different species, hence why I typically try so hard to avoid them. One dinner — I had one dinner with coworkers and within thirty-six hours, I feel like the protective little bubble that I have worked so hard to create has been permeated and is quickly dissolving. The part I'm struggling with the most is that I actually like Lauren and Lucca; it would be much easier if I didn't, and then I could just cut them out of my life. I know that's what I should do — for both their sakes, as well as my own.

Seeing Lucca's smiling face waiting for me outside of my room is bittersweet. There's no denying his face is nice to look at; it's actually light years better than nice — he's downright gorgeous. However, I know that no matter how many somersaults my belly does when he stares at me with those different colored eyes or how many times I dream about how soft his lips felt against mine, I will never be what he's looking for. How do you tell someone that you're not capable of love?

"Good morning, Miss Foster," he greets me as he hands me a hot cup of coffee. "I brought you your sugar and milk with a dash of java."

I accept it graciously after opening the door to let us both in. "Thank you very much, Mr. Ellis. That's awfully kind of you... not necessary, but kind."

He follows me inside, lingering around the keyboard as I put away my things. After just a couple of minutes, I'm settled and take a much needed drink of caffeine. Not meaning to, I moan with delight as the delicious, sugary liquid coats my taste buds and warms my chest as it travels through my body. His gaze snaps to my lips as the guttural sound escapes my mouth, and he begins to walk towards me.

"I'm glad you like it. I hoped I was making it to your specifications." He stops about a foot or two in front of me, purposely close but still far enough away to give me my space.

I look up at him and nod with a small smile. "It's perfect," I whisper.

"Go to dinner with me this weekend, Trina." His request is more of a demand than a statement.

"I — I can't," I stutter. "I have plans already."

He knows I'm lying, but he doesn't call me out on it. Instead, he says, "Then any weekend, the next one you aren't busy. If breakfast or lunch is better, we can do that. I don't care. I just want to see you again outside the walls of this school." Lifting his hand slowly, as to make sure I don't resist or back away, his thumb caresses my bottom lip. "I want to be close to these again."

I just stand there, mesmerized by his voice and his touch. Despite everything I've told myself, not just over the past two days, but over the past nine years, I nod my head yes and agree to see him again. He grins and I can see the joy on his face that my acceptance brought him, and unexpectedly, that in turn makes me even happier.

"I know that customarily the guy plans the date, especially if he's the one that did the asking, but I know you'll feel better if you make the arrangements." He reaches around me to grab a pen and notepad from my desk, making sure that his arm swipes up against my waist, and jots down his number. "You can text or call me, whichever you prefer, when you decide what day, time, and place you feel most comfortable with."

As he hands me the supplies back, his fingers linger against mine for just a moment before he makes his way towards the door. "I suppose I should get to my own class before the bell rings. I'll be waiting to hear from you, Miss Foster."

"It's Trina!" I call out after him. I don't think he hears me, but he sticks his head back in the doorway a moment later.

"Did you say something?" he asks.

I nod and bite my bottom lip to keep from beaming at him like an idiot. "I said 'it's Trina.' You don't need to call me Miss Foster."

He smirks as he replies, "You can still call me Mr. Ellis. I kinda like it." Teasingly, he waggles his eyebrows at me, and I laugh hard.

And then he disappears.

By the time school lets out that afternoon, I've gone back and forth in my head at least a hundred times on when and where I should meet Lucca again. There are thousands of restaurants in New York, but being in public with him makes me nervous. I'd rather not be visible in the public eye. I really wish that I could just have him over to my apartment so that I could cook for him, but that makes me feel even more vulnerable. Even though he knows I come from money, he really doesn't know how much money, plus I don't like the idea of him knowing where I live. This is our first — dare I say — date, and truth be told, I really don't know that much about him. Ruling out those two options, that really only leaves his place. Before exiting the building for the weekend, I grab my phone and type out a text.

Me: Dinner. Your place. Tonight.

I lock up the classroom and before I reach my car in the parking lot, I hear my phone ding with a text alert. Once I'm settled in the driver's seat with the door locked, I pull it out of my purse to read the response.

Lucca: Perfect. 7:00 ok? I'm on the corner of 10th St and 8th Ave, one block from Prospect Park. Call me when you're close and I'll come out to get you.

Me: Kk

The entire drive home I'm grinning like a fool. I know I shouldn't be so giddy about this; I shouldn't be going at all, but I just can't stay away from him. I'm not one to ever deny myself what I want because I can usually just buy whatever it is. The problem is I've never wanted a person — not like I want him.

It's nearly five o'clock by the time I get home, so I head straight for the shower to get ready. After a quick scrub from head to toe under water as hot as I can stand, I slip into my robe and run to the kitchen to pour a glass of wine. I need something to help calm my anxiety a bit. Once back in the bathroom, I blow dry my hair out straight and apply a little bit of mascara and lip gloss, very similar to how I looked when I went to dinner on Wednesday. I can't decide if I should wear my glasses or not. I put them on, take them off, and put them on again. I don't need them to see, but I feel like they are a big part of my *look* when I'm at school. I end up leaving them on; they're kind of like a security blanket.

After slipping on a comfortable but cute, black bra and panty set, I step into a black-and-gray-striped, long-sleeved maxi dress. The dress is one of my favorite things to wear because it's sexy in how it clings to my curves without looking slutty as the hemline sweeps the floor, and the scooped neckline is just low enough to hint at what hides beneath the soft cotton. I slide on some trendy black ballet flats and take one last look in the full-length mirror. Pleased with my appearance, I swallow the last of the wine in my glass and drop it in the sink before leaving for my first date in... well, in forever.

I ignore the strange looks I receive from both the guy behind the security desk and the doorman, and simply greet them with a "good evening" as I head out into the cool spring night. The walk to the subway is brief, and after a rather lengthy ride with several train changes later, I'm standing under the sign that reads 10th St.

Digging my phone out of my purse, I'm pleased to see that I'm about ten minutes early before I press the call button. Lucca answers on the second ring.

"Are you here?" he asks excitedly.

"I'm somewhere, I'm not sure if it's *here* or not," I joke.

"I'm on my way outside. Stay on the phone until I find you."

Seconds later I see him bounding out the front door of a red-bricked brownstone just a few yards down from where I'm standing. He spots me immediately and takes off in a jog in my direction. I hang up the phone, drop it in my purse, and meet him halfway.

"I'm so happy you came," he exclaims as he wraps me in a tight hug. His clean smell entices my nose, but the sight of him is just... wow. He's got on worn out, tattered jeans with frayed bottoms resting on his flip-flops and a simple, plain black t-shirt. His dark hair appears even messier than it normally does; it's still a little wet and it looks like he just jumped out of the shower and ran his fingers through it. I love that he didn't feel the need to get dressed up for me; the comfy, around-the-house look suits him perfectly.

We pull away from each other, but he grabs hold of my hand. His eyes travel up and down my body and the smile on his face tells me he's pleased with what he sees. "You look absolutely gorgeous, Trina."

"Thank you, Mr. Ellis, as do you," I respond cheekily.

Laughing softly, he tugs on my hand and pulls me towards his house. "Come on, let's go inside and get something to drink."

I follow him through the front door into a surprisingly well decorated home, especially for a place where three guys live. "Wow, this is really nice," I murmur as I take a look around the open-concept living room and kitchen area. The home is much bigger and nicer than I anticipated, and I'm curious how a guy on a teacher's salary can afford something like this. Maybe his cousin and other roommate pay a greater share...

"Not what you were expecting?" he asks as he pours two glasses of wine.

"I'm not sure what I imagined to be honest, but this isn't it. Did you guys have a professional decorate it for you?"

Chuckling, he walks over to where I'm standing in the middle of the room and hands me a wine glass. "No, my cousin just has a knack for this kind of thing. A little strange, I know, but I don't complain. I enjoy living in it."

Lucca then gives me a quick tour of the place, showing me each perfectly decorated room, including his which reveals a large cherry wood sleigh bed covered in fluffy bedding and throw pillows in a blend of blues. The works of art on the walls are all watercolor images of the beach and ocean, and the white gauzy curtains framing the window are the perfect accompaniment. The room is masculine but not stuffy; on the contrary, it's extremely bright and inviting. It's actually a perfect parallel to Lucca.

"I usually don't bring girls to my room on a first date. I just wanted to show you the house," he says in a low voice from behind me. I realize that I've been standing there for quite some time staring at his private sanctuary.

Embarrassed, I turn around to leave the room, but he doesn't move. "It's beautiful," I whisper, my face just inches from his.

"*You* are beautiful," he murmurs as he softly strokes my cheek with the back of his hand. I want him to kiss me so badly, but he doesn't. Instead, he rejoins our hands with fingers interlaced and leads me out of the room. "Dinner is almost ready. Are you hungry?"

I shake off the twinge of disappointment and follow him back into the kitchen. "Absolutely. Did you cook yourself or are we doing take out?"

He walks over to the oven and turns the light on inside. "Come over here and look."

I join him and stoop down to take a peek into the window. "Mmmm... lasagna?"

Placing his hand on the small of my back, he pulls me back upright and smiles. "Yes, it's my mama's secret recipe. I think I'll make her proud, but you be the judge." He opens the refrigerator and pulls out two bowls of Caesar salad and the bottle of wine. "Take a seat," he instructs and refills our glasses. "I'm going to get the lasagna out to cool some while we eat the salad."

I'm not used to obeying other's people commands. Ever since I was a teenager, I would actually challenge anyone who tried to tell me what to do, but again, for some incomprehensible reason, it doesn't bother me when he does it. I won't admit it to him or anyone else, but I kind of like the slightly dominating role that he's beginning to take with me. I like it, but it scares me.

A few minutes later we're both digging into the delicious dinner that he's prepared and talking about his baseball career that ended early due to injury. Everything's going great; we're laughing and joking about what he was like as a kid, until he asks the question.

"So what about your parents? What do they do?"

Instantly, I feel the knot in my stomach tighten and the color drain from my face. I stare down at my plate. "I don't have any family."

"What do you mean? At dinner the other night you talked about your dad's job bringing you into the city?"

This is exactly what I was afraid of, the reason I shouldn't have accepted his invitation in the first place. I know better than to think people won't want to know about my family or my childhood.

I lift my head, bringing my eyes to his. "I said I don't have any family."

I expect him to push me for answers, things to get really awkward, and the date to end not long after the dinner, but unexpectedly he smiles and says, "Well, good, I don't have to share you with anyone then. I expect to get you for all of the holidays, and that includes Christmas in Florida with my parents." Then he continues eating like it's no big deal.

My jaw drops open as I continue to stare at him. "Are you serious?"

He looks at me confused. "Of course I'm serious. Why wouldn't I be?"

"It's our first date, and not to mention it's the end of March! What makes you think we will be seeing each other at Christmas?" I scoff.

Calmly he sets his fork down on his plate and scoots his chair back away from the table. "Come here, Trina," he commands.

Now it's my turn to appear confused. "Excuse me?"

He gazes into my eyes, but it feels like he's talking to my soul. "I said, 'Come here, Trina.' Don't make me tell you again. I know you want to come, so come. Don't be stubborn."

For some baffling reason, I find myself getting out of my chair and walking over to him. He grabs my hips and gently pulls me down onto his lap. His strong hands cup under my jaw and our eyes lock on one another. "I told you that you wouldn't hold out two years before going out with me and you didn't make it two weeks. I told you not to fight the inevitable and so far, you haven't. Now when I tell you that you'll be spending Christmas, as well as all of the other holidays with me, trust me, you will."

I'm speechless. I want to argue with him, but he's right. And what's even more perplexing is the more he talks to me this way, the more sexually turned on I find myself.

He rests his forehead on mine. "Do I scare you?" he asks in a soft voice.

"Yes," I whisper. If he only knew in how many ways.

"I'll let you in on a little secret. You scare me, too," he says with a lopsided grin. "But I knew from the moment you bloodied my nose, I needed you as much you need me. I don't know how or why, but I knew." He stops talking to rub his nose up and down mine, and from the dampness between my legs, one would think it's the most erotic thing anyone's ever done. "We have a lot to learn about each other, but I assure you, nothing you can tell me will scare me away. I don't care why you don't have a family. I don't care what you've done in your past. All I'm concerned about is you and me from this point forward."

"But you don't understand," I try to explain, but he shuts me up as his lips come crashing onto mine. Unlike the sweet, gentle kiss from a couple of nights ago, this kiss is forceful and insistent. His tongue demands entrance to my mouth, which I give with no resistance, and then devours me. Within seconds we are lost in the most passionate kiss of my life– tongues curled around one another, teeth gnashing, each of our hands threaded in the other's hair. When I begin sucking and nibbling on his swollen lip, he pulls back, ripping our mouths apart.

"*That* is the only thing I need to understand," he mumbles as we both struggle to catch our breath. He kisses me again, this time slow and tender, returning the air to my lungs. I begin to wonder if I'm dreaming; this all seems entirely too good to be true, especially for my life.

We spend the rest of the evening cuddling on the couch, drinking wine, and watching a movie. I realize that no matter how sure of himself he seems, this whole fairytale can't last. I'll never be able to be honest with him about my past, and I still have other transgressions yet to commit. But for just a while, it's fun to pretend I'm a normal girl that deserves a happy ending.

Chapter Sixteen

Kat

(November Rain — Guns & Roses)

Even though Saturdays are supposed to be one of his nights off, Leo is insisting to come over this evening to discuss Daniel Saunders, among other things. It's a conversation I'm not looking forward to, but I know is unavoidable; he's not going to let this go.

I sleep in later than normal, finally rolling out of bed a little before noon. I have several errands that I need to run before he comes over, so I quickly throw on some jeans and a t-shirt and put my hair in a messy bun. I stop in the kitchen and grab a granola bar and bottle of water before grabbing my purse and sliding my feet in some flip-flops. Pausing for a moment as I look at the shoes, a tiny smile creeps over my face at the memory associated with them.

Once out of my building, I take off on foot, thankful for my prime location, and head towards the salon. The weather is unusually warm for the beginning of spring, but after the brutal winter we've had, I'm not complaining one bit. When I was a kid, I always dreaded fall and winter the most because that's when my dad would be gone — always either practicing or at a game. My mom would get really depressed during these times, and even though I didn't completely understand why, I just knew that our home was a happier place when he was home and we were all together. Now I realize that Momma most likely knew what he was up to all those nights he never came home, which were more frequent during the season.

Gratefully, I reach my destination before I can travel any further down memory lane. That horrifying afternoon plays through my dreams like a broken record, so I try my hardest not to allow it to torture me when I'm awake too. I plaster a smile on my face and walk into the salon, eager for an afternoon of pampering.

Several hours later, I walk back out on to the bustling street, feeling refreshed and revitalized. My hair has been trimmed and styled, my fingernails and toenails are the perfect shade of pink, and my muscles have been kneaded and massaged into submission. With a skip in my step, I make my way to the local grocery store to pick up a few things for the dinner I'm going to cook for Leo. It's been a long time since I cooked for anyone, but I've wanted to make a recipe I saw for traditional *osso bucco*. I figure tonight's as good as any; however, cooking an Italian dish for a guy who has an Italian version of Martha Stewart for a mom is a bit risky.

After the grocers and butcher shop, I walk hastily back to my apartment. Once inside, I empty all of the bags and begin preparing the veal shanks. As the butter melts, I open a bottle of 2008 Vina Cobos Cobos Malbec and pour an oversized glass. Reveling in the voluptuous and hearty blend of fruit and earthy flavors, I'm extremely pleased with the vintner's recommendation, knowing this will go perfect with the dish. I then move back to the stovetop where I finish browning the veal prior to adding the other ingredients before leaving it to simmer for about an hour and a half.

Glancing at the clock that reads half past six, I have about thirty minutes before he will be here. I scurry down to my bedroom to take a quick shower and change; I love getting massages but I hate the slick, oily feeling that it leaves on my skin. I hear the knock on the door just as I finish blow-drying my hair — I guess I spent a little longer in the shower than I planned. Hurrying to the front door to let Leo in, I don't think twice about him seeing me in just a robe; it's more than he sees me in most of the time anyhow.

I open the door with a smile, shocked to see him standing in the hallway holding a beautiful bouquet of flowers. He's beaming from ear to ear as I gawk at him.

"May I come in?" he asks, laughing softly.

"Oh, yeah," I sputter. "I'm sorry, I was just caught off guard with the flowers. Come on in; make yourself at home." All of a sudden this feels much more formal than just he and I hanging out for an evening while we eat and talk about things.

He follows me into the kitchen where I grab a vase and arrange the flowers in some water. "They're gorgeous, Leo. Thank you."

Sliding his arms around my waist from behind and pulling me into a tight embrace, he mumbles against my hair, "Not nearly as gorgeous as you, Katie-bug."

Twisting around in his arms, I cock my eyebrow at him curiously. "Why did you just call me that? What are you up to? Are you trying to sweeten me up to talk me out of my plan?"

He shakes his head and chuckles. "No, I know there aren't enough flowers in the world to talk you out of something that you've set your mind to. I just don't tell you how special I think you are often enough."

I give him a quick peck on the cheek and spin out of his grasp. "I don't pay you to tell me I'm special," I say as I pour him a glass of wine and refill my own.

His brows furrow in frustration as I hand him the goblet. "It's not about the money, don't even go there. I've known you since you were born; I don't think of you as my employer... you're one of my closest friends."

Feeling bad for cheapening our relationship, I apologize sincerely. "I'm sorry, Leo. I didn't mean it like that. You know how important you are to me. I've got a ton on my mind and I didn't mean to be rude to you, the one person who's stuck with me through everything." I stop and run the fingers of my free hand through my hair. "Can we start this evening over please? I'm making you *osso bucco*..." I plead, trying to tempt him with the thought of good food.

He relaxes his face and grins; he can never stay mad at me. "Of course we can. You cooking one of Mama's dishes in that flimsy little robe trumps anything."

I look down at my silky black ensemble, having completely forgotten that I didn't have time to get dressed before he arrived. "Oh, right. I meant to get dressed but you got here early," I explain with a soft laugh. "Do I need to change?"

"Absolutely not," he answers as he takes a big gulp of the wine. "But you do need to show me what smells so good."

Excitedly, I lift the cover on the skillet to show him the shanks, basting the meat again as he inspects the dish. "I hope it tastes as delicious as it looks and smells," he says approvingly.

"Well, I just hope I make Mama Rosa proud," I tease.

"I'll be the judge of that. There's no better critic of Italian food then yours truly." He chuckles and pats his very tone belly over his shirt.

"Shut up and take off your shoes. Pretend you're going to hang out a while." For the first time since he's arrived, I take a look at what he's wearing. "Why are you dressed in slacks and a dress shirt anyway?"

He looks down at his outfit with a frown and then back up at me. "I don't know. It's how I always dress."

"Yeah... when we're going out at night. Don't you ever just bum around in a t-shirt and jeans?"

"No, I'm a grown up and I dress like one," he barks. A look of disapproval and annoyance crosses his face.

Unsure of why his mood changed so suddenly, I probe carefully, "Are you insinuating that I don't dress like a grown up?"

He closes his eyes and shakes his head. "No, I'm sorry. I didn't mean to snap at you. I just haven't been sleeping well lately and I'm irritable." He forces a smile and finishes his wine. Quickly changing the subject, he asks, "How long until the food's finished? Should we talk about things now or over dinner?"

Groaning, I grab the bottle of wine and refill his glass. "We've got about an hour before dinner so I guess now is good. I just need to stay in here to keep basting the veal plus I need to start the *risotto* in about thirty minutes." I hop up on the counter and look at him. "So what do you want to know?"

He follows suit and sits on the counter opposite from me. "Let's start with Daniel Saunders. What do you plan on doing with the pictures you took of him?"

"Distributing them to the media, probably this Tuesday."

"What do you hope to gain from it?

"Causing a little bit of chaos in the governor's office and hopefully the mayor's too."

He nods and thinks for a minute. "What's after that? What's the end goal?"

"After that, I plan on doing the same thing to a couple more people in Robert's office until people start questioning his ability to control his own employees, much less a state. I want to fuck his life up, and knowing that being governor is the thing he had always been working for, I want it taken away from him," I explain with a half-truth.

Unfortunately, Leo knows me all too well. He raises his eyebrows at me in disbelief. "So that's the end goal to make him lose his job?"

I refuse to make eye contact with him or answer.

"Kat, you can NOT seduce your own father!" he yells at me, more forcefully than he has ever spoken to me.

Snapping my eyes up to his, I narrow them at him. "I don't plan on *seducing* him; that sick fucker would probably get off on doing his own daughter."

"So what then? What do you plan to do?" He jumps off of the counter and begins pacing around the kitchen. After a few laps, he stops right in front of me and asks the question I didn't want him to ask. "Are you going to kill him?"

I stare straight into his face. I can't lie to him. "I want to."

He wraps his strong arms around my shoulders and squeezes me tightly against him. Unable to control them, tears begin streaming down my face as the onslaught of emotions from the past nine years come ripping through me. He holds me as I cry, knowing that I need so badly to get it out. After I finally get a hold of myself and the sobs subside, he releases me enough to where he can look in my eyes. Bringing his hand up to my face, he tucks my hair behind my ears and cups my chin. "I know you *think* you want to kill him — and I'm not arguing that you want him dead — but I'm not sure you've really thought about the consequences of going through with it. It's not just the chance of getting caught, and you would be high on the list of suspects by the way, but it's living with yourself for the rest of your life with his blood on your hands. No matter how much you hate him, that's a huge burden to carry with you forever, and it's something you really need to think about."

I nod my head, agreeing with him on everything he's said, but it doesn't change the fact I want him gone. "I'll think about it more, but for now, I at least want to go forward with the first part of it."

"I'm okay with all of that, and I'll help you the best I can. You need to be extremely careful though. Once you leak the first story, you're going to have to cut back on your usual nightly activities. I know Manhattan has millions of people in it, but you can't take the chance of a story about a girl who picks guys up and leaves them cuffed in hotel rooms getting out. If you want to do this right, and not get caught, you're going to have to lie low for a while... and trust me."

"I know and I do," I murmur.

"My job is to keep you safe and out of trouble. Let me do my job."

I throw my arms around his neck and bury my head in his shoulder. "Thank you so much for understanding. I know I'm crazy, but I need to get the revenge on him that I told him I would."

"You're not crazy. I loved her too, ya know."

We continue to embrace for a couple of minutes, and I'm reminded why I could never live without Leo. He's the only one that gets me; he's the only one that can understand.

After the serious talk, we spend the rest of the evening eating and chatting as usual. The meal is good but it's no Mama Rosa's. I definitely need to work on the recipe again when I'm not so preoccupied with other things. As it's getting late, I yawn several times and he picks me up and carries me to bed.

"You need your rest, Miss Kat," he says as he lays me down in bed.

All of a sudden I feel awkward. I'm not sure if he's planning on pleasing me like he normally does or not, and I'm not really sure I want him to, but how do I tell him not to. It's not that it doesn't feel absolutely amazing, because it does, but things are different with me now... and I don't know how to explain that either.

Almost as if he can read my mind, he leans down and simply kisses my forehead. "Since we won't be going out as much in the evenings, just let me know what you want me to do. As always, my services are at your disposal."

He turns around to leave the room and despite the fact I didn't want him to try anything sexual, my feelings are a little hurt that he didn't. "Leo, why are you just leaving?"

He halts mid-stride, but doesn't turn around to answer. "Because it's what you want."

"How do you know?"

"It's my job to know."

"Did you follow me again last night?" I whisper nervously.

Still refusing to face me, he answers my question without answering my question. "He better be good to you, Katrina, or I'll kill him."

And without another word, he disappears.

Chapter Seventeen

Trina
(The Woman in You — Ben Harper)

I didn't hear from Lucca on Saturday, but he told me Friday night that he would be attending a function with his cousin and would be gone most of the day. I was so busy on Saturday anyway; it was probably for the best. However, Sunday morning I wake up to the sweetest text I've ever received.

Lucca: I woke up excited, thinking it was Monday and I'd get to see you, but instead I have to wait a whole 'nother day.

I actually giggle aloud when I read it. I haven't felt this way about a guy in so long, that I'm not even sure what's going on. All I've cared about for the last several years was getting a guy's attention, and once I had that and got what I wanted, I had no use for him any longer. Lucca, in so many ways, ignites something inside of me that I thought was lost forever, and the crazy thing about it, is I barely know him. When he asked if he scared me, I couldn't even begin to explain to him how much so. In just a few weeks of meeting and hanging out together a couple of times, he has me second-guessing so many things I thought I knew and the way I wanted my life to be.

I think about how I should respond for a minute before replying. I've never done this dating thing and I know there's supposed to be all of these stupid rules. I don't want to look desperate or overly eager, but I really want to see him today.

Me: Most normal people want the weekends to last longer, not wish for them to end.

I hop out of bed to go to the bathroom and brush my teeth, and by the time I get back, he's already texted back.

Lucca: What ever gave you the idea I was normal?

Climbing back under the covers, I get settled and turn the television on before I answer.

Me: Excellent point, Mr. Ellis, but nonetheless, it's still Sunday — all day long.

Lucca: What are your plans on this all-day-long Sunday?

Me: My current plans include seeing how long I can lie in this bed and do nothing too productive. Yesterday wore me out.

Lucca: Whose bed do you think is more comfortable?

Me: Huh???

Lucca: Which of our beds do you think is most comfy? It's not meant to be a trick question.

Me: Mine

Lucca: What's your address?

Me: I'm not giving you my address. You could be some crazy stalker/ serial killer.

Lucca: Then bring your cute ass over here. Let's be lazy in my bed together.

Again, I'm not sure how to answer this; I'm torn internally about what to do. I want to go spend the day with him, but I don't want to want to go. Groaning, I roll over and bury my face in the pillow. Why did I do this to myself? I have so many other stressors in my life that I really don't need to complicate it any more. The dinging of the phone pulls me from my feathery hiding hole.

Lucca: Stop over-thinking it and stop being stubborn. I'll see you in an hour.

Me: Stop being a pretentious jerk.

Even as I type out the last text, I'm getting out of bed to get ready. I tell myself I'm going to go over there and tell him that I don't appreciate him ordering me around. I'm not some submissive, dainty woman in need of saving; I'm a grown woman who controls my own thoughts and actions. I've taken care of myself for the past nine years just fine, and I sure as hell don't need a man to boss me around now.

I take a quick shower, not even bothering to apply any make-up or to fix my hair; a messy bun it is. I throw on some black yoga pants and a pink V-neck t-shirt with my sneakers. If he wants to see what my lazy is, he'll get it. I grab my phone off the bed and throw it in my purse before heading out the door.

After nearly an hour's worth of a subway ride there, I'm strolling up the sidewalk to ring the bell outside. The entire ride over I've been rehearsing what I'm going to say to him as soon as I see him, but when he opens the door in just a pair of plaid pajama pants hung low on his hips, every rational thought in my head disappears.

"Would you like to come in?" he asks as I stand there ogling him.

I blink hard and move my gaze up to his face. He knows exactly what he's doing. I don't say anything and just roll my eyes and walk past him inside the house. Strolling into the living room, I'm caught off guard by the two other guys lounging on the furniture playing a video game. They both look up at me with warm, inviting smiles.

"Hi, you must be Trina," the dark-haired guy on the couch greets me. Lucca comes up behind me and places his hands on my hips as the guy continues talking. "I'm Stephen, Lucca's cousin, and this is our other roommate, Bran."

"It's nice to meet you both. I hope I'm not intruding on your Sunday morning activities," I say politely.

"Oh please, you're no intrusion at all. We're happy to meet you; our boy here hasn't stopped talking about you since he started his new job. You've made quite the impression, beginning with the bloody nose," Stephen teases. I blush crimson.

Sliding by me into the kitchen, Lucca laughs. "Okay, that's enough of your mouth, cuz." He looks at me and asks, "Would you like something to drink? Water? Soda?"

"Water would be great."

He grabs the drinks from the refrigerator and then tilts his head towards the hallway. "Come on. Let's leave these two with saving the world from zombies."

Once we're in the room, he closes the door behind us and sets the drinks down on the bedside table. I'm trying hard not to stare at his chest but it's just right there in front of my face. I stand awkwardly in the middle of the room, waiting for him to tell me what to do. *Wait a minute! What did I just say?* Apparently, the pep talk I gave myself earlier was not very effective.

"Would you feel more comfortable if I put a shirt on?" he asks as he walks up to me.

"Yes," I whisper, even though I'm praying he doesn't.

"Why?" he challenges.

"Because you're walking around half naked and we barely know each other!" I scoff.

"We barely know each other but you agreed to come be lazy in my bed with me on this all-day-long Sunday."

"No... but..." I try to argue but he puts his finger over my lips to quiet me.

"We barely know each other but you sat in my lap a couple of nights ago and let me do this repeatedly." As he removes his finger from my mouth, he bends down and takes my lips in his, kissing me softly. My hands naturally move up to the back of his neck, threading through his dark tendrils as the kiss deepens. I moan into his mouth as our tongues touch and twirl against each other's. I'm thankful that his hands are gripping my hips firmly because I'm afraid I may melt into the floor.

When the kiss ends, his lips linger against mine as he mumbles, "I think we're getting to know each other pretty well, but I'll put a shirt on for you." He casually strolls over to his dresser, grabs a t-shirt, and slides it over his head. Turning around, he flashes me a huge smile. "Now get in bed before I throw you on it. We're supposed to be lazy, devil woman!"

Laughing hard, I step out of my sneakers and climb up on the mattress to where I'm propped up against all of the throw pillows. "Devil woman?! Why do you say that?"

He dives on top of the comforter, landing next to me, and rolls over onto his back. Gazing down at him, I'm once again mesmerized by his eyes. "You're a devil woman because you make me want to do very bad things," he says with an over-dramatic expression on his face.

I pretend to pout, sticking my bottom lip way out and crossing my arms over my chest. "I don't want to be a devil; I want to be an angel."

He begins to tickle my side, which causes me to slide down next to him as I attempt to fight him off. Stopping once I'm eye level with him, he taps the end of my nose with his finger. "You know the devil was once an angel," he says in a hushed voice.

"Yes, but he got kicked out of heaven," I whisper back.

"I promise I'll never kick you out of my heaven, no matter how bad you are." He grazes his lips across mine in a quick kiss before pushing himself up to a sitting position and grabbing the television remote. I lie there a few extra moments, wishing so much that his words were true, but I know they won't be.

"Now, come lay with me, *devil woman*, while we watch some movies," he commands. "I want to see how few times we can get out of bed today."

I cozily situate myself up against him like he requests and begin watching the television. I honestly don't expect to like the movie much because it's about vampires and shape-shifters, which is not my kind of thing whatsoever, but twenty minutes into it, and I'm completely enthralled. I've never thought of myself as a touchy-feely kind of person before, but I love how Lucca lazily strokes his fingertips up and down my arm and how he kisses my forehead at random moments. When I'm in his presence, I forget about everything else — all that has happened to me and the despicable things that I've done or have yet to do. He makes me feel safe from all that other bull shit, and even if it's temporary, it's the best feeling I've had in a really long time.

After the first movie, we pause for a quick bathroom break and to get refills on our drinks before starting the sequel. As we're getting back to how we were situated, he gives me a funny look. "What?" I ask with a nervous laugh. "Do I have something in my teeth or on my face?"

"Actually, no, you're missing something from your face — your glasses. Do you have contacts in today?"

His question is innocent enough, but it makes me feel extremely guilty. I choose not to lie to him. "No, I don't need glasses for vision. I just wear them more or less as a fashion accessory."

Grinning, he shakes his head. "Well, I must admit I do secretly like that smart librarian look that you rock at school; however, I love this natural side of you too." He peppers kisses across my jawbone until he reaches my mouth, where he begins to nibble lightly on my lip. "God, you are so fucking sweet."

I playfully push him off of me. "No, you pretentious jerk! I need more Lycans and vampires. You can't get me hooked on these characters and then withhold them."

"I'm the boss, devil woman. I tell you when we watch the movie and when we kiss," he grumbles, but he's already starting the next installment for me.

Chuckling, I lean over and whisper in his ear, "Thank you," and then peck his cheek before focusing back on the TV.

At ten o' clock that evening, I force myself to go home. We've spent the entire day in his bed, stopping only for bathroom breaks and to order food to be delivered. I have the strongest desire to stay the night, and not in a sexual way, but because I want to feel the same serenity while I sleep that I experience when I'm just next to him. But instead of asking me to stay, he offers to walk me down to the subway, but I insist that I'm more than fine. I've been in and around the city since I was a little girl. After telling one last time that I've had a great time, we kiss goodnight and I leave. When I get to the end of the block, I see a very familiar black SUV parked; and as I get closer, the driver jumps out and opens the back door for me.

"It's not safe for you to be out alone at this time of night. I'm taking you home," he growls.

I don't even try to argue with him; I just slide in the back seat with a scowl.

And we disappear.

Chapter Eighteen

Kat

(Never Say Never — The Fray)

Monday afternoon and evening I try my hardest to stay cool, calm, and collected, but I'm not doing a very good job. The excitement over releasing the pictures tonight has me feeling like a little kid on Christmas Eve, and time is creeping by at a snail's pace. I keep myself busy cooking homemade tortilla soup and sipping on a new *pinot grigio* my vintner just got in. Leo is joining me for dinner again even though I told him it wasn't necessary. I'm afraid he's going to drive me crazy over the next month or so that I need to lay low and not go out every night, and I'm curious to see if he's going to mention last night to me or not.

He arrives a little after eight o'clock, and thankfully, he's dressed a little more casual this time. I notice him smile when he sees that the flowers he brought over two nights ago are still on display in the middle of the kitchen table.

"Would you like a glass of wine or something else?" I ask him while he takes his shoes off and makes himself at home, sitting on a bar stool.

"Do you have any beer?"

I pad over to the refrigerator, grab him a bottle of dark ale, and hand it to him. "Leo, can I ask you a question?"

"If I said no, you would ask anyway, so I'm not sure why you're asking permission," he snickers.

I hop up on the kitchen counter, like I always do when I'm hanging out in the kitchen, and chuckle. "You're right. I would." I lean over and stir the chicken and broth in the crock pot before turning back to him. "What do you want to be when you grow up?"

He laughs so hard in response that he even spits out some of his drink. "Kat, I'm thirty-one. I *am* grown up.

Feeling a bit embarrassed because I always forget that he's quite a bit older than me, I ask the question in a different way. "You know what I mean. I'm sure driving me around at night so that I can fuck with the male population probably wasn't what you told your mom you wanted to do when you were a kid. What are your goals? Do you want a family of your own?"

He shrugs and curls his lip up a bit. "You've been my priority ever since I could remember. I don't really think about doing anything else. Sure, I've thought about having a family, but I don't think that's in the stars for me."

"Why? Because of me?" I figure it's best to just to ask what I really want to know.

His brown eyes stare me down, but I don't back down. "Do you do it because I'm your employer or for another reason?" I ask.

Tearing his eyes from mine, he gulps down the remainder of his beer and sets it down on the counter. He completely disregards my questions and changes the subject. "When are you sending out the pictures?"

I huff and slide down until my feet hit the floor. "Thanks for ignoring me," I snap as I walk out of the room. Retrieving my laptop from the office, I join him at the bar and set everything up. "I guess now is as good as time as any. Let me show you the ones I'm going to send and you take a final look over them."

As he's studying the photos, I do a final stir of the meal and pour myself another glass of wine. I look over at him and I am suddenly reminded of Leo sitting at the bar in my family's house the day I realized that my sperm donor really was an evil monster.

I came in from my swimming in the back yard to the delicious smell of spaghetti and garlic bread being prepared in the kitchen. "Mama Rosa, are you making my favorite?" I called out in my high-pitched thirteen-year-old voice.

"Of course, my sweet girl," she answered in her heavy Italian accent. "It will be ready in about twenty minutes. Go get changed."

93

I wandered into the kitchen, dripping water on the floor from my still-wet swimsuit. Mama Rosa was hovering over the stove while Leo was sitting up at the bar playing on his laptop. He looked up at me and flashed a big smile. "Hey Katie-bug, are you all ready for the Olympics now?" he teases me.

"Don't call me that! I'm not a bug!" I exclaimed, stomping my foot like a small child on the stone-tiled floor.

"Well, you look like one in that swim cap with those silly goggles on your head," he retorted.

I ripped the cap and goggles off, allowing my waist-length flaxen hair loose, and glared at him. "You're so mean! You're just jealous that I can outswim you and you're a boy."

Just at that moment, my dad walked in the back door with a scowl on his face. "Where is Stephanie?" he barked out at no one in particular. When none of us answered him, he focused on me, "I asked where your mother is, and why in the world are you standing here getting these floors soaked, Katrina?"

"I just came in from swimming, Dad. I don't know where Momma is, probably upstairs taking a nap."

"She's such a lazy bitch," he grumbled. As he pushed past me to head towards the stairs, he shoved me slightly, and because the floor was slippery, I fell to the ground.

Leo flew off of the barstool and got right up in my dad's face instantly. "Keep your hands off of her," he warned with a fury in his eyes that I had never seen from him before.

Despite the fact my dad was a professional football player and feared pretty much no one, he took a small step back from the passionate twenty-year-old before cautioning him. "Be careful, young man. I respect your attempt to be a hero, but remember I'm the reason that your mom has a job and a green card, and what allows you to go to college. Stay out of my family's business. This will be the only time I warn you." He didn't wait for Leo to respond before stomping out of the kitchen and bounding up the stairs to find my mom.

Both Leo and Rosa rushed to help me up and make sure I was okay, which I assured them I was. Completely flustered by the entire situation, I escaped to my room as quickly as possible and didn't come out for the rest of the night. Mama Rosa brought my dinner up to me, and thankfully, didn't mention what had happened earlier. That night, Leo snuck into my room to check on me and promised me he would never let anyone hurt me.

"Why are you staring at me like that?" he breaks my train of thought.

Closing my eyes, I shake my head and take a deep breath. "I was recalling the day that *he* pushed me down in the kitchen. You were sitting up at the bar, playing on a laptop, similar to the way you look right now."

"He was a piece of shit, Kat. Neither you nor your mom deserved the way he treated you guys."

"You know, up until that day, I had no idea what an asshole he was," I confess with an exasperated sigh. "I mean I knew Momma would be sad when he didn't come home at night, especially during the season when he was gone all of the time, but he was still my Dad. I still thought he was the greatest guy. But when he came home that day, it was like a switch had gone off in his head, and he just didn't care to pretend that he liked us anymore. I wish either he or we would've just left that day. Maybe then she would still be here..."

He hops off the stool and comes around to hold me in a tight embrace. "I know you miss her. I do too, and so does Mama."

"It's why I have no qualms about what I'm doing; I want to fuck up his world. He deserves every bad thing that ever happens to him, plus some."

Releasing me, he looks into my eyes. "Are you ready to send them then?"

I nod and walk over to the laptop. I already have the email drafted from the bogus account that I set up and ready to go. All I have to do is hit send and the pictures of Daniel Saunders — who is both the governor's head of communications and the mayor's son-in-law — in some rather compromising positions will be in the hands of several influential members of the New York media. Not wasting another second, I click the button to deliver them to chosen recipients, and all I can do is sit back and wait.

"I want you to take this laptop with you when you leave and make sure it's destroyed. I'm not sure what lengths they will go to in order to trace it back, but I just want to make sure we're covered."

"Of course, Miss Kat. I'll take care of it on my way home," he assures me.

Leo and I don't talk a whole lot over dinner. My mind races and my thoughts are scattered all over the place. After we finish eating, he helps me clean up the kitchen, and then I tell him that I'm tired and ready for bed. Nodding, he follows me back to my bedroom and waits for me to brush my teeth and change into my pajamas. Once I climb up onto the high mattress, he tucks me in under the covers and kisses my forehead.

"Good night, Leo. Thank you for taking care of me for the past nine years," I mumble sleepily.

"Yes ma'am, Miss Kat. I'll see you tomorrow."

And he disappears.

Tuesday morning I wake up extra early and turn on the local news immediately. Of course the meteorologist is on giving the five-day forecast — as if he knows what's going to happen tomorrow, much less in five days. I wait impatiently for him to finish weather-guessing and then the several minutes of commercials before the real newscasters are back on. Luckily, they begin to revisit the day's headlines and after touching on some national news, the first local story they cover about is the reveal of the X-rated photos of Mr. Daniel Saunders in what they call "more than compromising positions with someone who is obviously not his wife." They briefly discuss the negative backlash in both the mayor's and the governor's office. They also state that neither the Saunders' family, nor either political office, has issued a statement on the matter, and that they will have further coverage on the breaking story on the evening broadcast.

I pop out of bed as happy as can be. What a perfect way to start the day! A little part of me was scared that perhaps the story would be shoved under a rug or not get very much airtime, but I should've known better. People, especially those in a big city, love scandals; it makes for a great conversation topic with coworkers at the office or with friends over drinks at happy hour. I now know that no matter what happens with the story from this point on, I was successful in planting a seed of chaos.

Singing joyfully throughout the entire shower, when I get out, I quickly put my hair up in a bun and get dressed. I'm nearly thirty minutes earlier than normal as I walk through the lobby of my building to the parking garage. Sliding into the driver's seat of the modest car I've purchased to drive on a daily basis, I pull out onto Central Park West and begin my morning route to work, anxious to get back home as soon as possible to follow the news.

Chapter Nineteen

Trina
(Chances — Five for Fighting)

Pulling up to the school almost an hour before class begins, I wonder what in the world I was thinking leaving the apartment so early. Hurriedly, I grab my bag, exit the car, and rush into the building. Once I'm settled into my classroom, I pull out my iPad and begin searching the local news sites. I'm so engrossed in reading one of the articles that I don't even hear Lucca come into the room.

"Morning, Miss Foster," he greets me gleefully as he sets a cup of coffee milk on my desk. "You're here exceptionally early this morning."

Quickly turning off the device, hoping that he didn't see what I was looking at, I peer up at him with a cheerful smile. "Good morning to you, too, Mr. Ellis. I could say the same thing about you."

He pulls up the extra chair I keep to the side of my desk and sits down. "Yes, I have a meeting with Principal Matthews here in just a little bit, so I figured I should probably get a cup of coffee or three in me before that happens," he snickers.

Crinkling my nose with disgust at the name alone, I ask, "What about?"

"I can't tell you; it's top secret." He brings his hand up to his mouth and acts like he's zipping his lips shut.

"Ugh, I don't trust that man at all. He gives me the creeps."

Laughing, he leans forward a bit and taps me gently on the tip of my nose. "Not to worry, devil woman, I've got it under control. But you're smart in being suspicious of him, I don't trust him as far as I can throw him."

The vision of Lucca attempting to pick up Principal Matthews makes me chuckle. "You couldn't even lift him off of the floor!"

Covering his heart as if he'd been shot, he feigns injury. "You wound me with your words. My precious male ego may never recover from your wrath when you're finished with me."

"Something tells me that your ego has been pumped up enough over the years that little ol' me could hardly put a dent into it," I tease.

Shaking his head, he murmurs, "You have no idea what you could do to me." Abruptly, he glances down at his watch and then stands up. "I've gotta go do this, but I was wondering if you wanted to come over tonight?" He asks in a low voice. Thankfully, he's been very discreet about our budding relationship the last couple of days while at work. He understands and respects that I don't want to be the topic of the teacher gossip mill. I just hope that we can continue to stay under the radar.

Even though I'm eager to hang out with him again, I was looking forward to staying home this evening to get some things done. I gaze up into his persuasive eyes and my decision is made for me. "What time do you want me there?" I reply with a smile.

"You can come straight from here, if you want."

"Actually, I'd like to go home and change into something more comfortable, if that's okay?"

Nodding, he begins to make his way out of the room. "Sounds good." Just before leaving, he pauses and turns to look at me with a wicked grin. "Bring an overnight bag. I want to wake up tomorrow morning with you, Miss Foster."

And before I can think of an excuse as to why I can't, he disappears.

Throughout the day, I periodically check my iPad, continuing to follow the current local headlines. By the time I get off, I'm more than pleased with the way the day has gone, and now the anticipation of spending the night with Lucca is about to tip me over the excitement meter, if there was such a thing.

As soon as I get to my place, I rush in to take a shower, blow-dry my hair out straight, and change into a pair of jeans and a pink t-shirt. Throwing together a bag to take with me, I make sure to include pajamas, a change of underclothes, and an outfit for work tomorrow. Forty five minutes later, I'm heading back out the door on my way to Park Slope.

The trip to his house takes longer than normal due to the rush hour, but at a quarter past six, I'm standing outside, ringing the bell. His cousin, Stephen, opens the door to let me in.

"Hey, Trina. Come on in," he welcomes me. "Lucca had to run to the store real quick; he forgot something he needed for dinner."

"Hi, Stephen," I say, as I walk by him and into the house. "How was your day?"

We both walk into the great room and he continues on into the kitchen. "It was busy to say the least. Can I get you something to drink — wine, beer, soda?"

I feel a bit awkward being alone with him; I'm not sure how to act quite honestly. Other than Lucca and just a couple of others, I prefer to not even engage in conversation with males unless I know I'm completely in control of the situation; however, I know that I need to work on this, especially if I'm going to be hanging out here more. Stephen isn't going to hurt me. I know in my heart that Lucca would never allow that.

"Yes, a glass of wine would be great, thank you," I reply politely. "What line of work are you in?"

After pouring us both a glass, he hands me one and then takes a seat at the kitchen table with an exhausted sigh. "I work in the news room of NY1. The mayor's douchebag of a son-in-law decided to have an affair with some whore who documented the entire thing, and then sold the pictures to the press. I've spent all day following the story and news conferences."

I gasp for air while having a mouth full of wine, thus ending up in a choking fit as the liquid traveled down my windpipe. Coincidentally, Lucca picks that moment to walk through the door. He drops the bags he's carrying and rushes to where we are just as Stephen jumps up and comes over to help me.

"What's going on?" Lucca questions his cousin while patting my back and holding me close to him. "What happened?"

"I don't know, man. We were just talking and she started choking."

Regaining my composure with watery eyes and a few last coughs, I'm finally able to speak again. "Sorry, I just swallowed down the wrong path. My lungs didn't appreciate a drink of wine, I guess," I try to make light of the situation. I'm praying that Stephen doesn't revisit his day of work with Lucca. "I'm fine now." Smiling at Lucca, I give him a quick peck on the check in hopes to wipe the worried look off of his face.

Once he's certain I'm okay, he pulls me closer to him and kisses my hair. "I was afraid Stephen had gotten jealous already, and tried to kill you before I got home," he says jokingly.

Stephen playfully punches him in the arm. "Shut up, jerk. If I was going to kill anyone, it would be you, so that I could keep her for myself."

We all laugh at their banter while Lucca goes to pick up the groceries off of the floor. "I'm making Pork Milanese with squash and potatoes, if that's okay with everyone?"

"Sounds delicious. Bran won't be home tonight, so it's just the three of us," Stephen says as he walks towards the master bedroom. "I'm gonna shower and change into something more comfortable — be out in a bit."

With him out of the room, Lucca walks over to me and rests his hands on my hips, his eyes focused on mine. "I like coming home to you being here."

"Oh, I'm sure you'll get tired of me pretty soon," I say, half-teasing.

Furrowing his brow in a scowl, he asks, "Why do you do that?"

"Do what?"

"Assume we won't last very long." He stares at me so intently; I swear he's trying to read my thoughts.

"First off, I don't even know what *we* are," I reply.

"What do you mean what *we* are? We're Lucca and Trina — a couple that's spending time together and learning more about each other. I don't think *we* really need a label, but I thought I expressed my intentions at dinner on Friday."

"But how can you be so sure? You don't know anything about me. We've only been hanging out — you can't even call it dating because we don't go anywhere but here — for a week or so," I argue.

Without saying another word, he picks me up, and instinctively, I wrap my lean legs around his waist. He strides across the room until my back is flat against the wall and I am sandwiched between him and the sheetrock. His expression is intense and stern, but I'm not fearful whatsoever.

"Since the day we met, I knew that I had to have you," he says in a throaty growl, his face mere inches from mine. "And I don't just mean sexually, even though I'm very much looking forward to that at some point in the future." He presses his body a little more forcefully into mine as he says it. "But right now, I plan on learning everything there is to possibly know about you and spending every minute I can with you that you will allow. I've met many girls in my life, and even had serious relationships with a few of them, but I've never felt about them the way I feel when I'm with you."

Resting his forehead against mine, he brings one of his hands up to stroke my cheek with his thumb. "That is the honest to God truth, Trina. In the brief time that we've spent together, you bring out something in me that I never knew existed."

"What's that?" I whisper, completely enthralled in every word that's coming out of his mouth.

"Protectiveness." He leans in and softly sweeps his soft, full lips against mine. "I feel this overwhelming need to keep you close to me, to keep you safe from everything," Gently, he begins to nip at my bottom lip. "To blanket you in affection and adoration and to worship every inch of you, inside and out."

Moaning lightly, I tilt my hips so that I can grind my aching body against his hard body. "I've got a lot of demons you'll need to protect me from," I say breathlessly.

He smiles against my mouth and his eyes light up at my capitulation. "I don't mind a challenge, especially not when getting to keep you is the reward."

Completely lost in our own world, we don't even hear Stephen re-enter the room until he asks, "So I'm guessing dinner's still going to be a while?"

Lucca and I both start laughing as he releases his hold on me and I slide down the wall until my feet touch the ground. He kisses me once more on the forehead and then swats my ass as we both walk back over to the kitchen.

"Please don't stop on my account," Stephen remarks with a sly grin. "But you do have a bedroom for that kind of thing. That is, unless you'd like me to watch..."

"Get a life, jack ass," Lucca retorts while he begins to pull pots and pans out from the cabinets. "Or better yet, a girl of your own to harass."

I excuse myself to the bathroom to splash some cold water on my face. I'm more than a little worked up from the entire wall encounter. As much as I want to believe everything he said, it's hard for me to trust him. God knows that I want to. Oh, what I'd give to let go of the monsters in my mind that torment me on a daily basis and move forward with a normal life with Lucca. I'm terrified if I ever tell him the truth about me, he'll walk out of my life as quickly as he walked into it, but I know the longer I continue to lie to him, chances are that he'll do that anyway.

Dinner with the guys is a true delight. Just two years apart in age, the two of them together act more like brothers than cousins; they take turns telling me embarrassing stories of each other from when they grew up in south Florida. I learn about the time Lucca tied Stephen to a tree swing and left him there to pee in his pants, as well as the time Stephen made Lucca walk barefoot through dog poop. The three of us laugh until we are crying and our sides hurt, in addition to devouring the delicious meal that we all assisted in cooking. It surprises me immensely how natural it feels for the three of us to interact and hang out together.

We all help out in cleaning up the kitchen and loading the dishwasher, and then Lucca and I say good night to Stephen as we break off into the separate bedrooms. Once we are alone behind the closed door, I become a little apprehensive, unsure of what to expect. Thankfully, he senses my unease and immediately calms my nerves. He draws me into his warm body, enveloping me in his strong arms and nuzzling my neck.

"You don't need to worry, Trina. I'm not going to push you to do anything that you don't want to do, and that includes physical actions as well as talking about things you aren't ready to share. I *do* want to learn everything there is to know about you, but I realize that's going to take time. Most importantly, I want you to relax. When you're with me, I'll take care of the stress and worries."

He has no idea how much his reassurance means to me. I simply nod and squeeze him tightly against me. He pulls back a bit and flashes me the most genuine smile. I know that he's as happy as I am in this moment.

"I want you to change into your pjs while I grab us some drinks, and I'll meet you in that big, comfy bed in five minutes, okay?"

"Deal. Would you mind grabbing me some water?"

"Of course, anything for my devil woman," he jokes as he turns to leave the room.

Grabbing my overnight bag, I pull out the pale pink camisole and matching pink-and-navy-plaid pajama shorts that I brought with me. I quickly change into them and remove my bra to get completely comfortable. Crawling onto the bed, I situate myself on the side that I had sat on Sunday while we watched movies.

Minutes later he comes back into the room carrying a tray with two waters and a bowl of ice cream. He places it delicately on the foot of the bed and then strides across the room to his dresser. Unable to take my eyes off him, I stare as he unbuttons his shirt and allows it slide over his shoulders onto the floor. Next, he steps out of his shoes before unfastening and unzipping his jeans, which also fall to a pile on the floor. As he stands in front of me in just a pair of light blue boxers, I'm pretty sure I whimper aloud at his impressive physique. I want nothing more than to allow my fingers and mouth to play his body like the fine-tuned instrument it is. I know that the music we will make together will be nothing short of brilliant.

He pulls on a pair of pajama pants, similar to the ones he wore on Sunday and saunters back over to join me in the bed. Pulling the tray over to us, he hands me my glass of water and a coaster to set on the bedside table closest to me. He does the same, and then picks up the bowl of frozen yumminess.

"I hope you like ice cream. This actually comes from a little creamery located in a small town called Brenham, Texas. When I started going to school there and had this for the first time, I fell in love," he explains as he brings a spoonful of it to my mouth. "I order it online and have it overnighted here, just so I can have their Homemade Vanilla every night before I go to bed."

Parting my lips, I allow him to feed it to me and instantly I understand what he's talking about. There's no real way to explain the difference between it and other vanilla ice cream I've had except that it's richer and more flavorful. It's absolutely scrumptious. "Oh my, that's delectable," I tell him.

He shovels a spoonful in his mouth next and nods in agreement. "Okay, we're going to play a game. It's kind of like twenty questions, but each time you answer a question that I ask, you get a bite of ice cream, and the same goes for me." I shoot him a look of alarm; I'm not sure about this. "You don't have to answer the question if you don't want to, but you just skip out on your bite that round," he further explains. "Plus, I promise nothing too intrusive tonight. This is just a great way for us to get to learn more about each other."

With the stipulation that I can pass on anything I don't want to answer, I agree. I really want some more of that ice cream, not to mention I'm eager to find out more about Lucca. We start with easy questions like our favorite color (his blue, mine black), favorite foods (Italian for both of us), and place we'd most like to visit (London for me, Hawaii for him).

On my next turn, I ask him to tell me about his first real kiss, which he does without hesitation. Then he asks me the first question that makes me consider passing.

"Who was your first crush and how old were you?" he inquires innocently.

Pausing briefly before deciding to answer, I respond with complete honesty. "It was the son of our housekeeper and I was thirteen." He feeds me another bite, seemingly satisfied with the vague response

"Tell me about the longest relationship you've had," I take my turn.

"I dated a girl named Lindsay for almost two years during my freshman and sophomore years of college."

"Why did you guys break up?"

A pained look shoots across his face, but he quickly shakes his head and consumes another bite of ice cream. "Uh uh. My turn. I want to know the same thing — longest relationship?"

"Ummm... define relationship."

"Dating exclusively or boyfriend/ girlfriend. I don't want to know about any friends with benefits or fuck buddies," he grumbles. "I may go hunt them down tonight."

"Well, that would be however long we've been *us*," I reply embarrassed.

"What do you mean?" he asks, obviously confused.

When The Sun Goes Down

I look down at my hands in my lap, hoping he'll understand without me having to spell it out.

"Trina, what do you mean?" He uses his hand to tilt my chin back up.

I look up at him through my eyelashes. "I don't do relationships, Lucca. You would be the first."

Scooping a large bite onto the spoon, he lifts it to my lips. "Not would be — I *am*."

Tears of both sadness and joy prick the back of my eyes, and I fight them off with a smile. "I'm finished playing for tonight, if that's okay?"

"Can I ask one last question? If you don't want to answer, you don't have to," he requests.

"Sure."

"Are you a virgin?" His voice is almost a squeak.

I bust out laughing, partly because I can tell he was afraid to ask the question and partly because... well, because I'm not even close to being a virgin. "I'm not sure what you're hoping for, but the answer is no. I lost my virginity when I was seventeen."

Relief settles over his face and he feeds me the last of the nearly-melted dessert. "See, that wasn't so bad, was it? And look at everything we learned about each other. Now let's get some sleep, my little devil woman."

After moving the bowl and tray off of the bed, he turns off the lamp and we both lie down in the dark. I feel kind of silly because I'm not sure if I should cuddle up to him or which way I should face — I suck at this stuff. But again, almost as if he can read my thoughts, his hands grab my hips and he drags me across the sheets until I'm snuggled tightly to his body. Smoothing my hair down, he brings his mouth to mine and kisses me softly yet passionately. I know for a fact that I haven't felt this peaceful and relaxed in nearly a decade. I file everything to memory — the way his scent lingers in my nose, how perfectly his skin feels pressed against mine, the sugary, sweet taste of his lips, and the sound of his heart beating out a rhythm, a song only my soul can hear.

"Goodnight, Mr. Ellis. Thank you for tonight. I won't forget this for a long time."

"This is the first of many nights together." He kisses my lips one more time. "Good night, Trina."

And he doesn't disappear.

Chapter Twenty

Kat
(Secret — Maroon 5)

It's Friday evening and the Daniels Saunders' story is still getting airtime on the local news stations. The governor's office has placed him on a paid leave of absence pending further investigation of the situation; and his wife — as well as the mayor — have only spoken out to ask for privacy and understanding during this difficult time for their family. A tiny bit of guilt threatens to ruin my happiness, but I quickly swallow it back down, remembering that I didn't force him to do anything he wasn't more than willing to do. He actually approached me at the bar, knowing damn well what his intentions were. He's deserves everything he gets, and I've done his wife a favor if she truly had no idea what a cheating slime ball he is.

Feeling satisfied with the results of my first task, I focus on the next mission at hand. I pull up my laptop and begin to search through other employees that work in the governor's office. I narrow it down to two candidates — the assistant budget director and the crisis coordinator — both of which appear to be under the age of fifty and are photographed with wedding rings on. I'm having a difficult time finding much information on their personal lives, so I call up Travis to do some reconnaissance.

"Gorgeous girl, how are you?" he answers the phone.

"I'm good, Trav. How about you?"

"I'm just sitting here waiting for my dinner invitation that I was promised," he says teasingly.

"Mhmm. I bet you haven't left your place since the last time we talked."

He laughs and retorts, "You know it, sweet thing. Is that why you're calling today? Seeing when I'm free next? You know I keep a very busy calendar, Miss Kat."

"You're such an ass," I chuckle. "No, I'm actually calling because I have another job for you, if you're interested?"

"Always for you. Whatcha got?"

I give him the names of both men and ask him to get me any information he can. We agree on a time allotment and price, and as we're ending the call, I invite him over for dinner on Monday, telling him that he can bring the information then. I hang up the phone, hopeful that one of the two will work out for my plan, and get dressed to go out for the evening.

Chapter Twenty-One

Trina
(Fix You — Coldplay)

Lucca and I are going out on our first official date tonight. I feel like we're doing things a little bit backwards considering I've already spent the night at his house twice this week, but I've never been one to do things in the traditional style. I know it's irrational and more than a bit silly, but I've never done something like this with someone that I *really* like so I'm a little nervous about going out in public with him. The more time I spend we spend together, the more I start to develop real feelings for him, and I'm cognitively trying to push past the mental and emotional road blocks that emerge from my deep-rooted fear of getting hurt.

Taking a long look in the mirror before leaving, I realize he's never seen me dressed up like this. I'm wearing a fitted, backless champagne-colored dress that hits about mid-thigh with matching strappy heels. I've styled my hair in a simple chignon with stray ringlets falling loosely around my face in order to show off the back of the dress. My opaque eye make-up highlights my bright blue irises and I'm wearing a thin coat of shimmery pink lipstick to accentuate my full lips. I hope that he appreciates the stylish and sophisticated Trina as much as he seems to like the effortless and comfortably-dressed one. Then I wonder what in the world it is about him that makes me even care, but I do — way more than I should.

Our reservations are at 15 East at eight o'clock, and despite a somewhat heated argument with my driver, I get my way and take a taxi to the highly acclaimed sushi restaurant. Lucca is standing outside when the car pulls up, and I am in awe of how incredibly gorgeous he looks. Dressed in black slacks with a light blue dress shirt under a charcoal sports coat, his usually unkempt brown hair is somewhat tame and his often stubbly face is freshly shaved. After paying the driver, I exit the car and as soon as he sees me his radiant smile greets me. Those damn butterflies that I always read and hear about have apparently taken up residence in my stomach, and I rather like the way they make me feel — they're welcome to stay a while.

Rushing over to me, he slips his arms around my waist and draws me into him. "You truly are exquisite, Miss Foster," he whispers as he lightly kisses me just below the ear.

Goose bumps jacket my delicate skin his warm breath glides over it. "You clean up pretty nicely yourself, Mr. Ellis," I reply. "I'm more than impressed."

"I'm glad you approve." He releases me from his embrace and grabs my hand, leading me towards the door. "Are you hungry? Let's go in."

Grinning ear-to-ear, I happily shadow him to the building; however, just before I walk through the glass door a familiar black SUV turning the corner catches my eye. I pause briefly and look at the New Jersey plates to confirm my suspicion. Sighing internally, I turn around and redirect my attention to Lucca and focus on having an enjoyable dinner.

Two bottles of sake and nearly three hours later, we're nestled into a corner table lost in our own little world, thoroughly appreciating each other's company. Conversation between the two of us flows effortlessly, and the delicious seven course tasting menu that we both ordered doesn't disappoint. We casually mention to our server that we're on our first date and the manager brings us over a complimentary piece of their bittersweet chocolate cake and soba ice cream. We're both delighted with the thoughtful service, and of course the unexpected sweets.

He teases as he feeds me a bite of the dessert. "This is pretty good, but it's no Blue Bell Homemade Vanilla."

Laughing softly, I shake my head. "No, you're right; it's not. And it's not nearly as fun when we aren't playing Twenty Questions to go along with it."

He smirks at my response. "Ah, so you actually enjoyed baring your secrets to me?"

"I wouldn't go that far, but I haven't minded what we've talked about so far." I stick my finger in the cold ice cream and dab it on the end of his nose with a giggle. "My favorite part is learning more about you, though."

"You are a little devil! I can't believe you did that!" Using his napkin, he cleans his face, and I love that he can't stop smiling. "I should spank you for that later," he says in a low voice.

"Spank me? You must be drunk; there's no way in hell I'd let you do that," I retort.

A thoughtful expression crosses his face and he leans in closer to me. "Have you ever been spanked, Trina? As an adult that is?"

"Uh, that would be a negative. If you haven't figured it out yet, I'm not real comfortable around most people. And you already know that I've never had a serious relationship, so what would make you think that I'd allow some stranger to spank me? I like to be in control at all times — giving someone the go-ahead to slap my bare ass as hard as they can doesn't really fit in what I've got going."

He sits back in his chair and thinks intently for a moment without speaking. Then he raises his hand to my face and tucks a loose curl behind my ear before cupping my chin. His eyes pierce into mine as he states matter-of-factly. "I want to spank you. Tonight."

"Did you not just hear me? *No* one is spanking me." I feel like I should be outraged and incensed with his obvious disregard for my request, or non-request in this case. However, my body isn't on the same page as my brain because the butterflies from earlier in the night have morphed into baby dragons that are flapping around wildly and breathing their fire directly in the area where my thighs meet.

"Yes, I heard you, but I also saw the blush creeping up your neck and the tips of your ears when I first mentioned it." His voice has dropped several octaves and it's like he's bypassing the logical part of my brain completely and talking directly to my hormones. "And when I said the word 'tonight,' you started squirming around in your seat as those panties grew wet, all merely at the thought of me smacking that tight little ass of yours."

Body now aflame, I need to get out of this restaurant in a hurry. I don't even know what to say to him, so I sit there silently, but impatiently. Thankfully, he doesn't say anything else about it. He pays the bill and then leads me outside with a possessive hand on my lower back. The entire time we're walking, his words are echoing in my head. *I want to spank you. Tonight.* Over and over they torment me, until my body convinces my mind that I do indeed want to be spanked. *I've officially gone crazy.*

Once outside in the early April night, he abruptly stops walking and he lightly grabs my arm. Turning me around to face him, he asks as if he knows I've already agreed to his plan, "Are we staying at my house tonight?"

"We can go to mine. It's closer," I say softly. *I'm not just crazy; I'm certifiable.* I'm risking everything I've worked so hard for, but somehow I know that this feels right. The surprised look on his face pleases me, and instead of saying anything, he kisses me gently with an unspoken "thank you."

He goes to hail a cab, but I figure at this point, I'm going to really push his comfort zone, much like he's doing to me. I grab his arm and bring it back down to his side. "No, hold on." I grab my phone and send a quick text message.

In less than two minutes, the black Range Rover pulls up to where we're waiting. Leo jumps out of the driver's seat and comes around to open the door for us while Lucca stands frozen, unable to suppress the look of shock on his face. I step up to the SUV and climb into the backseat.

"Are you coming with me or not?" I ask sassily.

Shaking himself from his stupor, he slides in next to me and gives me a stern look. "Not just one spanking," he grumbles and my dragons begin to dance again.

Leo gets back in the car and looks at me in the rearview mirror, waiting for his instructions. "Home, Leo," I say. The sadness in his eyes is undisguisable and I know that he knows. He and I need to have a serious talk, but now isn't the time or place. I try to communicate that through my look, but he's already redirected his focus to the road.

"Lucca, this is Leo — my life-long friend and my driver. Leo, this is Lucca — one of my fellow teachers and my..." I pause not knowing what to call him.

"Boyfriend," Lucca finishes the sentence, shooting me a glare. "It' a pleasure to meet you, Leo. I appreciate you making sure Trina gets around safely."

"Nice to meet you, as well," Leo replies politely. "I'm sure I'll be seeing quite a bit more of you now that you and Miss Foster are seeing each other."

This really isn't how I intended the introduction between the two males in my life to go, but I'm relieved it's over and done with. The ride to my place is a short one, but tonight it feels as if it's taking hours. I can't wait to escape the awkward confines of the vehicle. Leo pulls right up to the door once we reach the building, and the door man is waiting to let us out.

"Goodnight, Leo. I'll message you tomorrow," I say as I exit the car.

"Goodnight, Miss Foster," he says despondently before driving away.

Lucca remains quiet as we walk through the lobby and ride the elevator up to my apartment, just observing everything around him. Once we're inside, I begin to feel apprehensive about my decision to bring him here; however, when he loops his arms around my waist from behind and tenderly kisses the top of my head, I begin to relax.

"So, this is my place," I say as we stand in the middle of the living room. "Make yourself comfortable. I'd give you the official tour, but I think it's pretty self-explanatory."

"It's a beautiful place, but I'm not interested in any tours right now," he whispers seductively in my ear as he playfully swats my ass. That's all it takes to send my body right back to the aroused state it was in at the restaurant.

Spinning around in his arms to face him, I draw my bottom lip in between my teeth and nibble softly. "What *are* you interested in, Mr. Ellis?"

He smirks and pulls my lip free of my bite with his thumb. "You, Miss Foster." Less than a second later, his mouth is on mine, kissing me fervently. The taste of his mouth is sweeter than any ice cream on the planet and the way his hands caress me sets my body ablaze.

Not wanting to take this any further in the living room, I reluctantly tear my mouth from his. "Bedroom," I slur as I drag him into my room.

Lucca kicks off his shoes, sheds his jacket, and unbuttons the top button of his shirt, making himself more comfortable, before sitting down on the ottoman at the end of my bed. "Come stand in front of me," he commands. I hurry over to stand in front of him, anxious to find out what he's going to do. I've never allowed anyone to be in control over me like this before, and I find it thrilling and exhilarating. I still don't know what it is about him that not only allows, but encourages, this kind of domination over me. There's something about him that makes me want to please him; it brings me an inner-calmness that I just can't explain.

"Turn around," he instructs.

Doing exactly as he says, I turn so that I'm facing away from him.

"Undress for me. Leave your panties on." My insides coil up tightly with his words.

I step out of my heels and kick them to the side, then unzip the side of my dress and allow it to fall to the floor. Standing in only a lacy red thong, I eagerly await what's next.

Ordering me to take a step back so that my ass is literally right in front of his face, he begins to lightly run his soft hands up and down the backs of my legs. I groan softly and slightly spread my legs as he nears the apex, and he stops, removing his hands.

"I want you stand there, perfectly still and quiet, while I study your gorgeous body. Do you understand?"

I nod my head which is followed by a hard slap on my ass cheek. "I expect a verbal response when I ask you a question. Do you understand?"

"Yes," I answer, not wanting another smack.

He slaps the other cheek. "Yes what?"

"Yes, sir." Again, I reply quickly.

For the next ten minutes, he studies my body — head to toe and front to back — with his eyes and hands, delicately sweeping his fingertips over every inch of my creamy skin, making comments such as "stunning" and "perfect" as he does his inspecrion. It takes everything in me not to move or say anything, but my desire to please him dictates my actions. The vulnerability I feel standing nearly naked in front of him, excites me in a way I never knew possible.

I'm facing him when he finishes, and he places one simple, sweet kiss on my belly. "Are you doing okay?" he asks sincerely.

"Yes, sir," I reply.

"Do you want me to continue?"

"Yes, sir."

"Look at me," he says softly.

Bringing my gaze down to his, a mix of passion and concern stare back at me. "I've never been into this kind of thing before. I'm not a Dom, or anything like that, and the last thing I ever want to do is hurt you," he clarifies. "But like I told you before, you bring out this side of me..." He shakes his head and chuckles. "Bend down here." Instantly, I drop to my knees so that we are eye-level with one another, and he continues. "I can't even explain what you do to me, but I *need* to take care of you. I know you've got demons deep inside that head of yours that you're dealing with, and I'm pretty sure that I scare you just as much as you scare me, but I think we're good together. I think we can fix each other if we just give this a chance." Cupping my face with his hands, his thumbs stroking back and forth across my cheek bones, he pulls me to him and captures my mouth with his in a tender kiss. "Let me fix you, Trina."

"I hope you can," I whisper back.

The kiss ends and we pick back up where we were. "Stand up, baby. I want to see you again." Eagerly, I get back to my feet and wait for his next command. He dips his finger into the elastic band of my thong and runs it back and forth across my lower abdomen. "Red lace, eh? You really are a devil woman, aren't you?" he asks with a smirk.

"Sometimes, sir," I answer truthfully.

"Do you deserve a spanking for your bad behavior?"

"Yes, sir." If he only knew.

He stands up, removing his belt and unbuttoning his shirt. I desperately want to reach out and touch his chest, but I don't. Sitting back down on the edge of the oversized stool, he pats his legs. "Bend over my lap," he instructs.

Throwing any lingering modesty I may with him have out the window, I position myself on his lap so that he has perfect access to my ass. Without any warning, his hand comes slamming down, leaving behind a sharp, stinging sensation. Before I even have a chance to react, the second slap makes contact, and naturally, I squirm at the hot pain. As I wriggle beneath his hand, my clit presses against his leg, sending a rush of heat and wetness to flood between my legs. He spanks me two more times before stopping to softly caress my inflamed cheeks. His hand dips down between my legs, lightly stroking the outside of my drenched panties.

"Despite your insistence to the contrary at dinner, I think you enjoy being spanked quite a bit," he says in a low voice. I lift my hips, pushing my pussy harder against his hand, wanting him to apply more pressure to the aching need that continues to grow. *Smack!* His hand makes contact again and I cry out. *Smack! Smack! Smack!* I'm a writhing mess in his lap; grinding myself on his thigh, I'm drunk with lust and begging him to spank me again and again as he alternates between slapping and rubbing my ass and juicy pussy.

Abruptly, he stops, and commands me to stand up. I stumble to my feet; my legs feeling as if they're made of Jell-O and I'm panting for breath. He rises to his feet in front of me, struggling to breathe as well. He hastily takes his pants and shirt off, tossing them aside, and then closes the gap between us. We begin to kiss feverishly, exploring each other's mouths while my hands weave through his tresses. His fingers glide the band of my panties down my legs, to reveal my smooth, hairless mound. He traces slow circles on the top of my pussy with his fingertip, and then slides it slightly lower to dip into the warm wetness of my slit. I gasp in pleasure, but his mouth swallows it as he continues to fuck me with his tongue. His index finger runs back and forth between my swollen clit and my soaked center, making sure it's all coated with my sweet juices. Then, he brings his hand up, pulling his mouth away from mine and traces the finger, wet with my arousal, around my full pouting lips, until they glisten. I smile softly at his glazed-over eyes. He lifts me up in his arms and walks me to the bed, sitting me in a somewhat upright position, my legs spread out in front of him.

"Stop me at any point you feel uncomfortable. I only want to please you, Trina," he whispers after he kisses my lips firmly.

He looks down at me for a minute before bending over to slide my panties the rest of the way down my legs, lifting each foot in turn until they're completely off. My eyes are fastened on the straining cock in his boxers, as he then kneels between my legs and brings the flimsy material to his face to deeply inhale my heady aroma before flinging them to the side. Leaning forward, he smiles up at me until his mouth is hovering right above one of my rosy nipples. He swoops down to take the peak in between his lips, moaning my name as he rolls it around in his mouth. One of his hands teases the nipple not being relished by his mouth, as the other hand travels down my tummy to rest against my hip. Whimpering with pleasure, I arch my hips up to grind my wet cunt against his tight stomach. I notice him shudder as he quickly switches sides to the other breast, suckling and nipping at the pebbled peak with his teeth. His hands skim the length my stomach, then around my back and down to my backside. He lifts me up so that my pussy nestles against his waistline, soaking his skin.

His mouth continues to ravage my breasts while his hands flex on my ass, pulling my cunt up to grind against him while my fingers are buried in his hair, holding his face against my nipples. He begins to kiss his way down my flat stomach, pausing to kiss my belly button- slowly tracing a circle around it with his tongue and then licking and kissing lower until his mouth hovers above my sweet spot. Flashing me a wicked grin, he lifts my thighs up and places them on his shoulders, so that my throbbing pussy is positioned directly in front of his face. He grabs my hips with both hands and tugs me down on the bed; the control he holds over his desire is slipping as his eyes grow heavy with lust and he licks his full lips. Not wasting another moment, he buries his face in between my legs and begins to make love to me with his mouth. His tongue is everywhere at once — flicking against my clit, nuzzling against my thighs, sliding into my sweet hole. His hands inch back down and begin to play with my bottom again, spreading the cheeks.

"Oh fuck, Lucca," I moan as he devours me. The combination of the sound of his kissing and slurping mixed with the pungent smell of sex and the incredible things he's doing with his mouth have me bucking and grinding furiously, my orgasm building rapidly. His index finger begins to trace slow circles against my puckered ass hole, teasing it as his tongue flicks, sucks, and nibbles my clit. I groan loudly and my body tenses , fluttering against his mouth, as I succumb to the pleasure and allow my release to flow freely against his tongue. He laps at my sweet juices until my body stops trembling and I relax in his hands, then softly kisses the inside of my thigh before moving back up my body.

"You taste unbelievably delicious, my little devil woman," he murmurs against my lips before kissing my deeply, sharing the erotic flavors of my orgasm with me.

"I need you, Lucca," I reply huskily. My thumbs hook inside the waistband of his boxers and I push them off, freeing his hard cock. He rises up on his elbow as I take the shaft in one hand and begin to stroke the length of it. Looking down in between our bodies, I use my thumb to rub the drop of pre-cum escaping the tip and rub it all over the purple head. I guide the tip of it to my slick pussy lips and run it up and down, coating it with my juices.

Growling like an animal, he grabs my hands and brings them up over my head, pinning them with one hand. With his free hand, he grabs his cock and lines it up with my slit. Slowly, he eases himself inside of me, my wet pussy gripping him snugly as his cock feeds my desirous core. "Oh my God, you feel amazing," he murmurs in between his shortened breaths.

He kisses my shoulder gently, hugging me close to him, and then begins to stroke in and out at a steady pace. I can feel my body stretching to fit around him as his throbbing cock grows larger inside of me. He grunts my name as his pace increases; the rhythmic sound of our bodies slapping against each other along with our labored breathing sparks the beginning of another orgasm growing deep inside my belly. He bites my shoulder lightly as he buries his cock completely inside of me. The ecstasy takes control of my body as he pulls out and slams into me again. Jerking and moaning, my body shudders as I lift my hips and fall over the edge. Feeling him join me as I soar into euphoric bliss, my walls clench around his shaft until I no longer feel him pulsating within me.

Still buried inside of me, he collapses, careful not to crush me with his weight. It takes several minutes for us both to gain control of our breathing and for our heart rates to return to a normal pace. He trails light kisses across my neck and shoulder as he lifts up his head to look at me. Pushing my sweaty hair back away from my face, he brings his mouth to mine in a gentle kiss. "My devil woman is indeed an angel," he drawls lazily.

I smile sleepily at him, still sensually intoxicated. "That was pretty heavenly," I agree. Slipping into a deep sleep, our bodies cling to each other and remain that way until we wake the following morning.

Chapter Twenty-Two

Kat
(Enjoy the Silence — Breaking Benjamin)

The weekend flies by in a blur and before I know it, Monday evening is upon me. Travis and Leo are both coming over for dinner, and up until about an hour ago, I had completely forgotten about it. I run to the local grocery store when I get home from work to grab some things for dinner and a couple bottles of wine.

The guys arrive within about five minutes of each other, and thankfully, Travis is first. I haven't seen Leo since Friday night, and we didn't part on exceptionally good terms. I owe him an explanation of what's going on or at least the full story because I'm sure he's figured most of it out.

"Oh, my lovely Kat, you look beautiful as always," Travis says as I greet him at the door. He's so over-the-top sometimes, but he's one of the few people I trust and would consider a friend. I don't know much about his life these days, and he doesn't know much about mine, but nonetheless, we've got some history over the past few years that keeps us close.

"Look at you, stranger," I exclaim, noting his purple-tipped spiky hair. "Did Halloween move to April and no one tell me?"

Picking me up in a warm embrace and twirling me around, he laughs hard. "No, it's called *style*; if you ever came out with me, you'd know what I'm talking about."

I playfully roll my eye as he sets me down on the floor. "Yeah, yeah... I'm more than fine with what I've got going on," I retort.

He follows me into the kitchen where he proceeds to help himself to a tasting of the beef stroganoff that's simmering on the stove. I slap at his hand when he attempts to dip it back in for a second time.

"Get your grubby fingers out of our dinner. Who knows where those hands have been!" I scold him.

"You're so mean to me," he retorts with a pout. "If I didn't know any better, I'd think you didn't like me."

A knock on the door interrupts our conversation. "Ooh, that's Leo! I'll get it," Travis says excitedly, bounding to the entrance.

Dropping the egg noodles into the boiling water, I hear the two male voices making their way into the kitchen, joking and laughing. I look up at them, my eyes catching Leo's and I can tell that he hasn't been sleeping well.

"Hey, Leo," I say overly-cheerful. "How was your day?"

"It was fine, thanks," he answers with a forced smile.

I'm not sure if Travis can pick up on the tension or not, but fortunately, he jumps in and starts talking to Leo about some motorcycle he's interested in buying. They continue to talk while I finish preparing the food, my mind wondering what's being served for dinner at a certain brownstone in Park Slope.

Dinner passes uneventfully; Travis carries most of the conversation as he catches us up on what's being going on with him since he obviously has much more of a social life than either Leo or me. After we put all of the dishes in the sink, Travis grabs the satchel that he brought with him and pulls out a notepad.

"Alright, I've got the information you requested. I'm not sure what kind of scoop you're looking for, but either way, I've got some good news and I've got some bad news," he explains. "First, there's this Michael James guy. He's the crisis coordinator, and he's obviously learned a thing or two from the dumb asses he's had to cover for, because he's squeaky clean. From everything I could tell, he goes to work and then straight home most days; and if he happens to leave the house in the evenings or on the weekends, he has his entire family in tow. He goes to church, coaches his son's baseball team... you get the picture."

"Yeah, he's not what I'm looking for. So tell me about the other one," I say disappointed.

Sniggering, he turns the page on the pad. "Mr. Jeffrey Lancaster is the polar opposite of the first guy. He's thirty-three, been divorced twice, and just recently got engaged again. This last woman was an *entertainer* that he got pregnant," he pauses, shakes his head, and looks up at me and then over at Leo. "The guy screams sleaze-ball just by looking at him, but I also found out some other pretty interesting information from one of my associates. He belongs to an extremely private, underground sex club called *Sequestered*. The place charges fifteen thousand dollars just for an initial membership fee and then has monthly dues of two thousand dollars. From what I've been told it caters to all sexual appetites. Some people just use it as a place to hook up with other rich people, but most members are rather deviant in their tastes. Now, my contact couldn't be one hundred percent, but when I showed her his picture, she thinks he's a switch, which means some nights he's a Dominant and other nights he's a submissive."

The entire time he's rattling off the details my mind is kicked into high gear. There are all sorts of possibilities with this situation; I need to get in that club.

"Perfect!" I cry out. "Trav, you've gotta get me in there. I'll pay whatever."

"I'm not so sure this is a good idea," Leo cuts in.

Swinging my head around at him, I look at him like he's gone crazy. "Why, in the hell, not? This couldn't be any better."

"It's not safe for you to go in there alone, Kat. I know you think you can handle yourself, but you've never been in a place like this," he argues. "And not to mention, I'm sure they're not going to let you walk around with a camera in a secretive place like that."

"I can figure something out there as long as Travis can get me in."

Travis pipes up with a smug smile. "I had a good feeling you were going to want that, so I've already worked something out, but there's a small issue."

"Okay..." I prod.

"The first time she can get you in is at Night of Serendipity, which is their semi-annual new member meet-and-greet sort of thing. These are the only two times a year that people can join, so this way no one will question your being there. In addition, all members are required to attend, so it also guarantees he will be there as well."

"When is it?" I ask anxiously.

"The last weekend in May."

"What?" I squeak. "That's like six or seven weeks from now."

Groaning, he runs his hands through his hair. "I knew that wouldn't make you very happy, little miss impatient, but it's the best I can do — and it's a sure thing."

I sit silent for a few minutes, processing everything he just said. It truly is a flawless set-up; the guy will be in prime form, served to me on a silver platter. And maybe waiting a little time in between each revelation will be better so that the incidents aren't linked to the same temptress. It also gives Trav's source more time to watch Mr. Lancaster and to find out additional information about his activities and preferences at the club.

"Okay, I'm in," I announce. "Can your girl continue to watch him and let us know more about his inclinations at the club? I'll make it worth her while."

Travis nods, but Leo remains silent. "It'll cost you ten thousand for entry and for her recon services up until the event. She'll provide me with weekly reports, as well as get me all the information of what you'll need to know and what will be expected of you that night."

"Can I get in, too?" Leo asks him. "I would feel better if I was at least inside with her, in case something happens."

I want to tell him that it's not necessary, that I can handle myself, but I know that he's right. Leo's main concern has always been about my safety and well-being; he won't let anything happen to me.

"It shouldn't be a problem; however, it may cost a little bit more money."

"I'll pay whatever. I want Leo in with me," I answer quickly. The slight smile that plays at Leo's mouth doesn't go unnoticed, and it makes me feel better. "In addition," I continue, "we'll both be using an alias so find out what kind of identification we'll need to show that night, so I can make sure we have those."

After we iron out all of the details, the conversation turns to us reliving memories from when Travis and I were in college together. The two of us kept poor Leo busy during those few years as we were always managing to get in some kind of trouble around the city. Thankfully, he saved our asses time and time again.

I get up to pour us all another glass of wine and look over at the two of them together. Despite the fact that Travis has moved on from us, I'm thankful that after everything we've been through, it's like old times when we get together. Well, like old times minus the sex. For a period of about six months during my sophomore year, the three of us slept together on a pretty regular basis. I'm pretty sure I am the only female Travis has ever had sex with, and I'm positive he's the only guy Leo has ever been with. The two of us were young and curious, not to mention we drank way too much and did too many drugs, while Leo basically just did whatever I wanted him to. Once Travis got into a serious relationship with another guy, he no longer joined us, but Leo and I were lovers until I graduated from college, until the night he turned me down. After that, we've continued to mess around sexually but I refused to have actual intercourse with him, and I've refrained from it with anyone else for the last two years — up until this past weekend.

The night grows late, and after we polish off the third bottle of wine, the guys both leave. It's a little weird saying goodbye to Leo in that manner, a quick kiss on the cheek at the door, but I suppose I'll get used to it. Tomorrow, I'll call him so that we can talk about everything that's been going on and my plans for the future — in all aspects of my life.

Falling into my bed, once I've stripped out of my clothes, I grab my phone to see that I've missed several text messages reminding me that someone is thinking of his devil woman.

Chapter Twenty-Three

Katrina

(Breathe Me — Sia)

The following afternoon, I text Leo and ask him to come over so that we can talk. Feeling a strain in our relationship is eating at me; I just want us to get everything out. He's at my apartment less than thirty minutes later and I greet him with a big hug.

"Thanks for coming so quickly," I say once we release each other and are walking into the kitchen. "Can I get you something to drink?"

"I'll have whatever you're having," he replies, sitting down at the dining room table.

I grab us each a beer and join him, nervous about how to start the conversation.

"Leo, we need to talk about what's going on," I begin. "I know you aren't happy with me right now..."

"It's not that I'm unhappy with you," he interrupts. "I'm worried about you, and I'm not sure you know what you're doing."

He stops talking and looks at me, waiting for a response. "Go ahead. Tell me what you see happening."

"For the last two years you've been focused on this plan to get revenge on your dad. You've basically been living a double life — the schoolteacher during the day and the seductress at night — and I've done everything I can to make sure they stayed separate. You've been smart about not getting involved with people because you knew that if you did, it would jeopardize what you're working towards." He takes a swig of his beer before continuing. "You finally put this plan into motion, beginning with the Saunders guy, but at the same time you go and get involved with some douche from your day life. I don't know what this guy knows and what he doesn't know, but he's bound to want some answers about who you are."

"He's not a douche, his name is Lucca," I spat.

"I *know* his name," he grumbles. "Anyhow, I just don't understand it. I'm neither stupid nor naive, Katrina. Even though you've always said that you would never fall in love and all of that, I knew it was bound to happen. I honestly didn't think you would risk everything until after this mission of yours is complete."

Slumping back in my chair, I groan, knowing he's right. "I didn't plan on this, Leo. He just kind of appeared in my life. And I don't know how to explain it... he has this effect on me that makes me do things I would've never done before."

"Look, you can't help what you feel. Believe me, I of all people know that," he says with a frustrated sigh. "But I think you need to choose — either abandon the thing with your dad and focus on moving on with your life or break things off with this guy, at least until you're finished with all of this other stuff. If you continue to try to do both, I promise things are going to get messy and you're going to end up getting hurt or hurting him. You've already let your guard down so much with him. You brought him here for God's sake! It's my job to make sure you're safe and protected, but your behavior these past couple of weeks has made that really fucking hard."

"I know and I'm sorry. Again, I never planned for this. My intentions were to continue on as I've been doing, but this just kinda happened... *he* just kinda happened."

"So you tell him that you've got some family issues that you really need to focus on, and that you can't get involved right now. Once everything is resolved, you'd love to give it a go then. If your feelings for each other are real, they should still be there in a few months. I mean, come on, you've known each other for like a minute, it's not like you're in love with him. Be smart about this."

Everything he says makes sense. I've been acting ridiculous allowing some guy I hardly even know to derail my plan of revenge — revenge that my mom deserves. I know that's not Lucca's intentions, but nonetheless, his presence in my life distracts me and makes me act reckless. I realize that I have to let Lucca go before he finds out the truth; thinking I could carry out my plan and walk back into his waiting arms is just a fantasy. Leo's right. I should've never gotten involved with him to begin with, I should've never brought him to my home, and I damn sure shouldn't have let him spank and fuck me. Angry at myself for acting so foolish and irresponsible, I finish my beer and slam the bottle on the table.

"You're right!" I exclaim incensed. "I've had a complete lapse of judgment recently, and I need to regain control of myself. I can't believe how thoughtless and careless I've been. I'm really sorry, Leo."

Smiling, he leans over and places his hand on top of mine. "Don't be too hard on yourself. I know you were forced to grow up way too early, but you forget that you're still young and figuring stuff out. Shit, I'm thirty-one and I'm still learning."

I nod in agreement, but I know we still have one more thing to talk about. "There's still something else we need to discuss."

"Okay, what is it? Are you rethinking the sex club thing?"

"No, not that. Leo, I need to be honest about my feelings for you." I chew on my lip nervously, not sure exactly how to word this. "You have been in my life since the day I was born. I grew up having the biggest crush on you, and once we became sexually active, I thought we would be together forever. You've put up with my experimental phase during college, you've watched and helped me seduce guys on a daily basis for the last couple of years, and you've never once tried to control or even question my behavior. I know that you're always here for me, whatever I need, and I've taken advantage of that. I never meant to belittle you, but I know I've acted selfish and extremely inconsiderate even though you've always put me first. I'm sorry for that."

"No need to apologize. I just told you that I realize you are young and still figuring out what you want in life. I don't fault you for that," he says with an understanding expression in his eye.

"Don't make excuses for me. Ever since Momma's been gone, I've used her death to act however I want, and I know that it's not right," I argue. "I *do* love you, Leo. I've always loved you, but we won't ever be together as a couple. I hope you can understand this, but you know too much about me. Once I take care of him and I feel like vengeance has been served, I want to put these past nine years behind me and I want to forget about the person I've been. She wouldn't want me to be this manipulative bitch that I've become — I know that." I can't help but start crying as I think about her and knowing that she'd be ashamed of the things I've done and the way I've treated him.

Getting out of his chair, he comes over and picks me up out of mine, then sits back down cradling me in his lap. "Don't cry, Katie-bug. It kills me to see you like this," he whispers, holding me tightly against his body. "Don't ever worry about me. I love you in a way that I can't explain, but I've known for a long time that I'm not the one for you. I've made it my job to take care of you until that one comes along. I'm a big boy and am well aware of what I'm doing, and I won't abandon you. Just think of me as your nightlight until the day comes when the sun rises again in that fragile little heart of yours."

Chapter Twenty-Four

Trina

(Goodbye My Lover ~ James Blunt)

Knowing what I need to do, and actually doing it, are two very different things. Letting Lucca go, at least for now, is the best thing for both of us. I need to focus on other aspects of my life, and until I have closure with those, it's not fair to him for me to continually deceive him or keep him in the dark. I can't give him all of me, and he deserves more.

Tuesday night when I go to bed, I'm rehearsing exactly what I'm going to say to him, but the minute I see his face Wednesday morning, I know it's the last thing I want to do. I purposely avoid him throughout the day; however, when the final bell rings that afternoon, he's in my classroom before I can escape.

"What's going on, Trina?" he asks demandingly as he walks in.

Looking up at him from my desk, his expression tells me that he senses something's wrong. "Well, hello to you, too," I reply.

"Don't lie to me. I know you're hiding from me and I want to know why. We spend all weekend together, taking a pretty big step in our relationship I might add, and ever since Monday, you've been acting weird. You've been 'busy' the last two nights so that I couldn't see you or talk to you, without any explanation of what you're doing, and then today, you've been downright elusive. What did I do wrong?" His tone is more hurt than angry, and I feel awful knowing what I'm about to do.

"I can't do this, Lucca, especially not here. There are thing about me that you don't understand — that you can never understand — and quite honestly, I don't owe you an explanation for what I do. There's a reason that before you I didn't make friends with people or go out for happy hour with other teachers, and it's not simply because I'm a recluse. It's better for me if I'm alone, and it's better for you, too." It's taking everything inside of me not to break down, but I've got to do this. "You're a real sweet guy, and I have a great time when we're together, but I don't want to hurt you, and I *promise* you I will if we continue this."

"*I'm a real sweet guy*? Are you kidding me?" He runs his fingers through his hair, obviously extremely frustrated. "Do you have any idea how I feel about you, Trina? Everything I've told you has been one hundred percent true. I know that you've got issues with your past; I don't know what they are, but it's nothing I can't work with. I want to protect you, to take care of you; it's this feeling that I've never had before but it's like I *need* to. Do you know that meeting I had with Principal Matthews last week was me asking him, begging him, to keep me on here permanently next year just so that I could be close to you? And it's not to smother you, control you, or anything else other than the fact I *need* to be near you."

No longer able to hold back the tears, his words cut deep inside of me. The pained look draped across his face kills me. I don't want to end this; I want him to take care of me, but unfortunately, that's just not the reality of my situation. Standing up abruptly, I grab my purse and look at him one last time.

"I'm really sorry. This isn't what I want, but it's what has to be done. I'm not the girl you think I am, and you deserve better than me," I choke out through my sobs. "Goodbye, Lucca."

Then without another word, I brush past him, leaving him standing there speechless.

And I disappear.

Chapter Twenty-Five

Katrina

(Bleeding Out — Imagine Dragons)

Life isn't fair. I wish he would've killed me the same day that he took her life. I pay for his actions every damn day, and I'm tired of it — tired of the nightmares, tired of pretending I'm okay, tired of living this fucking life. I finally find someone that makes me forget about all of it, someone who breathes promise into this dark and hopeless heart of mine, and I have to say goodbye to him. Now, I not only want revenge for Momma, but also for Lucca and what might have been.

I can't wait to kill that fucker.

Chapter Twenty-Six

Trina

(Dreaming With a Broken Heart — John Mayer)

The day after I walked out on Lucca, I resign from my teaching position — effective immediately. As much as I love my kids, I can't fathom seeing him every day. I know that I'll break down and give into him; after all, it's what I really want to do. I tell the security desk at my apartment building that absolutely no one is allowed access to my place except for Leo. I know they wouldn't allow a stranger access anyway, but I feel I need to make a point of it.

I don't get out of bed for the first week. Leo comes over and makes me eat, but that's about all I'm willing to do. I've turned my phone off in case Lucca or Lauren tries to reach me. I cry all day and every night, and my nightmares are no longer about the sperm donor, but now it's Lucca and he's always just out of my reach. I can't listen to music anymore because every song reminds me of him somehow.

I contemplate going back to therapy, but that would mean getting out of bed. I know I shouldn't be so distraught over some guy that was only in my life for a blink of an eye, but as much as I try to convince myself of that, I fail miserably. Of course, this can't even come close to comparing to what it was like to lose Momma, but I feel like a small sliver of light had begun to shine on me again, and I was forced to close the shade and block it out.

I miss my kids. I miss music. I miss Lauren. And mostly, I miss Lucca.

Chapter Twenty-Seven

Katrina

(Soldier — Gavin DeGraw)

At the three week point of being home, I finally leave the apartment, but only because I have to go to the doctor for my annual check-up. Emerging from the security of my bed, I throw on the first clothes I can find, not caring in the least bit what I look like. I hide behind a pair of big sunglasses and make my way downstairs to where Leo waits with the car.

"Good to see you joining the living," he says in an attempt to make me smile, but I'm not amused.

"I'd rather be dead," I reply without feeling as I slide into the passenger seat of the SUV.

"She would want you to live, and live happily, Katrina," he scolds me before closing the door.

We don't speak for the rest of the trip. I know that he only wants what's best for me, but I'm struggling far worse than I ever imagined I would. I hate to be awake because I think about everything I'm missing out on, and I hate to be asleep because two different colored eyes and the sensations that he made me feel taunt me.

Pulling up to the professional building, he lets me out at the front door and I tell him that I'll text him when I'm finished. After waiting to be seen for nearly thirty minutes, I finally go back to an examination room, first stopping to check my weight and blood pressure. The doctor enters the room a few minutes later and she begins to caution me about my weight being below normal. She then begins going through a panel of questions about my health over the past year; thankfully, I've been well despite a common cold here and there. It's surprising that I haven't been sick more frequently since I was around small children all day long.

When she gets to the part about my sexual activities, I honestly report that I have indeed been sexually active, even if it was for just a three day period, and that I didn't use any protection. At the time with Lucca, it had felt so natural, that I didn't even think about asking him to wear a condom. And up until this moment, I've been so lost in my sadness and despair that I haven't even thought about the repercussions. Immediately, she has me take a pregnancy test and orders a full scope of blood work to check for every STD possible. Once I return to the room from the lab, the results from the test are in, and thankfully, it's negative. She finishes the exam, tells me that her office will call me if anything comes back irregular on the other tests, and advises me to gain some weight before sending me on my way.

Leo is waiting for me as soon as I walk back outside. "How'd everything go?" he asks with concern.

"I'm not pregnant," I reply deadpan.

"Well, I really wasn't expecting you to be, but that's a positive thing."

"Mhmm," I mumble as I stare out the window.

"Did she say anything else?"

His questions are really starting to get on my nerves. "She told me to eat more," I snap. "Anything else you want to know?"

Inhaling a deep breath, he shakes his head. "No. Sorry for caring, Katrina. I won't ask anything else, but I'm not going to let you push me away. I know you're hurting, and I'm here when you need me."

Instantly I feel bad for jumping on him; Leo's my rock and it's not his fault I'm in this place in life. If it wasn't for him, I probably would've gotten myself killed long ago, if not done it myself. "I'm sorry for snapping at you. I didn't think this would be so hard, Leo. I know it doesn't make any sense, but I miss him so much. There was just something about him…"

"You know your only other option is to tell him the truth."

I can't help but laugh at the preposterousness of his statement. "Yeah, right. How would that conversation go? 'Hey, Lucca. So here's the deal — my dad murdered my mom a few years ago so I'm planning on killing him sometime soon. You still wanna be my boyfriend?'"

Scowling at me, he growls, "Not like that. I just meant telling him about what happened."

I wave my hand to dismiss his idea. "I'm not sure what good that would do. Plus, after the way I just vanished from his life, I'm sure he never wants to talk to me again."

Mercifully, we arrive at my apartment; I'm finished with this conversation. Talking about him just makes me miss him more. "Well, if you want the opportunity, it's waiting for you right over there," he says nodding his head to the left of the building's front door.

My gaze flies to where he's looking and sitting on a bench is a despondent-but-hopeful-looking Lucca. Not bothering to ask any questions about why, what, or how, I jump out of the vehicle and rush over to him. As soon as he sees me, he stands up and braces himself as I lunge towards him. Catching me in his arms, he holds cuddles me against his body as I cry tears of happiness and overwhelming relief.

Chapter Twenty-Eight

Trina

(Patient Love — Passenger)

There are no words to describe the feelings pumping through my body as Lucca holds me snugly to him. I honestly thought I'd never see his beautiful eyes again, never inhale his clean-rain scent, and definitely never taste his lips on mine again. However, when his mouth finds mine, I know that I can't let him go again — I need him like I my lungs need air to breathe.

We stand there on the street, people passing by as if we don't exist, kissing, smiling, and reveling being in each other's presence again. We don't say anything for at least five minutes; we're just there — together.

Finally, I say to him, "We need to talk, Lucca. I've got so much to tell you."

Beaming, he nods his head emphatically. "Me too. Where do you want to go?"

I look around to see if Leo is still by the car, and he is, with a sad smile on his face. I wave at him, grinning like an idiot, and he waves back at me before ducking back into the driver's seat. "Let's go for a walk in the park. I could use the fresh air."

He grabs my hand and leads me around the building to where we can enter Central Park. Once we are strolling down one of the pathways, I take a deep breath before I begin telling my story.

"Lucca, what I'm about to tell you, I've never told another living soul. Leo knows the story because he lived the nightmare with me, but other than that, no one knows this. I'm taking a huge risk here because there's a good chance after what I tell you, you're going to walk away from me and never look back."

"Trina, there's nothing you could say that could make me turn my back on you. I've been absolutely miserable the past three weeks. I can't eat; I can't sleep; I can't focus on anything. I've been worried sick about you."

"Wait until I'm finished before deciding that, but please know, that if you choose to walk away, I won't fault you. At least I'll know that I laid it all out and was completely honest with you." He squeezes my hand for reassurance, and I launch into the full story.

"I was born Katrina Michelle Green, the only child to Stephanie Foster Green and Robert Allen Green. Like I've told you before, I grew up in an extremely affluent New Jersey suburb. My mom's family, the Foster's, are what most people call *old money,* and my dad..." I swallow hard; this is more difficult than I thought. "My dad was first known for his football career."

He gasps, realizing what I'm about to tell him. "Oh, Trina, I had no idea," he says softly. "I used to watch him on TV when I was a kid."

"There's no way you could've. I didn't want you to; I don't want anyone to," I admit regrettably. "Let's go sit down over on that park bench, and I'll tell you the truth about what happened that day."

Once we are comfortably seated facing one another, he insists that I drape my legs over his lap, and I continue. "I was fourteen and my mom and I were on a vacation together, but we decided to come home early because I wasn't feeling well. Leo had picked us up at the airport and taken us to the house. Everything seemed normal, we walked in through the front door, and she called out to my dad to see if he was home. There wasn't an answer at first, so she started to walk up the stairs towards her bedroom, when my dad appeared at the top of the landing. He was stark naked and was holding a gun. He didn't say a single word — he just shot her. I screamed out at him at the same time Leo walked inside carrying our luggage. The next thing I knew Leo picked me up and ran outside with me."

Lucca pulls me close, tenderly stroking my hair, and kisses away the tears freely flowing down my face. "You don't have to say anything else. I'm sorry that you had to relive that."

"There was another woman there with him, of course." I can't stop now; as hard as it is to talk about, I'm finding it equally therapeutic. "And he claimed that he thought it was a burglar breaking in because we weren't supposed to be home for a couple of days, but I know he saw it was her... He saw that it was her and pulled the trigger anyway. Who's to say if he wouldn't have killed me too if Leo hadn't been there?"

"Leo's a pretty great guy," he murmurs into my hair.

I'm a little perplexed at why he would say that, especially considering my and Leo's relationship, but I have to keep going. I've got to tell him everything. "So from that day on, I've had no real relationship with him. He was arrested, but released on bond shortly thereafter, and he never came back to the house. Rosa — our housekeeper and Leo's mom — raised me from that point on... or at least she tried to. A depressed teenager with no real parental figures, combined with a limitless bank account is a bad mixture, and it was finally Leo who got me to pull my shit together and straighten up somewhat. I moved to the city when I graduated high school because I couldn't bear to be in that house any longer — everything that reminded me of her made me sad and everything that reminded me of him filled me with rage."

"Why do you think that story would make me leave? I'm heartbroken for you and what you had to go through as a kid, but I don't blame you," he says compassionately.

"I'm not finished," I blurt out. "I've done some really horrible things since then."

Tilting his head, confused, he asks, "Like what? You know I haven't been perfect either. People make mistakes.. The important thing is that you learn from them and don't repeat them."

"For the past two years, I've been planning a way to get revenge on my dad, and now that's he been elected governor, I've started putting that plan in motion."

"Revenge how?"

"I want to torture him — make his life a nightmare like he did to her for the years leading up to her murder — but eventually, I want him dead," I state matter-of-factly. "I want to kill him."

"Babe, you don't really mean that. You know him dying isn't going to make her come back?" His voice tells me that he doesn't believe I'll go through with it. "

When The Sun Goes Down

"I know it won't bring her back, but I think I don't think I'll ever be over it until he's gone." No one can understand the depth of hatred that I have for that man.

I can see the concern set in on his face as he processes all of this information. "What's your plan?"

"Right now, I just want to wreak havoc on his political career. He always wanted to hold some high office, so he used his popularity to get elected, and now, I want to show everyone that he can't control his office much less a state. I haven't thought much past that."

"Did you have something to do with that Saunders' guy and his sex scandal?" he asks, the pieces coming together in his head.

"Yes," I reply bluntly without offering any more information.

"And you're planning to do more of that?"

"Yes."

"Does Leo know about this?"

"Yes."

Rubbing his face with his hands, he sighs heavily. "Can I ask the nature of your and Leo's relationship?" he asks, wincing. He knows the answer before I even open my mouth.

"Are you sure you want to know this?"

"I want to know everything about you, Katrina. I'm absolutely and completely wrapped up in you and I need to know what I'm dealing with. Like I told you before we began this talk, there's nothing you can say that's going to make me walk away from you, and when you get scared again and try to run away, I'm gonna persistently pursue you just like I did this time. I need to protect you."

"Okay," I say with a shrug, unsure of what he means by that. "Leo and I started having sex when I was seventeen, and though I wasn't exclusively with him, we continued our relationship up until recently. I love him, but in a different way. He's basically allowed me to use him as a security blanket for the past nine years, doing anything necessary to keep me happy and safe. We've discussed this not too long ago, and I've apologized to him for how I've treated him."

"How recently?" he questions.

"How recently what?"

"You said you've continued your relationship up until recently. When did you stop?"

"I haven't touched him since the first time you and I kissed," I answer honestly.

"Do you have any desire to be with him again?"

Shaking my head, I reply, "No, I don't want to hurt him anymore. Plus, there's only one person I want."

He grabs my face and kisses me hard. "Even though I understand why you feel the way you do, I'm never going to support you killing someone, and I honestly hope that there'll be something I can say or do to keep you from going through with it. Everything else I can come to terms with; I just need to know what's going on. I promise to be both patient and understanding while you do whatever you need in order to get closure with this, but please don't shut me out again. I want to talk more about this later, but the important thing is I'm not leaving your side."

I nod and nuzzle my face into his neck. I can't believe I just told him all of that, and even more so, I can't believe that he didn't run away screaming. We stay like that for several minutes before we begin to walk back to my place.

Neither of us says much of anything, both lost in our own thoughts, until I see a patch of dandelions just off of the pathway. I go over and pick two from the ground, handing one to him. "Time to make a wish," I tell him.

Grinning he takes the stem attached to the fluffy white flower. "On the count of three — ready? One. Two. Three."

Together we blow the downy seeds into the wind, allowing them to float away with our dreams on their tail. I look over at him and I know it's a moment I will never forget. The gentle sunshine — bathing my face with its rays — feels almost as good as the warmth radiating inside of me from having Lucca nearby, knowing that even after finding out the truth, he still wants to be with me.

"What did you wish for?" he asks, playfully nudging my shoulder with his.

"I can't tell you or it won't come true!" I exclaim.

"Oh, that's just an old wives' tale. Come on, I'll tell you mine if you tell me yours."

"Nope!" I call out as I run away from him. "Never!"

Chasing after me, it takes him no time to catch me and tackle me into the grass. He tickles me relentlessly, but I refuse to give in. Pinning me to the ground, he lowers himself to whisper in my ear, "I'll just have to spank it out of you later, *devil woman*."

Chapter Twenty-Nine

Katrina

(Secrets — One Republic)

Over the next several weeks, Lucca and I spend quite a bit of time hanging out in the evenings and weekends when he's not at work. I try hard to limit it to two or three times a week, so that we don't smother or grow tired of one another, but it's hard because I'm so comfortable and content when I'm with him. We haven't discussed my dad again since the day at the park, and that's perfectly fine with me. I love the way he's gentle and affectionate with me, but at the same time assertive and aggressive without being callous, especially in bed. Since I became sexually active as a teenager, I've always been the dominant one because I thought I needed that power. I'm now learning there's something overwhelmingly liberating in relinquishing control, but I know it has to be with the right person.

Now that I'm not spending my days hiding under my covers, I've started working on a few different projects to better myself as a person. First, with the insistence of both Leo and Lucca, I've started seeing my therapist, Dr. Donias, again. My grieving process after my mom died was a little different than most, because in essence, I lost both of my parents that day. I hadn't even realized how much guilt I've been carrying around with me since we'd returned early from the trip due to my illness. Accepting the fact that my father deserves one hundred percent of the responsibility is the first step I had to overcome. I tell her about my wishing his life was ruined, and often hoping that he died, but of course, I fail to mention I've seriously contemplated killing him or my involvement in the Saunders' photo scandal.

We're really focusing on my control issues as well. As much as she thinks that Leo is a terrific friend and applauds his selflessness in pretty much taking care of me over the past near-decade, she says his submission to me one hundred percent of the time only fuels the issue. It allows me to think that my behaviors are acceptable and appropriate. I tell her about him orally pleasuring me each night after I've had my way with some random guy, and she makes me realize how deplorable and offensive that is. I apologize to him constantly, but he always shrugs it off and tells me that all he wants is for me to be happy.

I never thought I'd be the type of person to read self-help books, much less get anything out of them, but Dr. Donias has recommended some really good ones, along with some helpful websites. I recognize why I feel the need to control everything — I believe I can manipulate the outcome of a situation based on what I think is the best thing for myself. Contrary to that belief though, I don't always know what the best thing for myself is, *and* I'll never be able to control other people's thoughts and actions; so basically, I'm setting myself up for eventual disappointment and failure. She is a huge fan of Lucca, and thinks he's a positive influence as I attempt to tackle the art of surrender. I've got a long way to go before I get there, but I'm moving in the right direction at least.

The other project that I've been working on during the day is taking online business classes. Since I obviously won't be getting another teaching job in the New York public school system anytime soon — they tend to frown upon immediate resignations with no good reason — I've been thinking about opening a private music school for underprivileged kids at some point in the future. I have the capital to get it started, but I don't know much about running a business, and it's something I would want to be hands on with not just hire people to run the school for me. Feeling the satisfaction in giving back to those children — similar to how I felt when I was at the school — is something that I'm striving towards.

I've definitely made huge progress in this short amount of time, but I've not given up on my plan. Not one bit. The Night of Serendipity at *Sequestered* is this coming Saturday, and I have full intentions of attending and hopefully finding Mr. Jeffrey Lancaster engaged in disgracefully unacceptable acts of debauchery.

Chapter Thirty

Kat
(My Body is a Cage — Arcade Fire)

The day has finally arrived and Travis has come through like always, giving me almost ten pages of Lancaster's ins and outs. As I sit in my bubble bath, pouring over the various notes tracking his behavior, it appears that he is very much the switch. I see the pattern clear as day; every other meeting he switches dominant-submissive-dominant-submissive, like clockwork. Assuming he doesn't deviate from this, he will be submissive for the new member induction.

"Perfect," I think to myself. Pulling the drain on my bubble bath, my routine comes back to me as if I did it yesterday. I grab the plush towel and pat myself dry.

"Kanebo Sensai, why are you so heavenly?" I whisper to myself with a grin as my skin screams in delight.

I slip on my black silk robe and lightly dance into the kitchen. Grabbing the Chevalier-Montrachet, something immediately feels off, and as I turn the bottle into the glass, only two drops seep out. Frustrated momentarily, I reach to the bottom rack of the wine chiller, a bottle of Domaine de la Romanée-Conti, my favorite burgundy, waits for me. I pop the cork, pour myself a quarter glass, and head back to the bathroom.

The eyeliner and mascara go on a little extra thick tonight. After applying a dab of blush, I playfully pop myself with shimmery powder. My mouth salivates as the cherry lip gloss glides on seamlessly, and I take just a small taste.

"Mmm, perfect!" I grin widely and blow a kiss at the mirror.

The wine goes down more easily than usual as I blow-dry my hair and then straighten it with the flat-iron. Gently shimmying the robe off my shoulders, I giggle at myself as I hang it back in its place; I've not felt this kind of excitement in quite a while. I fling open the closet and pull out my chosen outfit for the night, a silver-studded, black leather lace-up corset with a matching leather miniskirt. The skirt goes on without a hitch, but the corset I'm going to need help cinching up. As I'm putting on the black stilettos, I hear a knock at the door.

Lucca is escorting me instead of Leo. Once he found out about the plan, he insisted he be there for security purposes. Thankfully, Leo didn't balk at his request — not that he has the final say anyhow — but instead, gives us both pointers for things to look out for. He'll still be helping out in other ways. I'm concerned Lucca's jealousy may get the best of him if he sees me with another guy, but he swears to me he understands I'm there to do a job, and that unless he thinks I'm in danger, he won't interfere. We've discussed things I won't do, which is primarily intercourse with someone else.

Rushing to the entrance, an extremely handsome Lucca — dressed in an all-black designer suit — waits for me with a smile. I've seen him dressed up once before, but this is on another level. He looks like he just walked off a Gucci billboard in Times Square, and now I'm wondering if I'll be the one to get jealous if another woman approaches him.

"Wow," we say in unison, then burst out in laughter.

"Come in, come in. I'm almost ready," I say, kissing him hard on the mouth. "You look fantastic."

Following me inside, he squeezes my ass through the miniskirt. "I think I like you dressed in leather, devil woman."

"Anytime you'd like, Mr. Ellis," I quip back.

Prior to today, I had tiny surveillance cameras sewn into my corset and attached to his tie. We've been told that we'll not be allowed to bring anything inside with us — no purses, jackets, wallets, or anything else — only the clothes we're wearing, so I've gone through great expense to have these undetectable devices attached to our clothing. Leo will be monitoring the feed from a nearby parking lot. Only one hour of footage is recordable, so he'll determine on the laptop when to begin.

When The Sun Goes Down

Ever since Lucca and I got back together, my relationship with Leo has been improving as well. I think he sees the positive changes in me, and is truly happy that I seem to be getting my life somewhat together. The two of them get along better than I could've ever hoped for — not that they are best friends and go out for beers without me, but they both appreciate the role the other plays. I need both of them in my life and they both accept that. The three of us working together as a team tonight brings me great joy.

Half an hour later, we pull up to what appears to be another dingy warehouse in the industrial part of Queens. If it wasn't for the other luxury cars in front of us, waiting their turn to pull up to the valet attendants, I'd definitely think we are in the wrong place. Once it's our turn, the doors are opened and we are ushered into the building. The first room we enter is a check-in room where a busty redhead confirms our identification and collects all our personal belongings. Satisfied with the results after running our names through the computer system, she looks up at us and smiles. "Ah, two new inductees. Welcome to the club, and I hope you enjoy your Night of Serendipity."

The plan is to present ourselves as a couple in which he likes to watch me dominate other men, but we're going to play it by ear. Neither of us knows what to expect except for what Travis has told us; I trust Lucca to stay by my side and intervene if things get carried away. The nervous energy buzzing through my body continues to grow at a rapid pace the closer we get to being inside.

We're then buzzed through a massive gray door, where we're then transported into another universe. I can't help but to stand there gaping at my surroundings, but Lucca quickly nudges my shoulder to get me to move. The main area of the warehouse has been transformed to look like we're walking outside in the streets of Paris — complete with cobblestone roads, light posts with street signs in French, and stars twinkling overhead. A full bar spans the width of the room across the back wall, and while some people amble around the open area, others lounge around bistro tables and on benches. Most of the men are dressed in suits, but the women's ensembles range from sequined cocktail dresses to stark naked. Several of the men have their partners on a leash, which is something I've never seen in real-life before, and again, I have to consciously tell myself not to stare.

Lucca guides me by the elbow towards the bar and orders us each a drink. Taking it from him without even paying attention to what it was, I take a big mouthful from the rocks glass and relish the warmth sliding down the back of my throat as I swallow. It's just the jolt I need to refocus myself on the mission. The first thing we need to do is locate Jeffrey Lancaster, so we begin to mingle with the other guests, never straying far from one another.

About twenty minutes after we arrive, a gentleman's voice booms over a public address system, welcoming everyone and explaining that each of the faux store fronts on one side of the room are entrances to different "themed" rooms, while the ones on the opposite side are either private rooms or viewing rooms. Things begin to grow a little more interesting shortly after the announcement; some of the less modest people begin to perform random sex acts out in front of everyone, while others wander behind closed doors. I still haven't seen *him* yet, and I begin to grow a bit worried that he's not going to show.

As if he can hear my thoughts, Lucca's gruff voice whispers into my ear before kissing the back of my neck, "Don't look, but I've spotted him at your nine o' clock. He's not alone."

Smiling, I continue to half-pay attention to the conversation between the two couples in front of us, until I can manage to direct my focus to where Jeffrey stands without him noticing. Based on the way she's dressed, the woman he's paired up with is most definitely a Domme. I'm not sure how this plays into our plan, but I'm hopeful that perhaps they'll do all the work for us. As they begin to move towards the themed rooms, I catch Lucca's gaze and communicate to him I want to follow them. Excusing myself from the discussion, we trail far enough behind them to not look suspicious, but once they go into one of the rooms, my stomach tightens into a hard knot. It's the moment of truth.

Nodding my head, we disappear behind the same door into a room like I've never quite seen before. It's what I imagine a BDSM dungeon would look like; there are several St. Andrew's crosses mounted to the walls, pommel-horse-looking contraptions and other restraint tables are scattered across the room, and one wall is lined with every type of whip, belt, chain, and flogger one could possibly imagine. Loud music fills the space, muffling out the screams and the sound of leather whipping against bare flesh. Numerous couples are engaged in various activities, while several others are sitting on love seats and chairs watching.

Picking up on my apprehension, Lucca leads me to one of the loungers where we can sit down to observe for a while. Jeffrey and his partner head straight to one of the empty crosses. He quickly strips and places his clothes on a side table before getting on his knees, his eyes fixated on the floor as he waits for her. She chooses her instruments of pleasure and pain and seductively walks back over to him. Then, not bothering to remove her leather one-piece jumpsuit, she straps a black collar around his neck that is attached to a metal chain and proceeds to walk him around the room like a dog. Stopping in front of each of the couples who are viewing, she allows them to pet him before moving on to the next one. When she reaches us, she instructs him to halt and greets each of us with a smile.

"Would you like to pet my dog?" she asks me sweetly.

As much as I don't want to, I'm afraid of what she'll say or do if I refuse. Reaching out hesitantly, I barely touch the top of his head.

"Do you not like my pet? Has he been a bad dog?" she asks me.

"I... I'm not sure," I answer warily. "I'm not familiar with his behaviors."

Tilting her head at me, she says in a disapproving tone, "I think you know that he's been bad and aren't telling me. Is that the case?"

I shake my head no. She leans forward, places her hand under my chin, and smiles reasuringly. "It's okay, sweetie; you don't have to say anything. He likes to be punished. Come with me," she instructs me. Then spinning around on her heeled boot, she drags him back to the cross and restrains him to it.

Hesitantly, I stand up and follow her, giving Lucca one last *you-better-not-let-anything-happen-to*-me look. Once I'm standing next to her, she hands me a cat o' nine tails and grins wickedly. "You're too timid and stiff. Being here is about letting it all go — no rules, no inhibitions, and no one to pass judgment. I could feel the tension radiating from you sitting over there with your partner, so I'm going to give you the opportunity to take it out on mine."

"Are you sure?" I ask, still in disbelief.

"Absolutely. Like I told you, he enjoys it. Plus, tonight is all about teaching our new members. So... have at it; he's all yours."

"Can I watch you first?" I ask, looking down at the intimidating adult toy in my hands.

Laughing, she grabs a whip similar to the one she's handed me. "With pleasure, doll."

My eyes are fixated on the two of them over the next five minutes as she beats the shit out of him and he begs for more. I'm in shock watching the scene play out in front of me. She stops and looks at me, indicating that it's my turn. Cautiously I step up to him and begin to mimic her actions. The first few swats lack any power behind them, but as she urges me on, I begin to hit him harder and harder. Before I know it, I'm envisioning him as my father, and I'm unleashing all of my pent up emotions. For ten solid minutes, I deliver blow after blow on his bare skin, leaving slashes and welts all over his body. I'm pouring in sweat, and my adrenaline is higher than it's ever been when I force myself to stop and hand her back the whip.

"Don't you feel better?" she asks, chuckling.

"You have no idea," I reply through labored breaths.

"Now I want to watch you fuck your boy. We can leave dog here; he's not going anywhere."

Leading me back over to Lucca, she looks at him and says, "Stand and strip. My friend here is ready to fuck you."

Being the dominant personality that he is, I'm afraid he's going to tell her no, but he stands up and removes his clothes quickly. Seeing him naked in front of me and ready for the taking, sends my already humming body into overdrive. I barely notice her unlacing my corset or my skirt being unzipped; my eyes are locked on Lucca's Adonis-like body and raging erection. From behind me, she helps me step out of my shoes and skirt, and then slides the top the rest of the way off. I know there are other people in the room — some of them possibly watching — but I can't find it in myself to care right now. I need to feel Lucca inside me now.

He sits back down on the small sofa, his eyes glued to mine, and I climb up to straddle his lap, my dripping pussy hovering right above his cock. Then, without wasting another second, I impale myself on top of him, taking the entire shaft in one thrust. Moaning, he throws his head back into the cushion as his hands clutch my hips. I lift up off of him, only to repeat the motion. Over and over again, I bury his hard cock deep inside of me; frantically and feverishly, I ride him until I feel that sweet release take over my body. I can tell he's at his breaking point as well, and with an unspoken word between the two of us, our bodies detonate together, and I shatter into a million pieces on top of him.

"Great job. The first one with an audience is always the hardest," a female voice says low in my ear.

I had completely tuned out everyone else by the end, and I can't move my limp body right now, even if I'd want to. I hear her heels on the floor walking away from us, and I nuzzle my face into Lucca's neck.

"Are you okay?" he whispers as he rubs his hands up and down my back, comforting me.

Nodding slightly against him, "I'm perfect," I answer.

Once we redress, we exit the smaller room and rejoin the large crowd in the main area. Not wanting to leave immediately and look suspicious, we have another drink and mingle about a little longer. I'm itching to get out of there; even after having that mind-blowing orgasm, watching the other people engage in intimacies has me all hot-and-bothered again almost immediately. I know Lucca's feeling it too because he can't keep his hands and mouth off of me.

Finally, we leave the party and rush back to my apartment. Leo texts that he'll bring over the footage the following day, so as soon as we get through the front door, we shed our clothes and become a tangled mess of limbs, and gasp through mouths that can't be fed fast enough. We somehow stumble our way into my bedroom; however, once we're in there, he puts the brakes on our frantic movements and begins to make slow and deliberate love to me.

After he makes my body tremble, quiver, and quake, time and time again, we both collapse onto the pillows, breathlessly. Once I can speak again, I ask him cautiously, "What did you think about tonight?"

He pulls me closer to him so that my head is lying on his chest so he can run his fingers through my hair. "At first, I was kind of in shock. Even though I knew that's what we were going to, actually seeing it in front of my own eyes was a little different. Then I got really nervous for you when she took you over to whip Lancaster, but once you got into it, I could see your frustration and rage letting loose. Your eyes had this glazed-over look when you came back to me, and I was so hot for you. I knew you were high on the adrenaline, and I've never been so turned on."

He pauses to kiss the top of my head and move his caressing hand to my back. Chuckling softly, he admits, "I've never had sex with an audience before, so that was exciting — I'm not gonna lie. But you know, once we got into it, I completely forgot they were there. I was just so into you, and your body buzzing all around me it was like nothing I've ever experienced. I'm not sure it's anything I want to ever do again, because now that I think about it, I hate the thought of other people getting to see the look on your face when you come. That's something I want to keep to myself from now on."

I purr softly as I squeeze him around the waist. "Me too," is all I say, hoping he understands everything I mean with those two words. Snuggling me tightly to his warm body as I begin to drift off, he kisses my closed eyelids and then my forehead, whispering, "Good night, devil woman. I love you."

"Me too," I whisper again.

Chapter Thirty-One

Katrina

(Arms — Christina Perri)

For the first time in a long time, I feel hopeful. Things seem to be falling into place for me, and even though I'm a bit leery of how smoothly everything is going, I'm embracing my optimistically positive attitude. It's been a few days since the night at the sex club, and the pictures have been cropped and are ready to be released. Lucca's cousin, Stephen, is using his job at the news station to leak the photos next week. I'm nervous about bringing someone into the circle of trust, but Lucca swears to me he has full faith in him. I believe that he wouldn't let anything happen to me, and if I was emailing them in, even from a fake account, the possibility of getting caught still remains.

Lucca comes over straight after work; I'm not sure what's going on, but he texted earlier saying he needed to talk to me. I hope all is still good to go with the plan. He arrives just as I'm finishing up my online classes for the day. I turn off my computer and hurry to greet him at the door.

"Hey, handsome." I welcome him with a sweet kiss.

"Now that's what I like to come home to after a day of dealing with twenty second graders who've already mentally checked out for the summer," he says, grinning widely.

"Only a few more weeks, babe. You're almost there."

We walk in to the kitchen and I grab us each a beer from the refrigerator before continuing on to the living room.

I sit down on the couch and wait for him to start talking, except he says nothing. I can tell his mind's somewhere else and he's definitely worried about something.

"So are you gonna tell me what you needed to talk to me about? Not that I mind you coming over just to hang out, but you appear to be pretty preoccupied," I prompt him.

Sighing loudly, he says, "Matthews called me into his office today. I assumed it was about my request to stay on at the school for next year, but instead he wanted to talk about you."

"About me?" Even as I speak the words, I can feel the bile rising up in my chest.

Running his hands through his messy hair, which I've now learned is his go-to move when he's anxious about something, he groans. "He asked if I still talked to you anymore, and of course, I lied and said I don't. Of course, I was suspicious of why he called me down only to ask me that, so I questioned him. At first, he tried to play it off, like he was simply curious, but after a little ummm... *coercing*," Lucca pauses briefly and looks down at his hands, obviously leaving out some details, "he admitted that he's been getting paid to monitor and report on your actions. He *claims* he doesn't know who's behind it, but I'm not sure I believe him."

"I know *exactly* who's behind it," I growl as I stand up and begin to pace the room. "I can't fucking believe this. That piece of shit is having me watched!?!?" Infuriated by the news, I grab my phone and text Leo a shortened version of the story.

Me: Sperm donor's been paying the principal to watch me and report back.

"Who are you calling? What are you doing? Calm down and think about things before you react, Katrina," Lucca warns me.

"I'm just letting Leo know what's going on. They may be watching him too."

My mind races as I wonder what all he knows. *Has he had me followed at night? Does he know it was me behind the Saunders photos? If so, why didn't he contact me or out me?* I knew things were going way too perfectly; it was only a matter of time before they began to fall apart. I had even considered dropping the whole plan of revenge after this next anticipated scandal. The happiness I've discovered in spending time with

Lucca, and the possibility of starting my very own music school vastly surpasses that of bringing random men to their knees and even the thought of retaliating against *him*. But now... now that I've found out he's paying people to spy on me, I no longer aspire only to follow through with attempting to get him ousted from office... I want to settle the score.

Counting backwards from ten while taking deep breaths, I settle myself down a bit. I need to appear like I'm handling this news with a cool and even-tempered head. Leo knocks on the door five minutes later without even texting back. He storms in and joins Lucca in the living room. I grab three more beers, tossing each of the guys one, and plop down in the recliner with my own.

"I'm not really sure what we can do at this point," I say calmly. "Leo, if you can keep your eyes open for anyone possibly doing surveillance here, that would be great. Interview all of the security people and door men in the building; he's probably paying one of them too."

I turn my attention to Lucca. "All you can do is be aware of people following you. I don't think he's planning on hurting me. He's probably just making sure I don't do anything to him or his family, but I want to make sure he isn't trying to get to the people I lo-" I cut myself short and clear my throat, finishing with, "care about."

They both nod in agreement, and we all sit there lost in our own thoughts, no one with much to say. Leo leaves a little bit later, claiming he's having dinner with his mom. I tell him to give her a hug and kiss for me, and I promise I'll visit her soon. Lucca stays a while longer, but he's made plans to play basketball with some friends at seven. He offers to cancel and stay with me, but I really want to be alone right now. Making me promise I won't do anything to the asshole until I consult with him first, Lucca kisses me and then leaves.

As soon as I'm sure he's had time to make it out of my building, I pick up my phone and dial Travis' number.

"Hey, doll. How was the club?" He always answers and just starts talking.

"It was great. I owe you big time... wait, I already paid you for that," I say half-jokingly.

"Awesome, glad I could help. Whatcha got for me today?"

"This favor is a little bit different than my usual ones. I've got to keep my distance from this one, but I need information and surveillance pictures of someone. I'm pretty sure his personal life includes some non-socially acceptable behavior, but if not, I need you to create some. He won't say no."

"I can make anything happen for you, K," he replies confidently. "What's his name?"

With an evil gleam in my eyes, I answer, "Paul Matthews. He's the principal of an elementary school in Brooklyn."

A few days later, and I still can't stop thinking about *him*. I've realized my life will never be okay as long as he's lurking around. I need him dead.

Plotting out a murder is extremely difficult, especially if you hope to not get caught. I've pinpointed July twenty-fifth on the calendar. It's the night of the Governor's Summer Masquerade Ball, and it just so happens to be the ninth anniversary of my mom's death. It's almost as if fate has set this up for me.

Now, I have approximately a month-and-a-half to figure out how to pull it off. I've considered hiring someone to do it, but that would be too impersonal. I want him to know I'm cashing in on my promise from the courtroom all those years ago. Shooting him seems the easiest route, and the most fitting, but I'd have to deal with obtaining an untraceable gun, as well as finding the opportune time to pull it off. Poisoning him is another option I'm considering, but I need to do a little more research on what exactly I could use.

Meanwhile, things between Lucca and I continue to progress brilliantly. Now that he's such a big part of my life, I'm not sure how I ever functioned without him. *Not well, obviously.* I'm staying the night at his place tonight, which has become our usual Friday routine, and as soon as the clock hits three o'clock, I walk out the door with my overnight bag.

Leo's waiting to drive me over there; we've all become a bit paranoid of people watching or following us. Lucca's walking up just as I jump out of the SUV, and after saying bye to Leo, I rush to greet him. After welcoming hugs and kisses, we disappear into his house and begin to cook dinner together.

After eating some of the best chicken cordon bleu I've ever had, he and I play *Quelf* with Stephen and Bran. Laughing late into the night, we turn into the bedroom after Lucca turns out victorious, both holding a bowl of vanilla ice cream. We settle into bed and dig into the creamy goodness I now look forward to each time I stay here.

I'm not sure where the thought comes from, but I blurt out. "What happened to Lindsay?"

"Lindsay?" He chokes on his bite, obviously not expecting me to ask about her. "What do you mean?"

"The first time we played Twenty Questions here, you told me that you dated a girl named Lindsay for two years when you first started college, but when I asked why you guys broke up, you said it was your turn to ask a question. Then I got sidetracked, and we never discussed it again. Actually, you've told me a lot about your childhood and your parents, but you never discuss your college years. Why is that?"

Refusing to make eye contact with me, he picks at an imaginary loose thread in the sheets. "After everything I've told you, there should be nothing that you can't tell me, Lucca. For God's sake, my dad murdered my mom; I don't think you can scare me away!" I huff, my feelings hurt a bit.

Twisting in the bed to face me, he sets the cold bowl down, and grabs my hands. The somber look on his face warns me that the story to come is not going to be easy for him to tell. I squeeze his hands to show my support. "I'm here for you, babe. I promise, I'm not going anywhere," I reassure him just as he had done for me.

"The summer between my sophomore and junior year at UT," he begins the story, "Lindsay and I were at a party, and we got in an argument over her wanting to leave early. The previous few weeks she'd been really over-dramatic and grouchy; she never wanted to do anything except stay at her apartment. So I — being the asshole of a boyfriend I was — asked someone else to drive her home, because I couldn't be bothered with leaving the good time. Little did I know or care to realize, the person I asked to drive her home had been drinking quite a bit. So to make a terribly long and heartbreaking story short, the girl lost control of her car on the drive and hit a tree. The girl was killed instantly and Lindsay was in a coma for a little over a week before she died as well."

Understandably, he begins to cry while recalling the horrific details of the night. I wrap my arms around him and he buries his face into my chest. "Why did you never tell me about this?

I'm so sorry, babe." Rubbing his back and rocking him slightly against me, I try to soothe and console him.

Without looking up at me, he continues the story. "She was three months pregnant with our child, and I didn't even know. I found out at the hospital. I lost her and the baby, and I was devastated. I should've been the one protecting her, making sure she got home safely, but instead I pawned her off on a drunk driver — who I killed as well — just so I could stay with my buddies to drink more beer."

I understand the responsibility that he feels over his decisions and the outcome that they led to. Feeling like your actions caused someone's death is an overwhelming weight that lives with you forever, especially if that person is someone you loved. "It's not your fault, Lucca. You've got to let go of the blame."

He pulls back from me and stares deep into my eyes, his still wet with tears. "I've been through just as much counseling as you have, if not more, and I've finally accepted that — somewhat. It doesn't make it much easier to talk about, and I don't think I'll ever be able to fully forgive myself. The truth is what it is."

"Is this why you feel the need to protect me? Am I Lindsay's replacement?" As soon as the words escape my lips, I feel guilty for the selfish questions. He's pouring his heart out to me, finally opening up about what haunts him, and I'm asking how it pertains to me.

Before I can apologize for my self-centered thoughts, he reaches up to stroke my cheek and shakes his head. "Lindsay and I were teenagers in love, and as horrible as I feel that neither she nor the baby are here, I know in my heart she wasn't my *one*. I would've been a man and taken care of her and our baby though, if things didn't end up the way they did. After her, I refused to date for quite some time. Sure, I partied and fucked around with girls, but most of the time I was so drunk trying to forget everything, I'd wake up with someone and have no idea what her name was." I cringe at his words. Despite my less than stellar past, I hate to think about him acting like a male whore and sleeping with a lot of girls, but I more than understand the escape from his reality that he was seeking.

"After that happened, I always said I'd never fall in love and get married," he says softly, "because I knew how terribly painful it was to lose someone I knew *wasn't* my soul mate, I didn't ever want to find the one that is. The way I figured it is if I never found her, I'd never have to know how it feels to lose her. But the day I laid eyes on you, Katrina, I knew there was something different about you. I knew I needed to peel back the hard outer layers you had strategically wrapped yourself in, and find the real you. And now that I have, I know I was right- you're my *one*. Everything that I thought I believed before has changed. I'll risk losing you, if it means getting to love you, even for a little while."

"I already told you — I'm not going anywhere. I won't disappear on you."

Usually, he and I cuddle quite a bit at night, at least until we fall asleep, but tonight feels different. I can't get close enough to him; it's almost as if I want to crawl inside his skin and blanket him in my love. Intertwining my legs with his and enveloping him in my arms, I do the best I can. I kiss him tenderly on the lips, mumbling for the first time, "I love you, Lucca Ellis."

Chapter Thirty-Two

Kat
(All These Things That I've Done ~ The Killers)

As promised, Stephen anonymously leaks the Lancaster photos as an exclusive story on the airwaves of NY1 a week-and-a-half after the night at *Sequestered*. Due to the shocking nature of them, the story takes off like wildfire and spreads throughout the New York media at a rapid pace. By lunchtime on this beautiful Tuesday in early June, the governor's office has already fired their assistant budget director and issued statements apologizing for his actions. The governor himself schedules a press conference for the afternoon to discuss increased appropriate behavior, and to conduct training measures being put into place for his employees.

Many news outlets are beginning to question electing a beloved sports star as the governor of the great state of New York based on popularity alone instead of someone with a solid and proven political background. Governor Green only spent one term in the Unites States Congress, and during his time there, he did nothing politically noteworthy. I'm more than satisfied by the upheaval these photos have caused for the governor. Any moment of discomfort he has to endure, pleases me greatly. However, as I sit and watch the story developing on my television, I'm sure of two things...

First, my days of being *Kat* are over — there's nothing about that lifestyle I desire any longer. With the help of Lucca, Leo, and Dr. Donias, I've matured more in the past three months than I had in the last three years combined. Sometimes in life, you just reach a moment of clarity, and all of a sudden, you can plainly see the path you're supposed to be on, laid out right in front of you. My moment began when I smacked Lucca in the face with a door, but was fully realized the day I came clean to him about everything in my past, and he didn't run away from me.

And second, there's still one major roadblock that stands in the way of me traveling down my path. No amount of scandals or bad press about *that man* is going to alleviate this problem. He. Must. Die.

Chapter Thirty-Three

Katrina

(River of Deceit — Mad Season)

Surprisingly, it's fairly easy to learn how to kill someone with poison online. There are several websites dedicated solely to this topic and there's even a three minute long video on YouTube called *How to Fatally Poison Someone*. I'm curious about how many of the over thirty-one thousand people who've watched this have actually gone through with it. Not that I'll be following the narrator's steps exactly, but I can promise you, this is one girl who will be added to the list of follow-throughs.

I've spent the last several weeks researching all different kinds of poisons. First, I need to choose if I want the death to be immediate or a drawn out process. My choice is instantaneous; I don't want to take the chance he can get medical help that will save him. Second, I must determine the method of administering the poison. Since I plan to do this at the ball, I think serving it in a drink will be the easiest way. And finally, I have to find out which of these poisons I can easily and anonymously obtain. Because no one else knows of my plan, I've got to be extremely discrete about this entire thing, and as of this morning, I've narrowed my possibilities down to aconite, cyanide, and arsenic. Unfortunately, I'm forced to put my research away, as Lucca's coming over so we can go out to lunch. The ball is about a month away, so I still have a little time to work everything out.

When The Sun Goes Down

When Lucca texts that he's downstairs just after twelve, I slide my feet in some flip-flops, grab my purse, and head out the door. As soon as I step foot outside, the heat slaps me in the face, and I'm thankful I threw my hair up in a ponytail instead of taking the time to fix it. Unable to locate him at first, I finally see him squatting a little ways down on the sidewalk petting a dog. He doesn't see me at first, so I stand there and watch him with the furry, four-legged animal; there's a look of longing on his face, but I'm not sure if it's because he's remembering a pet he had as a child, if it's because he wants one now, or both. Eventually, he notices me and stands up with a big smile spreading across his face. Hurrying over to where I stand, he hugs and kisses me hello.

"Hey there, beautiful girl. How's your day been?"

"Even better now that you're here," I reply as a smack him lightly on the butt. "So, what's the plan?"

"I thought we could pick up some sandwiches, chips, and maybe even a little pasta salad from the deli up the street, and then take it to the park to enjoy some of this nice, warm, and sunny weather."

"Sounds perfect."

Walking hand-in-hand, we make our way to get the food and then settle in an open, grassy area in the park. After the harsh winter we had, the high temperatures and bright, blue sky are very much appreciated in these early days of summer. I'm sure by mid-August I'll be begging for sweater-weather days, but for now, I stretch out on the ground and bask in the rays.

"Now this is more what I'm used to," Lucca says.

I turn to look in his face and he's beaming up at the sky. "What do you mean? The weather, or having picnics?"

"The weather," he answers. "For a boy who grew up in Florida and went to school in Texas, throwing me into the northeast in the middle of winter wasn't the easiest of adjustments. Other than going on skiing trips, I'd never seen snow before I got here, at least not the kind that sticks to the ground."

"Well, get ready, 'cause it's going to get hot here. You'll have more heat than you can take before too long," I warn him.

"Not possible. I wish I could live somewhere where it's in the eighties and nineties year-round. I don't mind a little rain now and then, but I prefer days I can spend my non-working time outdoors."

"Then why did you choose New York for your Teach for America placement?" I ask curiously.

He shrugs and picks a blade of grass from the soil. "I don't know. I wanted to get out of Texas and leave all of the bad memories there, but I didn't want to go back home and live with or near my parents. So when I came to visit Stephen last summer, he suggested I try the city out for a change of pace. I thought it was a good opportunity — I'd have a couple of roommates I already knew; plus, I think most people wonder what it'd be like to live here at least some point in their life. Of course, it was hot here then, and I didn't think too much into the cold, wet future."

"So you've been miserable since you've been here?" I try not to express the hurt feelings in my tone, but I obviously fail.

Scooting closer to me, he chuckles and twirls a strand of my ponytail around his finger. "Don't put words in my mouth, devil woman. I've been far from miserable, and I'm pretty sure you know that." He leans in and leaves a trail of gentle kisses from the base of my neck up to my ear. "I'd live through a thousand blizzards if it meant I got to be with you," he whispers.

His breath against my sensitive skin wakes up the baby dragons in my belly, and they begin to flutter about. "Do you plan on staying here when your two year contract is up?" I question him.

"Honestly, I'd prefer to live somewhere with a few more warm days and fewer people, but if you tell me you're never leaving here, I'll stay to be with you. I'm not disappearing on you either, Katrina."

"I'd be willing to relocate," I reply softly. Once everything's said and done, it'll probably be best for me to restart my life somewhere that no one knows who I am and I'm not reminded of my father's fucked up legacy. "I've been here my whole life; it'd be nice to start over fresh in a new place."

"Start over after what?" He pulls back a bit and looks at me inquisitively.

Careful to word my answer without lying, but not clue him in on my other plans, I give him a small smile. "You know, now that I'm ready to move on and let the past nine years go. I want to focus on opening the music school, and then one day, I'd like to start a family of my own."

Apparently pleased with my answer, he pulls me into his lap, my back pressed against his chest with his arms lazily looped around my waist, and nuzzles into my neck again. "I think that's a great idea. Where would you like to live?"

"I'm not sure since I haven't given it much thought, but I could do something down south. Ideally, where do you see yourself in ten years, Lucca?"

"Married with a few little rug-rats running around, living somewhere near the water, coaching baseball, maybe a dog or two in the backyard," he replies. "What about you?"

"Married with a few little rug-rats running around, living near the water, teaching music, maybe a dog or two in the backyard," I answer cheekily.

He tightens his arms around my mid-section and playfully bites my shoulder. "Would you like to meet my parents?"

Shocked at the question, I twist around in his arms to face him. "Say what?"

"I asked if you'd like to meet my parents. They've invited us to come and stay with them for the week of Fourth of July," he answers with a sneaky look on his face.

"*Us?* They know about me?" I balk.

"Of course they know about you, You're the girl I'm in love with. Was I not supposed to tell them?"

I shake my head, feeling all giddy inside. "No, that's fine. I just didn't know that you had. Did you tell them...?" Suddenly, the dread sets in with the realization that he'll obviously have to tell his parents about my past.

Cupping my face, he kisses the tip of my nose. "Stop worrying. I haven't told them anything about any of that, and they haven't asked. That's your story to tell whenever and however you want to. My parents are good people; I think you'll like them quite a bit, but I should warn you — they're quite excited about meeting you."

"Why haven't you told me this?" I push the uneasy feeling down and allow the enthusiasm about the possible trip to take over.

"I didn't want to freak you out and make you run the other way. Plus, I hadn't told you everything about Lindsay and the baby yet, and I wanted everything out in the open between us before we took our relationship to the next level." A little more than a twinge of guilt plays at the back of my mind. I truly want all of these things with Lucca, but as long as Robert Green is on this earth, I'm not sure I can fully give him all of me. Once he's dead, no matter how stealthily I pull it off, Lucca and Leo will both know I'm the one who did it. I pray that they'll be able to understand and forgive me.

"I'd love to go with you! I've never been to Florida before," I exclaim excitedly. "I'm nervous they won't like me, but I guess we might as well find out now.

He pushes me back until I fall in the grass, giggling as he hovers over me and peppers kisses all over my face. "I'll book our flights tonight. You're going to love Sunny Isles, and they're gonna love you."

Not long after we finish our talk, we walk back to my apartment where we spend the remainder of the afternoon and evening lying around, watching movies, and him telling me more about where he grew up. We reserve our flights online; we're scheduled to leave on July second and to return on July ninth. I'm excited about our first trip together and about meeting his family and friends; I've never done anything like this before. As we fall asleep together, I hope and wonder if — someday — we'll have the life we talked about today in the park. It's slowly becoming the dream I'm working towards, but I'm afraid he'll view me differently once he knows I'm a murderer.

Chapter Thirty-Four

Trina
(Happy — Pharrell Willimas)

Tonight, I'm having Lauren over to my place for dinner. I haven't seen her since I resigned from my position three months ago, and I'm finally ready to come clean to her about my past and let her know who I am. I've thought long and hard about doing this, but Dr. Donias believes that it'll help me let go of some of the guilt I've been harboring over our relationship, and my lack of honesty with one of the dew people who made an effort to be my friend. After this evening, *Trina* will be no more. From this point on, everyone that I care about in my life will know me as Katrina; however, I will never use *his* last name. I legally had my name changed to my mom's maiden name as soon as I became an adult; I never want to be associated with him again.

Lauren arrives right on time, and as soon as I open the door she begins to scream and hug me as she jumps around the foyer. Laughing at her usual over-the-top dramatics, I hug her back and welcome her.

"I'm so glad you're here! Please, come in," I say, closing the door behind her.

"Oh my God, Trina! Look at you... look at this place! Holy cow, I thought I'd never see you again!"

She follows me into the kitchen, where I have some tequila lime chicken breasts baking in the oven and some long grain rice simmering on the stove. "Can I get you something to drink? Wine, beer, or liquor? I've got it all."

"I'll have some white wine, please," she says and takes a seat at the bar, continuing to look around the apartment.

I grab a bottle out of the fridge, pour us each a glass, and hand her one. "Feel free to take a look around, if you'd like. It's not all that big."

"Not all that big? Are you fucking kidding me? This is like twice the size of my place — and I have a roommate! It's really beautiful, Trina."

Taking in a deep breath, I pray this goes over well. "Actually, Lauren, my name is Katrina, not Trina."

Her brow furrows in confusion, but before she can even ask, I take a deep breath and begin to tell her the story. Beginning with growing up a spoiled, rich brat in Jersey, to my dad murdering my mom, then my wild and rebellious teenaged and college years, and ending with my lifestyle (both day and night) over the past two years; I tell her almost everything. I explain why I was so leery of making friends and going out with her, and then of course, I fill her in on the entire Lucca story. I don't tell her about my involvement with either of the sex photo scandals, but she's smart enough to probably figure it out. After I'm finished, I lean back on the counter and take a long drink of wine, waiting for her to reply.

"So you and Lucca are still together? That's awesome! I'm so happy for you both!"

"Out of everything I just told you, that's your only comment?" I ask, laughing softly.

Waving her hand in front of her face, she says, "Pssh! I don't care about that other shit. I mean, I'm very sorry that you lost your mom, that's terrible, but like you said, you're moving on with your life now. I don't care who you're related to or what you've done. Katrina, you're my friend and I want you to be happy."

"Well, I really appreciate that. You're one of the very few that I have, and I've missed you dearly." I walk over and loop my arm around her shoulders, squeezing her to me. "I finally remember what *happy* feels like."

Dinner is ready shortly after that, so we sit and talk over the good food and a couple bottles of wine. She brings me up-to-date with her dating life and everything that's going on with the gossip circle at the school. Also, she heard about Lucca roughing up

Principal Matthews before summer let out, but claims no one knew what had happened. Happy she brought up that subject, it allows me to transition nicely into the next subject.

"About Principal Matthews, Lauren," I say softly, "there's some things you need to know about him, and unfortunately, they're not all that great. The issue between Lucca and him was because we found out my father was basically paying him to spy on me. When I found this out, I hired someone to do surveillance on Principal Matthews, and I discovered that his extra-curricular activities would be frowned upon in the teaching community."

"I'm not surprised," she responds as she finishes her glass of wine. "He's hit on me more than a couple of times, like I'm gonna change my answer from no. He's a sleaze-ball through and through."

Standing up from the table, I walk over to one of the kitchen drawers and pull out the large manila envelope Travis had dropped off a couple of days ago. I sit back down and slide it over to her. "You can open it now if you'd like, or you can wait until you're ready to use it. The photos inside show him engaging in sex acts with females *and* males that appear to be minors. I'm not sure of the kids' ages, but I'd guess they're around sixteen. Even if they are eighteen and legal, they aren't his wife. I hope you choose to take these to the school board saying they were anonymously delivered to you and ruin his life, but they're in your hands now."

"Wow... okay. I wish I could say I'm shocked, but I'm not." Grabbing the envelope, she sticks it inside her purse. "Don't you worry; I'll make sure he gets what's coming to him."

I smile widely at her and get up to pour us one more glass. We continue to talk about other things for another hour or so, but as it grows late, she gets ready to leave. We say our goodbyes and promise to get together again soon, right after I get back from my trip. Once she's gone, I tidy up the kitchen a bit and then tipsily stumble to my room where I fall straight into bed. Only three more days until I'll be soaking up the Florida sun...

Chapter Thirty-Five

Katrina

(Fireflies — Ron Pope)

"I'm going to meet his parents tomorrow, Leo," I say excitedly in between bites of steak. "I still can't believe I'm doing this!"

"I'm really happy for you, Katrina. You deserve a little vacation; you haven't been on one in years. Plus, I really like Lucca — he's a good guy and I know that he truly loves you." He smiles warmly at me. "I've got all of your flight information, plus the phone numbers to his parents' house in case I can't get a hold of you."

Beaming back at him, I'm reminded of how blessed I am to have Leo in my life. It's the night before we're both leaving to go out of town and we're having dinner at Peter Luger's in Brooklyn — my absolute favorite restaurant in all of New York. This will be the first time since the last trip I took with Momma that I've been away from Leo for more than a couple of days.

"Tell me again where you and Mama Rosa are going."

"We're flying into Palermo and then driving to San Vito lo Capo. I've got us booked at one of the hotels directly on the beach for twelve days," he replies, obviously proud of himself. "From there, I've got several day trips around the country planned, but most of the time, I want her to relax and enjoy herself."

"And she knows she's going to Italy, but none of the details, right?"

Nodding, he finishes chewing the bite he just put in his mouth, and then wipes his face with a napkin. "Yeah, I wish I didn't even have to tell her that much, but I needed to get her traveling paperwork in order, and to make arrangements for the house while we'll be gone. Her sister and my cousins are meeting us there too, and I know she's going to be shocked to see them."

"That's so awesome. You're such a good son; I know she appreciates your thoughtfulness. And not to mention, you deserve some time off too. I know I've been a pain in your ass for quite some time," I say sincerely.

"Stop it. You know you're my family. I'd do anything to keep you safe and out of trouble- anything at all..." His voice trails off and he looks down at his plate, lost in thought.

We finish our meal shortly after, and he still hasn't said anything else. "Earth to Leo — are you still with me?" I ask concerned.

He looks up at me and gives me a forced smile. "Always. I'm always with you, Katie-bug."

Crinkling my nose at him, I make a funny face. "You're acting weird. Is everything okay?" He's actually been acting strange for the past couple of weeks, but the only other time I asked, he assured me everything was fine.

"I'm sorry; I've just a lot on my mind with the trip tomorrow and all. It's like I'm mentally running through check lists, making sure I've got everything ready to go."

"No biggie, I completely understand. I've been doing the same thing for a couple of days now. I'm so nervous about what his parents are going to think about me. I'm making sure I pack the right clothes and all that kinda stuff — first impressions are vital."

"They'd be foolish not to love you. All you need to worry about is being yourself."

This time his smile is genuine, and I reach across the table to give his hand a quick squeeze. "Thank you."

After paying our bill, we drive home in comfortable silence. As he pulls up to the front door of my building, he surprises me and jumps out of the car. Instead of letting the doorman open my door, he jogs around the front of the car and lets me out. Scooping me up in a giant bear hug, he whispers in my ear, "Be smart and be safe, Katrina. I know it's going to work out perfectly for you. I love you always."

"I love you too, Leo," I choke, holding back tears. I'm not sure why we're both getting so emotional, but it feels more profound than a goodbye for a couple of weeks apart.

He releases me and returns to the car, never looking back.

And then he disappears.

Chapter Thirty-Six

Katrina

(Wanted — Hunter Hayes)

Waking well before my alarm sounds, I'm up, dressed, and bouncing around my apartment when Lucca arrives a little after nine. My bags have been packed for several days; all I have to do is throw my toiletries and flat iron inside once I finish using them this morning. I'm pretty sure I've over-packed, but we're going to be there for a full week, and I've got no clue what we'll be doing.

I smother him in kisses as he comes through the front door, unable to contain my jubilee. Laughing, he picks me up and twirls me around.

"Good morning, love. I'm glad to see you're in a good mood," he says, lowering me back down until my feet hit the ground.

Embarrassed that perhaps I'm a little too excited, I chew on my lip nervously. "Yeah, sorry. I'll tone it down a bit before we get there — I promise."

"You better not," he warns me with a swat across my butt cheeks. "Just wait until you see my mom; she's gonna be the same way. She's been straight driving me crazy this last week. I think she's afraid we aren't going to come or something."

His words make me feel better, even if he's just saying them for my benefit. "Good! Are you all ready? Where are your bags?"

"I'm not bringing anything; everything I need is already there — clothes, shoes, bathroom stuff. And I assumed that you'd have enough for both of us." Looking around the room, he eyes my pile of luggage and starts to laugh. "You do know we're just going for a week, right? Not a year."

"Yes, smart ass, I'm well aware. I don't want to be ill-prepared," I say with a smack to his muscular bicep.

Groaning, he picks up two of the larger suitcases and mumbles. "You and my mom are going to get along famously." I snicker and grab the other one, along with my carry-on bag. I hope he's right.

Thankfully, our flight from JFK to Miami is direct. I spend the three hours flipping through magazines and checking the time while Lucca sleeps the majority of the trip. The plane touches down in the Sunshine State at two-thirty on the dot, and I know that for sure because I happen to be staring at my watch for the five hundredth time since we took off.

Shaking him awake, I whisper in his ear, "Wake up, sleepyhead. It's show time." He quickly comes to and begins to unbuckle his seatbelt. Then, we impatiently wait for the people in the few rows ahead of us to exit the plane. He grabs my carry-on from me and ushers me to go in front of him. As we walk through the airport to the baggage claim area where his parents will be waiting, he holds my hand tightly and the grin never leaves his face. I, on the other hand, grow more and more nervous with every step we take closer to them. I'm no longer sure I want to go through with this. By the time we get to the area filled with luggage carousels, he's practically dragging me along.

Abruptly, he stops walking and turns to face me. "Stop overthinking this, Katrina. Relax and be yourself; they're gonna love you. Trust me on this." He kisses me firmly on the lips, and then resumes his path through the crowd of people.

When I see his parents, I know it's them from the pictures I've seen at his place. He's the spitting image of his dad, only thirty years younger and with no gray hair. His mom is even prettier than her photos — she's a petite woman with straight, copper-colored hair and bright blue eyes. As soon as they see us, they begin to move towards us and greet us with huge, radiant smiles. Lucca embraces them both, giving his mom a sweet kiss on the cheek as I stand off to the side a bit. Then he motions for me to step over to them.

"Mom, Dad, I'd like to introduce you to my girlfriend, Katrina," he says cheerfully.

Wasting no time, his dad wraps me in a tight hug and then passes me off to his wife, who does the same. As she frees me from her arms, she says, "It's so nice to finally meet you, Katrina. Lucca has told us so many wonderful things about you."

"Likewise, Mrs. Ellis, the pleasure is all mine. I'm so thankful for you and Mr. Ellis to have us at your house this week."

His dad interjects, "No need for formalities with us, Katrina. It's Sarah and Christian, and our house will always be Lucca's home too. Y'all are welcome to come down whenever you want." I'm pretty sure I'm glowing from the inside out, relieved at their friendly nature and the overall comforting vibe I've picked up on immediately.

After the introductions, we gather my bags and head to their car in the parking garage. I'm a little surprised that they drive a Range Rover almost identical to mine, except that it's gray instead of black. I shoot Lucca an inquisitive look, but he's busy talking with his dad about something I think that has to do with fishing. Lucca packs my suitcases in the back and we all pile in the SUV for the half hour drive to their house.

Conversation flows easily between the four of us during the ride. We mainly talk about all of the places Lucca wants to take me to see while we're there. His parents make several other suggestions which are added to the list, and again, I'm surrounded with a feeling of joy. When we turn into the Sunny Isles area, my focus drifts away from talking and more to looking out the window. I'm taking in the entire coastal resort vibe as well as the glimpses of the ocean I keep getting; however, when we turn into a private gated community with some of the biggest houses I've ever seen, which is saying a lot considering where I grew up. I can't help my mouth from gaping open.

Lucca has always talked about the great relationship his parents have and how supportive they'd always been of him while growing up, but he's never mentioned what they did for a living, or their financial status. I guess I never asked because I hate when people asked me about mine, but apparently, I should've.

"This is it. We're home," Christian announces, pulling into the driveway of a house that resembles a luxurious Mediterranean villa. I try to get Lucca's attention, but he's purposely not making eye contact with me. "Sarah, go ahead and give Katrina the tour while Lucca and I unload the car."

She nods and grabs my elbow, leading me towards the front door. "I'm not sure what Lucca told you about our home, but he and Christian actually designed it themselves when he was in high school. He only lived here for a year before going off to college, but I know he feels a connection with it since he helped in so many ways during the build," she explains as we walk through the grand foyer.

After familiarizing me with the great room, which encompasses the kitchen, dining room, and living area, she shows me the master suite and then leads me upstairs to the game room and other bedrooms. Opening the final door, she says, "And this is your and Lucca's room. Take a look around; I'm going to go make sure the guys got everything."

At first, I'm caught off-guard because I assumed that we'd be sleeping in separate rooms, but that train of thought gets lost when I see the massive bedroom. It's like a larger version of his room in New York — an oversized sleigh bed swathed in blue linens adorned with lots of throw pillows is the focal point, tasteful ocean-inspired art hangs on the walls, and an obscenely large flat screen television hangs on the wall opposite the bed. However, in this room, instead of a windows are French doors draped in sheer light blue fabric that lead out onto a balcony. After looking around the room, I immediately head towards the doors, open them, and walk outside. The space is large enough for a patio table and two chairs and it looks out over the immaculately landscaped backyard and pool area which leads to a boat dock.

Two large hands slide around my waist from behind and that clean, soapy smell I'm completely in love with teases my nose. Nibbling on my neck and ear lobe, Lucca asks in a low voice, "So, do you approve, Ms. Foster?"

Closing my eyes and laying my head back on his shoulder, I ask, "Why didn't you tell me?"

"Tell you what?."

"That your parents live like this. You've always made it seem like you didn't come from money; you even made that comment about needing a sugar momma the first night we had dinner," I protest.

He spins me around by my hips so that we're staring into each other's eyes. "Would it have made a difference? If anything, you probably would've been more hesitant to go out with me because you associate people with money with greed and narcissism — not that those stereotypes aren't usually correct, but it's not the case with my family. Neither of my parents came from affluent backgrounds; they met in college, got married shortly after, and they've worked extremely hard to get to this point in life. They've always promoted hard work, determination, and appreciation in me which is why I'm working for an internship in the field of teaching. I want to be a baseball coach, so they expect me to follow the path that anyone else with the same dream would travel down."

Leaning down, he gently rubs his nose against mine. "I didn't want you to make assumptions about me off of my background, just like you didn't want me to judge you off of yours. You know the real me, so none of this should make any difference."

Looping my arms around his neck, I bring my mouth to his in a tender but meaningful kiss. "You're right; it doesn't. And I think the place is gorgeous; I can't believe you helped design it."

"Oh, Mom's already told you, has she?" he asks with a chuckle.

"Mhmm. I get the feeling she's pretty proud of you."

He cuddles me up against his body and kisses my forehead. "Let's go grab some lunch and then I'll show you around outside. You're gonna love the boat."

After eating a light lunch with his parents, Lucca walks me around the property as promised. I can't decide which is prettier, the outside or the inside of the house, but I know I could definitely get used to living in a place like this. We head down to where the boat is docked, and I can tell he's getting more excited with each step. As we approach the wooden platform, he begins to tell me all about the vessel. I'll be the first to admit I know absolutely nothing about boats. It looks pretty enough — it's mostly white, with a red stripe running down the side of it, and it's bigger than a canoe, but smaller than a cruise ship. He's going on and on about the specs and telling me how versatile it is; I can tell he's really proud of it.

"The only time I've ever been on a boat was when I went on a cruise with my mom. I think I was maybe eleven or twelve," I tell him.

He looks at me with disbelief. "Are you kidding? Oh my God, I love to be on the boat. I grew up fishing and jet skiing with my parents. Nearly every weekend in the summer we'd be out on the water in some form."

"It sounds like fun," I say enthusiastically. "Are we going to go out on it while we're here?"

"Of course! We can do whatever you'd like. I can try to teach you how to ski or wakeboard if you want. And the night of the fourth, we'll go out and watch the fireworks over the water. It's incredible."

I wish I could bottle up the happiness exuding from him in this moment. His smile isn't limited to his lips, it's radiating from his eyes and voice as well. "Sounds perfect," I reply as I step forward and capture his mouth with mine, wanting to taste his joy.

Chapter Thirty-Seven

Katrina

(You Found Me — The Fray)
(Kiss ME — Ed Sheeran)
(Never Stop — SafetySuit)

Our first full day in Florida, Lucca drives me up and down the coast, showing me places he used to go as a kid, his high school, his favorite beach, and all sorts of other memorable locations. We have an incredible time together, singing along with the radio and stopping to explore whenever we get the whim. I've never taken a long road trip with anyone before. If I traveled with my parents, we always flew to our destination, but after spending a good six hours driving around with him today, I think it would be something fun for the two of us to do in the future.

For dinner, we eat with his parents at *Il Mulino*, an Italian restaurant inside the Acqualina Resort. The company and conversation are even better than the food, which speaks volumes because the *chicken franchese* I order may be even better than Mama Rosa's. The Ellis' love to talk about their son and all of the things he did growing up, but they do it in a way that shows how proud they are rather than bragging or boastful. Watching the three of them together, it's obvious the amount of love that exists in their home. Christian and Sarah still find ways to touch each other all the time, whether it be with a quick hand squeeze or a sweet kiss, just something to display their affection for one another. I don't ever remember seeing my parents act like that.

As we are driving back to the house, his mom is playing around on her phone in the passenger-side front seat and asks, "Do you know what the name Katrina means?"

"No, I'm not sure if anyone's ever told me," I reply truthfully.

"It means *pure*. I'm sure your mom looked it up when she was choosing your name," she says with a warm smile. "You should ask her sometime. Do you have a middle name?"

"It's Michelle — Katrina Michelle. I was named after her favorite aunt, but I'm sure you're right. Thank you for telling me." I still haven't told his parents about my family situation, and this night is going so well, I really don't want to ruin it with the horrific story. Lucca squeezes my hand as a show of support and I give him a weak smile with a shake of my head.

Unaware of our silent conversation in the backseat, she continues talking as she types something into her phone, obviously looking up the meaning of my name talking. "Ah, Michelle means a *gift from God*. That's a beautiful name. When I was expecting, I scoured over books after books of names, trying to find the perfect one. When I saw that Lucca meant *bringer of the light*, I knew immediately it was the one. I was going through a really dark time because I was having issues conceiving, but when I finally accepted that it just wasn't meant to be for me, I got pregnant. And ever since then, he truly has been the light of my life."

"Oh Mom, stop," he teases. "You're embarrassing me."

"I'm not telling Katrina anything she doesn't know. Your father and I feel blessed that we have such an amazing son; there's nothing wrong with that," she argues.

My heart melts a little at her kind words, and as I fall asleep later, the idea that the meaning of our names has some higher significance bounces around my thoughts.

The following day is the Fourth of July, and thankfully, the weather is beautiful once again for all of the planned festivities. The small community they live in truly goes all out for the summer holiday. Numerous food stands serving barbeque, shrimp skewers, corn dogs, and funnel cakes line the waterfront, and there are bounce houses and face painting stations for the kids and organized volleyball tournaments and games of cornhole for the adults on the beach itself. Most of the families set up an area of blankets and lounge chairs close to the shoreline and go back and forth from playing in the ocean to the food and activities.

Lucca and I are having a blast as we walk up and down the beach, stuffing our faces with delicious food and chasing it with fruity frozen cocktails. Being able to stare at him shirtless all day, wearing only his blue-and-white-checkered board shorts is a bonus, but I'm finding that the rest of the female population thinks the same.

"What's wrong?" he asks me, a teasing tone in his voice, as we pass by one of the volleyball games.

"Nothing," I fib.

Nudging his hip against mine, he laughs. "Liar- now spill. What's got your bikini bottoms in a ruffle?"

I look down at my solid-red bikini which is indeed ruffled across the triangle tops and the butt. "My suit was made with ruffles, silly," I attempt to change the subject.

He stops walking and turns to me. Lifting my chin up so that I'm gazing into his eyes, he asks again, "What's wrong, Katrina?"

Crinkling my nose playfully, I whine, "All of those girls are ogling you, and I don't like it." Rarely in my life have I felt jealous or envious of people, especially over a guy, but he makes me feel things I've never experienced or even thought about. Most of those feelings are pleasurable and gratifying, but this one — not so much. And I hate that I sound like an insecure, whiny kid.

He bursts out laughing, which is neither the reaction I expected nor wanted. "Please tell me you're joking."

Saying nothing, I pull my stare away from his and look down at the sand as I dig my toes into the warm, gritty beach.

"Katrina, look at me now," he commands in a low, but serious voice.

Obediently, I bring my eyes back to his. He cups my face gently and lowers his mouth to mine, capturing it in a soft kiss. "You think I don't notice every male on this beach gawking at you? I do, but I don't worry myself with that. I know you belong to me, just like you should know I belong to you. I see no one but you, no matter where we are. Learn that and accept it. I'm far from perfect; I know that I can be a stubborn jerk sometimes, among other things, but one thing you never have to worry about is me being unfaithful to you. Do you understand that?"

I nod as his words excite the baby dragons in my tummy. "Yes," I answer, knowing he expects a verbal response. "I understand, and I feel the same way."

"Good, now I'll race you to the water. Last one in has to wash the other's laundry when we get back home." Laughing hard, he takes off running towards the shoreline and I follow closely on his heels, all thoughts of insecurity washed away.

Obviously, with his head start and long legs, he beats me by a landslide. Splashing me as I enter the refreshing blue waters, he cackles, "Ha-ha, you've gotta do my laundry!"

I hurl myself at him, making him fall back into the incoming wave, and start laughing. "No problem, silly boy! My building has a cleaning service that does door-to-door pickups," I taunt, sticking my tongue out.

"Oh, you think you're so clever, don't you?" he asks, regaining his footing. Then he grabs me by the waist and begins tickling me before dunking me.

The rest of the afternoon we spend fooling around, bantering back and forth and sneaking kisses in here and there. I can't remember the last time I felt so carefree and relaxed, and even though we still have five days left, I'm already dreading going home.

Returning back to the house, Lucca and I take a short nap, as we're both exhausted from the day in the water and sun. Once we wake up, we shower and get dressed for the nighttime celebration with more food, drinks, live music, and fireworks. Since I had my hair up all day, I spend a little extra time and fix it to wear it down for the evening. After applying a little bit of mascara, and a thin layer of coconut oil to my sun-kissed face, I step into a pale yellow, cotton sundress that hits a few inches above my knee. Lucca helps me zip it up from behind, kissing the back of neck when he's finished before I slide my feet into some sparkly, brown flip-flops. He's wearing a light blue, Guevara-style shirt with tan linen shorts and dock shoes. His hair is a wild, unkempt mess, and his skin is already bronzed from the couple of days we've been here. I'm pretty sure he's never looked sexier than he does tonight.

"Are you ready to go, babe?" I ask excitedly.

Looking me up and down, a mischievous smile spreads across his face. "I'm rethinking leaving the house tonight. Maybe we should just stay here and make our own fireworks."

I shake my head, giggling, and begin to walk out of the bedroom. "Uh-uh. You promised me my first ride on the boat tonight, and I'm keeping you to it."

His face lights up when I mention the boat. "Oh, yeah, I've gotta get you out on the water. You're going to love it," he says, patting my ass just before we head down the stairs.

We meet up with his parents in the kitchen area where they have drinks already made for us to take on our walk into town. Much like during the daytime, it appears most of the locals are taking part in the holiday celebrations. The four of us stroll around the streets, talking and laughing like I've always been a part of their family. It's astonishing to me how comfortable and at ease they make me feel. At one point his mom even slips her arm around my waist as we're talking about different beaches that we've traveled to. No one can or will ever replace my mom, but Sarah Ellis is doing a phenomenal job of making me feel like a daughter again.

A couple of hours later, Lucca and I return to the house while his parents head over to sit with some friends of theirs for drinks and to watch the show. They tell us to have a great time and give us both quick pecks on the cheek. As we walk hand-in-hand down the street, I feel like I'm floating I'm so blissful. I'm overjoyed that I agreed to come on this trip with him.

"I really like your parents," I say sincerely. "They've been so welcoming."

He beams back at me. "They really like you, too. I told you there was no reason to be nervous."

We walk up to the house and he says, "I need to grab a few things from inside, and then I'll be ready. Go to the bathroom or whatever else you need to do. You may want to grab a hair tie or something, because it gets windy out there."

I do exactly as he says and run upstairs to use the restroom and snag a ponytail holder. When I come back down, he's walking in the back door — once again with a look on his face like he's up to something.

"All set?" he asks.

I nod and follow him back outside to the boat slip. He climbs onto the boat first, and then helps me do the same. Excitement and nervousness both have my stomach flopping around, but his confidence and composure help to alleviate any uncertainties I have. After pushing a bunch of buttons, and adjusting some other levers that apparently start the engine, we back away from the dock. He's standing in front of the control panel and steering wheel while I'm sitting in the co-captain's chair in awe of what he's doing.

Before long, we are out of the little canal that runs along the back of the homes and out in the open waters. There are a lot of other boats out, obviously with the same plan that we have, so we aren't able to travel at too high of a speed, not that I really care to anyways. We ride for about ten or fifteen minutes until we pull into a little cove away from the rest of the traffic. I'm still sitting there, taking everything in, when he kills the motor and pushes a button that I think drops the anchor.

"Hopefully, we can stay hidden back here," he says as he turns to me with a huge smile on his face. "I want to keep you all to myself tonight."

Standing up next to him, I wrap my arms around his waist and lift up on my tiptoes to kiss him. "I'm always just yours."

"That's my girl," he mumbles against my mouth. "Now, I have a surprise for you."

"What kind of surprise?" I ask enthusiastically.

"Hold on, let me show you." Walking to the back of the boat, he grabs a container and a cooler. He pulls a large blanket out and spreads it across the open area in the front *V*-shaped part of the vessel. "Come sit up here," he instructs.

I hurry over to where he is and take a seat on the soft fabric, anxious to see what he's planned. First, he brings over the cooler and sets it next to me; then, he walks back over to the captain's area, and suddenly, music begins playing. Joining me on the blanket, he grins at me as he pulls out a bottle of wine with two glasses and a plate of fruit and cheese.

"I brought us some refreshments for the show, and I thought a little music would be nice."

Graciously, I accept the glass from him and pop a few grapes into my mouth. "Nice indeed. Thank you for making this so special for me."

He leans over and kisses the tip of my nose. "Take a few drinks and then I want you to lie down and look up."

Doing as he says, I take a few sips of my wine and then set it to the side as I lie on my back. "Wow" is the only word I can muster. I have never seen so many stars in my life. The entire night sky is covered in the twinkling beauties, and the sight is truly breathtaking. He lies down right next to me and takes my hand in his. Neither of us says anything for a while; words really aren't necessary. At one point I hear him humming along to the song playing through the speakers, which is one of my favorite Ed Sheeran songs, and I pray he covers me up, cuddles me in, and kisses me like he wants to be loved, just like the lyrics say.

When the fireworks show starts a short time later, I feel like my heart is going to explode with euphoric rapture, much like the pyrotechnics lighting up the heavens. We lie there and watch every color in the rainbow adorn the already awe-inspiring sky for quite a while. Then, as if he knows what song is about to come on, he turns onto his side, propping himself up on his elbow and begins to sing.

"This is my love song to you; let every woman know I'm yours," he begins to serenade me with the most heart-felt song I've ever heard. His voice isn't perfect, but his tone and pitch are the last things I'm focused on. Our eyes are locked onto one another, staring deep into each other's soul, and I'm completely captivated by the words he's singing to me. When he gets to the chorus, giant crocodile tears of joy begin to trickle down my cheeks. I'm simply overwhelmed at the man lying in front of me and the love I feel for him. As the song comes to an end, he brings his lips to mine in a kiss so passionate and intense that the colorful blasts overhead are jealous.

Without wasting another moment, I transition from being flat on my back to sitting on top of him, straddling his hips. Nothing on the planet could keep me from making love to him right now. My digits are fumbling at his shirt buttons as our tongues continue to dance with the music. After he helps my shaking hands remove his clothes, he lifts the hem of my dress and dips his fingers into the waistband of my white panties. Slowly he runs the tips of them across my lower abdomen, awakening the baby dragons and causing me to flood immediately.

He begins to kiss his way down my neck as I tangle my fingers in his hair and grind against him, frustrated at the thin piece of cotton acting as a barrier between his body and mine. Unexpectedly, with his mouth never leaving my skin, he grabs the front of my panties and yanks hard, ripping them off of me. Rising up slightly, I grab his hard cock and line it up with the entrance to my aching core. Slowly lowering myself down on top of him, I bite down on his shoulder to keep from screaming out as he fills me. Grasping my hip bones with his strong hands, he lifts me up and down on his throbbing shaft in a rhythmic tempo.

Our bodies move as one to the melody under the starlit summer sky, and accompanied with the exhilaration of the entire night, we rapidly reach our release together. Breathlessly collapsing against his body, he wraps his arms around my waist and holds me so close I can feel his heart pounding against my chest.

"This is what I wished for that day in the park, Katrina," he whispers into my hair. "You and me. Always."

It's in this moment I know I can't go through with killing my father. His actions have stolen so many things from me, and I've wasted way too much of my life concentrating on him and getting my revenge. There's a good chance if I were to carry out the plan that I'd get caught, and that would keep me away from the life awaiting me -my life with Lucca. I won't allow that asshole or anyone else to stand in the way of that. I've finally found the one who brings light to my life — Lucca Ellis is my sunshine.

Chapter Thirty-Eight

Katrina

(Time of Our Lives — Tyrone Wells)
(Forever and Always — Parachute)

The rest of our vacation in Florida is spent frolicking in the sand, surf, and sun, and unfortunately, the day that we have to return to New York comes way too quickly. Even though I know that we'll see them again at Thanksgiving, saying goodbye to Sarah and Christian is much harder than I expected, and I can't help but get choked up as we walk away from them in the airport towards our departure gate. Lucca keeps me close to him, attempting to console me by rubbing my back and playing with my hair. I want his two year internship to be over with now so that we can stay in Florida, and I tell him as much.

"The time will go by fast, Katrina. I promise," he assures me. "If when that time comes, you still want to move down here, that's what we'll do. I'll go wherever makes you happy."

Despite being sad about leaving the Sunshine State and the Ellis', my heart is still overflowing with bliss as we board the plane and settle into our seats. I'm more excited than I ever thought possible about my future with Lucca. This trip together has given me all of the assurance I need about what path I should follow. In addition, I'm excited to get back into my business classes so when we do move in a couple of years, I'll have everything lined up and ready to go. I can't wait to see Leo to tell him how right he was about me needing this vacation. Finally, I've let go of the hatred and animosity that I've carried with me for almost a decade, and I'm truly ready to move forward — no more looking back. Lucca has freed me from my past.

Over the three hour plane ride, we play a few card games and then look through the *SkyMall* magazine together, laughing at some of the ridiculous items and making note of a few of the things that look pretty cool. We discuss our plans for the rest of the summer, and when we found out that neither of us has ever been to Las Vegas, I tell him I'll be booking that trip for us as soon as we get home. I've always been curious as to what all the hype is about, plus I really want to do one of those gondola rides at the Venetian that I've seen on commercials.

Before I know it, we are landing at JFK airport; the trip is officially over, but we both still have huge smiles plastered across our faces. Once we're off the plane, he carries my tote bag for me as we make our way holding hands through the airport towards the baggage claim area. About halfway there, he says he needs to use the restroom, so I wait for him out in the terminal. As I'm standing there, I casually look up at one of the televisions scattered throughout the airport, and the first thing I see is the large headline plastered across the bottom of the screen: *Breaking News: Governor Robert Green Found Dead, Apparent Suicide*. Nausea , extreme dizziness, and an overwhelming heat takes over my body. Then everything goes black.

The next thing I know, Lucca is crouched down, hovering over me, begging me, "Please wake up, Katrina. Please."

I look around, trying to grasp my bearings, and I notice lots of people walking by and staring at us. Then I realize that I'm in the airport and I remember...

"Oh, thank God, you're okay," he says, exhaling a sigh of relief. "We gotta get you out of here, babe, before someone recognizes you. Your picture has flashed on the TV several times. The media is going crazy trying to find you."

"So you saw? My dad? It's really true?" I whisper as he helps me stand up on my wobbly legs.

Wrapping his free arm around my shoulder, he pulls me into a tight embrace. "I'm so sorry, Katrina."

We begin walking at a steady pace towards the baggage claim area. I can't even begin to make sense of the thoughts and emotions running through me — it's almost like I'm having a system overload and, in turn, am shutting down. Sitting on a bench with my eyes fixated on the ground, Lucca gathers the luggage from the carousel, and then leads me outside to grab a taxi. He gives the driver his address instead of mine — and even though I'm not sure why — I go along with whatever. He leans over and explains in a soft voice, "I'm sure the reporters are camped out at your place."

Nodding, I lay my head on his shoulder and pass out until the car comes to a stop. He nudges me awake once we are outside of his home, and after paying the driver and retrieving my bags from the trunk, we hurry inside. Unsure of what to do next, I try to call Leo, but get a "cannot connect your call at this time," which I assume is because he's out of the country.

"I think you should just call the Manhattan police station, babe. Tell them who you are, and that we just got back in town and saw the news reports. I'll call Stephen to find out what he knows; I'm sure he's at work."

I find the number online and dial it with shaky hands. Immediately, I'm transferred to Detective Conner, who gets the address of where I am, and informs me that he and his partner are on their way. All that I can do now is sit and wait.

"I can't believe this," I say as I run my fingers through my hair. I've wanted him dead for so long, and now that he is, I don't know what to feel. I'm not happy, I'm not sad, I'm not relieved... I'm just numb.

"All Stephen knows is that they found him in his home office with a gunshot wound to the head and that there was a suicide note. He said he'll call if he finds out anything else, but of course everyone's being hush-hush about it." Lucca picks me up and sets me in his lap, after hanging up his phone. He rocks me gently back and forth, kissing the top of my head. "Just tell me what you need me to do, babe. I'll do anything. I feel completely helpless right now, and all I want to do is make sure you're alright."

Clinging to him, I bury my face in his chest, finding comfort in his scent and the feel of his warm body against mine. "I'll be alright. I simply want to get through all of this as quickly as possible. I'd just told myself today that after this week I knew was finally ready to move on from him and all of the years I've spent loathing him and wanting revenge. I guess he heard me."

Lucca makes me a cup of hot green tea while we wait, and even though I probably shouldn't, I sit and watch the news recapping what they know about the governor's death and the coverage of the immediate swearing in of the lieutenant governor. Nearly twenty minutes later, there's a knock at the door, and Lucca gets up to let in the policemen. Detective Conner and Detective Rayburn join me in the living room where they extend their condolences before sitting down.

"Miss Foster, there has been quite a bit of speculation about your involvement in the death of Governor Green from the media," Conner begins. "Your disdain for your father has not been a secret ever since his trial for your mother's murder; you even legally changed your name to rid of any association with him several years ago."

"Yes," I agree solemnly. "I've had extremely limited contact with him ever since I witnessed him shooting my mom. Surely, you can understand that."

"I can indeed, but you should understand why people would think you were involved after you publicly announced your intent to get revenge on him," he quips.

"I was fourteen years old, and I'd just lost my mother, detective," I snap back, not appreciating his tone. "Am I being officially questioned here? If I need to call my attorney, I'd be more than happy to get her here quickly. From our earlier phone conversation, you made it seem like you were coming over simply to report on the findings at the scene."

The other officer, Detective Rayburn, cuts in as he picks up on the growing hostility in my voice. "Miss Foster, we aren't questioning you at all. I apologize if we've made you feel like that." He pauses to grimace at his partner. "We know that you've been out of town for the last week. We've pulled Governor Green's phone and computer records, and it doesn't appear that you've had any contact with him any time recently. There doesn't appear to be any foul play whatsoever in this case, but as you can imagine, with the high profile nature of something like this, our top forensic specialists began investigating immediately and everything looks to be what it seems — a cut and dry suicide. However, please understand that it will take us quite some time to finalize and close out this case."

"Okay, thank you for clarifying that for me. Is there anything else I need to do?"

Detective Conner's voice softens a little. "Not at this time; if we need you for any reason, we'll contact you. Again, I'm sorry for your loss, and I apologize for my previous behavior. It's been a bit of a stressful day, none of which is your fault."

The two men stand up and begin to walk towards the door. "I apologize in advance for the onslaught of media attention that you're about to receive. Feel free to say what you wish, but know that you don't owe anyone anything. If any other evidence comes to light, we'll be sure to contact you first thing," Rayburn says before they let themselves out of the house.

A little while after they're gone, Lucca makes me dinner, and it isn't until it's sitting directly in front of my face, that I realize how hungry I am. I've literally been sitting in the same spot on the couch, watching television for hours, not saying much of anything.

"Do you want to talk about it?" Lucca asks calmly as I take the last bite of my soup. "Talk about anything at all?"

I smile slightly at him. "I'm going to be fine, Lucca. Actually, I'm going to be better than fine. It's not how I envisioned I would get it, and I can't even say that I'm happy or pleased that he's dead, but finally, I feel closure. I know the truth about him killing my mom, and even though I was ready to move on, I'll never forgive him. I'll be happy when it all blows over and we can go back to being us. You're my future and you're what I care about. I just hope this doesn't freak you out and send you running," I admit honestly.

Sitting down on the couch next to me, he takes the food tray off of my lap and sets it on the glass coffee table. He pulls me onto his lap, slides his hands around the back of my neck, and brings my face down to his so that my forehead is resting on his. "I will never disappear on you, Katrina. You are mine and I am yours, and I'll never stop loving you."

Later in the evening, we take a long bubble bath together, and he takes complete care of me — washing my hair and body, drying me off with a towel, and then carrying me back to bed. I don't deserve someone as amazing as him, but I plan on keeping him forever nonetheless. As we fall asleep in each other's arms, I hope I never have to go to bed without him again.

Several days later, once some of the madness has calmed down a bit, we go to my apartment so that I can get some more clothes and a few other personal items. Lucca doesn't want me here long — especially not alone — and I don't mind continuing to stay with him at his place. I know it's not the permanent solution, but right now, I can't imagine falling asleep without him.

As I'm digging through my closet, gathering some dresses and blouses, an envelope, taped to the wall back behind where my clothes hang, catches my eye. Equally curious and nervous as to what it is, I pull it down and wander out into my bedroom. Sitting down on my bed, I pull the paper out and begin to read the handwritten letter over and over again. I can't help but to weep until the page is covered in tear stains, my heart filling with sorrow.

My sweet Katie-bug,

From the moment you came into my life, I've tried my best to keep you out of trouble and I've loved you unconditionally. What I did this morning was the ultimate to act to serve both purposes. I know what you were planning to do, and because I love you so much, I couldn't allow you go through with it. Please forgive me for lying to you, but I did what I had to do.

Momma Rosa is safe and with her family, where she belongs. Maybe one day in the future, I'll be able to reunite with her, but I urge you not to try and contact her. It's for the safety and security of you both. I'm going away to somewhere you won't be able to find me. Please don't waste your time or money trying to do so — this is what I have to do.

My wish for you now is to move on with your life. It's time for you to put your past behind you and focus on the future. You've found a good man in Lucca, and I have no doubt that he loves you dearly. He's the one that will take care of you the way you deserve.

I will never forget what we've shared — I had the time of my life each moment I got to spend with you. I loved you yesterday, I love you today, and I will love you tomorrow.

Always yours,

L

Completely engrossed in the letter, I'm unaware that Lucca has come into the room and read the message over my shoulder. His strong arms loop around my waist and he slides me over in between his legs. Cuddling me tightly until my uncontrollable sobs turn into faint sniffles, he kisses the top of my head and whispers, "We'll find him one day, baby. I promise you we will."

My body is fragile and weak while my heart is heavy and overwhelmed with sorrow, but one thing I'm sure of — Lucca loves me and he'll never leave my side.

"You are the light that keeps me from being afraid of the dark, Lucca Ellis. I love you, forever and always," I whisper as I fall asleep, humming *You Are My Sunshine* to him.

Epilogue
Two Years Later

Leo

Staring out into the turquoise waters of the Adriatic Sea, I drink my morning coffee on the small patio of my Zlatni Rat beachside condo, listening to the sound of the children playing under the early rays of sun. Croatia is the last place on earth I thought I'd spend the rest of my life, but it's one of the few countries that doesn't have an extradition treaty with the United States and it offers mile and miles of beaches. It's not that anyone from the States is looking for me — at least not to my knowledge anyway — but I figured better safe than sorry when everything happened with that asshole, Green.

Convincing him to commit suicide wasn't nearly as difficult as I thought it would be. When I gave him the option of me killing him, his wife, and his son or him taking his own life, he really surprised the fuck out of me and chose the latter. I'm glad he didn't call my bluff, because there was no way I could've taken that baby's life. After I watched him take his own gun from the desk drawer in his high-rise apartment and blow his brains out, I left as quietly and stealth-like as I had entered, knowing it wouldn't take long before someone found him. Thanks to Travis and his contact I was able to bypass the buildings video surveillance and got a key to the home; I was waiting for Green when he waltzed into his office early that Wednesday morning.

Since I had already gotten Mama set up with her family back in her hometown a few days prior, I immediately left the country and set up a comfortable little life here. I made sure the entire event took place while Katrina was gone so she would have an air-tight alibi; and as much as it killed me to do it the way I did, without giving her a proper goodbye, I had faith that she had found the life she deserved with Lucca.

Turning my iPad on, I pull up the local New York news websites where I continue to monitor the headlines, just to make sure that nothing is ever mentioned about his death not being a suicide. To date, everything appears to be going as planned. I enter in the words *Governor Green* in the search bar — expecting the typical "no search results found" to pop up — but instead one article appears. Sucking in a deep breath, I click on the link to read the short announcement.

Former Governor Green's Daughter to Marry

Katrina Michelle Foster, the much-talked-about-daughter of the late Governor Robert Green and his previously deceased wife Stephanie Foster, is set to wed her fiancé, Lucca Christian Ellis, over the Fourth of July weekend in Sunny Isles Beach, Florida, where the couple will continue to reside after their planned honeymoon in San Vito lo Capo, Italy.

I can't help but chuckle when I see where they're taking her honeymoon; I bet money she's going to see Mama while she's there. A warm feeling of joy fills my chest knowing that the two of them made it. As much as I loved her, I knew from the first time I saw her with him that he was the one for her, and I cared more about her happiness than I did my own. Even at thirty-three, I still have hope that someday I'll find my one true love, but until then, I have a wedding to attend.

Acknowledgements

A huge thank you to my family for their continued support throughout this entire year as I've embarked on this journey that I never planned on taking, especially my husband and my girls who have had to deal with my hours upon hours of time spent in the cave. They keep a smile on my face and remind me of why I am doing this. I love you all so very much.

To the best betas/ support group a girl could have ~ Trina, Kirsten, Steph, Sarah, Michelle, Shelly, Toski, and Jennifer: Thank you for the incredible amount of time and effort that you've put into both this book and my sanity. I couldn't do it without you, and all of my characters would end up dead in every project.

Shelly: In addition to being a kick-ass beta, you're an extraordinarily fantastic assistant that I never knew I needed. There aren't enough thanks in the world for all you do for me. Love you big, woman!

My editors ~ Kayla & Mandi: Thank you, *thank you*, and THANK YOU; I love semi-colons almost as I love both of you.

Hang Le: You've truly outdone yourself with this cover! Thank you for everything!

Nicki: Here we go again, my sister from another mister. Thank you for believing in me and for the hour-long bitch sessions.

My bubble of friends ~ you know who you are: Cookie bouquets, cupcakes, chocolates, and wine deliveries... now this is what true friendships are made of.

My mom & Lenora: For everything, always. I love you more than you could ever know.

The bloggers: You ladies are the reason that I'm getting to pursue this dream. Thank you from the bottom of my heart for the time you spend — not only reading, but reviewing and promoting as well.

Kassi Bland Cooper: For fitting me in, for dealing with my crazy, for making it beautiful!!! Thank you!

My baby street team: Huge thanks for pimping me and all of the teasers photos! You ladies are so dear to me.

When the Sun Goes Down Playlist

Mysterious Ways ~ U2
The Only Time ~ Nine Inch Nails
In the Fade ~ Queens of the Stone Age
Destrokk ~ MGMT
My Same ~ Adele
Ain't No Sunshine ~ Bill Withers
Addicted to Love ~ Skylar Grey
Sail ~ AWOLNATION
Can't Get You off My Mind ~ Lenny Kravitz
Better Living Through Chemistry ~ Queens of the Stone Age
Head Full of Doubt/Road Full of Promise ~ The Avett Brothers
Been Caught Stealing ~ Jane's Addiction
Calm Like a Bomb ~ Rage Against the Machine
S&M ~ Rihanna
Glad You Came ~ The Wanted
November Rain ~ Guns & Roses
The Woman in You ~ Ben Harper
Never Say Never ~ The Fray
Chances ~ Five for Fighting
Secret ~ Maroon 5
Fix You ~ Coldplay
Enjoy the Silence ~ Breaking Benjamin
Breathe Me ~ Sia
Goodbye My Lover ~ James Blunt
Bleeding Out ~ Imagine Dragons
Dreaming with a Broken Heart ~ John Mayer
Soldier ~ Gavin DeGraw
Patient Love ~ Passenger
Secrets ~ One Republic
My Body is a Cage ~ Arcade Fire
Arms ~ Christina Perri
All These Things That I've Done ~ The Killers

Erin Noelle

River of Deceit ~ Mad Season
Happy ~ Pharell Williams
Fireflies ~ Ron Pope
You Found Me ~The Fray
Kiss Me ~Ed Sheeran
Never Stop ~ SafetySuit
Time of Our Lives ~ Tyrone Wells
Forever and Always ~ Parachute

About the Author

Erin Noelle is a Texas native, where she lives with her husband and two young daughters. While earning her degree in History at the University of Houston, she rediscovered her love for reading that was first instilled by her grandmother when she was a young child. A lover of happily-ever-afters, both historical and current, Erin is an avid reader of all romance novels. In 2013, she published the Book Boyfriend Series, which included books Metamorphosis, Ambrosia, and Euphoria. Her books have been a part of the USA Today Bestselling list and/ or the Amazon and Barnes & Noble overall Top 100. You can follow her on Facebook @ www.facebook.com/erin.noelle.98, her blog @ www.erinnoelleauthor.com, and on Twitter @authorenoelle.

Beautiful Ink

A Forever Inked Novel
Nicole Reed
Coming Spring 2014

Prologue

"Do as I say, when I say it," he forcefully commands. "Turn around and put your hands on the chair behind you."

I slowly pivot on the balls of my feet. He doesn't have to tell me to grip it tightly: my fingers curve over the back of the metal chair instinctively. Thousands of tiny chill bumps cover me in dread at the thought of my naked body on display. My heart throbs in a frantic rhythm, this moment the torturous accumulation of years of anxiety and apprehension.

His heavy breathing sounds frighteningly close. "You are not allowed to fuckin' move."

My eyes clamp shut. I am afraid of the consequences I have wrought. My tongue darts out of my dry mouth, wetting my cracked lips. I should have taken the water when he offered it earlier. The last harrowing fifteen hours have been an emotional train wreck, and just when I think things can't get any worse, they do.

I don't hear a whisper of the leather until it rips into the center of my back. The cracking sound against my skin reverberates all around me.

"Ahhh," I cry out, the white-hot pain sucking the air out of my lungs. There must be small metal spikes lining the belt, because they stab excruciatingly into my flesh. I almost let go of the chair, until I remember his words not to move.

"That's for the year I woulda gave you my name," he says, directly into my ear, but loud enough for everyone else to hear.

I didn't think I could shed another tear, but at the sound of the pain laced through his voice, my eyes swim with them. Even after this, it kills me to know that I hurt him. Many seconds pass before the next strike slams across my sensitive butt cheeks. My knees go weak, making it harder for me to stand. A cry escapes me from another assault of the metal and leather, this one stinging worse than the last. I dig my fingers into the cold metal of the chair, silently praying that I can hold myself up.

"That's for the year I woulda made our dreams come true."

So many memories assault me along with his belt, memories both sensual and evil. I want to open my eyes, but I fear what I would see in his gaze. The grief in his voice already rocks me to my core.

My screams echo around the room when he delivers two consecutive swings of the belt. His torture finally beats my body down, and my knees buckle, roughly sending me to the concrete floor. My eyes open in time to see red splatter across my arms, staining my already colorful skin. His unerring aim catches the exact spot as the first, slicing deeper into my flesh. I choke back the bile that threatens to erupt.

"Get up," he growls.

I force myself back to my feet, bowing my head, and bracing myself for his words as much as his strikes. My tears represent the agony of defeat that I don't want to give him.

"That's for the goddamn year," his voice breaks midsentence. "I woulda gave you my child."

Any inner strength I have left vanishes at the words torn from his mouth. His feet stand before me now and I have to see him. My eyes lift from the ground to stare directly into his dark, penetrating gaze. The room and those in it fall away and I only see him. This was once my friend. My family. My lover. My savior.

"*Our* child," he whispers through gritted teeth. He leans down to deliver a tender kiss upon my chapped lips, his tongue soothing them. His actions surprise me, the antithesis of his words. I watch him move slowly back. The look of desolation in his eyes is more than I can bear, so I close mine.

His backhand catches me completely off-guard. The searing pain explodes across my jawline up to my eye and has me staggering backward. The chair scrapes against the floor, following me several inches. I stare at the blood-splattered ground, blinking my vision back into focus. I hear the sound of his heavy shit-kickers as he moves behind me once again.

The voice in my head screams enough. I am too close to my breaking point. I wouldn't have lived through the earlier offer of the bullet to my brain, but I am not sure I will physically or mentally survive this agonizing persecution.

The next whip of his belt catches me against the soft flesh of my legs and on the underside of my rear. Quivering uncontrollably, I completely lose my balance, finally relinquishing the chair. He jerks my elbow up, making it easier to steady myself. His foot kicks out to knock the chair across the room away from us. My stomach threatens to rebel at the feel of something wet and warm running from my back, down the crease of my ass, slowly over my legs. I glance down to see drops of crimson silently rolling over my feet to encircle them. He tosses the belt so that it lands in it.

Our joint harsh panting is the only sound between us. He painfully tugs me backward to him, further lacerating my torn skin. The smooth texture of the leather rubbing against my back prompts another scream of pain. His jeans roughly grind against my buttocks.

"No," I say over and over, but make no attempt to move, knowing it would cause him to order more of this torture.

"Do you know what it's like to pretend it's your face on every girl I kiss?" The sound of his husky voice whispers softly against my ear. "Wanting it to be your body under me every time that I fuck someone."

A violent tremor racks my system. His words are making me sick and I whimper as I feel his fingers brush across my wounds. They tenderly wrap around my body, and I look down to notice him painting the letters "HHMC" across my heaving chest in my own crimson blood.

"Blood in and blood out," he says, kissing my neck in between his words. "Your fuckin' choice. But know this: it is forever now my blood that runs through your veins. And I will drown you in it before I let you escape me again."

Made in the USA
Charleston, SC
06 November 2014